RANDOM ACTS OF MURDER

Holly Anna Paladin Mystery Series
Book 1

by Christy Barritt

Random Acts of Murder: A Novel
Copyright 2014 by Christy Barritt

Published by River Heights Press

Cover design by The Killion Group

Dedication:
When I started writing this book in 2012, I didn't know
that my dear sister-in-law Ann Barritt would soon be
diagnosed with cancer and given a year to live. Before
she died in 2014, she asked that everyone do one
random act of kindness in her name. This book is
dedicated to Ann and the legacy she left behind.

CHAPTER 1

This had to be my worst idea ever.

Before I lost my courage, I rushed inside the house, turned the locks, and leaned against the door. I tried to steady my breathing and push away the regret that threatened to consume me—regret at my decision to do this.

A dark, silent house stared back at me, almost taunting me.

It was too late to turn back now. I was in. I'd already broken the law. I might as well follow through with the rest of the plan.

"Are you in, Retro Girl?" My friend Jamie's voice sounded through my Bluetooth headset.

"I'm in, Girl Genius." Jamie had picked her code name herself.

"Everything clear?" she asked.

"What's clear is the fact that I'd make a terrible, terrible criminal."

"That's a good thing, Hol—I mean Retro Girl. Be careful."

I nodded. "Roger that."

In the delirium of a restless night, this whole scheme had seemed brilliant. But the fact remained that, in order to execute my plan, I'd just broken into someone's home. I'd utilized the skills my locksmith father had taught me, though I was certain he'd never dreamed I'd use them this way. I'd become a masked vigilante of good deeds, only without the mask.

My heart slammed at a quick beat into my chest, each thump reverberating all the way down to my bones. I pinched the skin between my eyebrows as I tried to rationalize my actions. This wasn't just a haphazard stranger's home. And I wasn't breaking in for nefarious reasons. That was the good news.

The bad news had generated my new life mantra: engaging in random acts of kindness whenever possible. And not just any ordinary random acts of kindness. *Extreme* random acts of kindness. Life was too short to do anything halfheartedly, after all.

To lay it all out, I'd just broken into the home of Katrina Dawson, one of my former social work clients—but only so I could clean her house and surprise her. I wanted to help. The idea had started innocently enough when I'd sneaked in to clean my brother's house—a drive-by good deed, as I'd called it. He'd been thrilled, especially when he'd found the nice, anonymous note I'd left, explaining I didn't seek recognition but only wanted to make his day brighter.

Cleaning Katrina's house would help her and add a touch of quality to her life. I knew it would. She was a single mom, she couldn't catch a break when it came to getting a decent job, and with a whole gaggle of kids, she barely had time to brush her teeth, let alone clean her home.

A clean residence could do wonders for a person's spirit.

"You still okay, Retro Girl?" Jamie asked in my ear.

"I guess. What's it look like outside?"

"It's all clear. A neighbor three doors down just

went inside. He didn't even look my way. Good thing I'm driving the ghettomobile. It blends right in."

"Here goes nothing, Girl Genius."

I took a deep breath, grabbed my bucket of cleaning supplies, and plunged into the darkness. I planned to focus on the kitchen and bathroom since they usually needed the most attention.

I pushed up the sleeves of my black T-shirt. I'd abandoned my trademark dress in favor of something more sensible. I didn't want to draw any unnecessary attention to myself in the run-down neighborhood. Pulling up in my '64 1/2 powder-blue Mustang—Sally, as I affectionately called her—and stepping out with a vintage frilly dress on just wasn't a smart idea.

I could do this, I told myself, a feeling of false security washing over me. I'd clean, leave a sweet note explaining I was a friend doing a random act of kindness, and then I'd hop in the van and head home. I was making a big deal out of nothing.

That's what I told myself, at least.

I waited until I was away from the front windows before I turned a light on. Before I'd come inside, I'd put my gloves on. I never cleaned without them. Nothing was less appealing than smelling bleach on your hands three days after the fact. Plus, since I was officially breaking in, the gloves just seemed like a good idea.

I set my bucket on the countertop and looked at the mess around me. Dirty dishes in the sink. Junk on every visible surface—everything from schoolbooks to groceries to toys. There was something splattered on the linoleum floor, crayon marks on the wall, and this morning's breakfast—at least, I assumed the food was from today — was still on the little table in the corner.

The house smelled like it hadn't been cleaned in a while, a mix of trash that desperately needed to be taken out, rotting food on the plates in the sink, and laundry that had been sitting for too long. I'd noticed that on my last visit here. But the main thing I'd noticed had been the look of hopelessness in Katrina's eyes. Hopelessness about changing her life, about getting ahead, about catching any breaks. No one should have to feel like that.

As I picked up my first plate, ready to wash it, I realized that I was breaching an uncountable number of professional standards. The good thing was that, even if I was fired from my job as a social worker, it wouldn't matter.

"Girl, what is that noise?" Jamie asked.

"It's the water running."

"Well, can't you help a sister out and turn it down some? My ears will be ringing for the rest of the night."

Just then, I bristled. Why did I feel like someone was watching me? The thought was crazy. I was the only one here. I'd watched Katrina and her family leave earlier. She worked the graveyard shift and took her kids to a sitter's.

"Girl Genius, something doesn't feel right."

"You broke into someone's house. Maybe that's it."

"But I broke in with good intentions, so that makes it okay, right?"

Jamie chuckled. "You just keep telling yourself that, Retro Girl."

Three months ago, my job and my reputation would have mattered. Three months ago, I'd had a different outlook on life. I'd thought I had forever left.

—

8

But sometimes a routine visit to the doctor changed a girl's view and made her realize that she could take chances, that life was too short not to take risks.

My name is Holly Paladin, I'm twenty-eight years old, and I've been given a year to live.

The introduction played over and over again in my mind, much like a broken movie reel. In my head, I also had the same accent as Inigo Montoya from *The Princess Bride*, but that was an entirely different issue.

But this wasn't a movie. This was my life. I only had one year to leave a mark. One year to embrace what I loved. One year to let my loved ones know how much they meant to me.

There was a lot I wouldn't be able to do, so I decided to focus primarily on one task: changing the world. At least, changing one or two people's worlds.

That's why I washed the dishes in the sink.

That's why I collected the trash and placed it by the front door.

That's why I wiped down the counters and the stove and the refrigerator.

When I stepped back, the kitchen looked spotless.

I smiled, feeling satisfied. This *had* been a good idea. I just had to make peace with myself about the implications of my means. I knew my motives were golden.

Now I just had to do the bathroom. I'd clean the whole house, if I could. I'd wipe the windows, scrub the baseboards, and start some laundry. But that would take more time than I had.

I stepped into the hallway, went down two doors, and reached inside the bathroom. Just as my fingers connected with the light switch, I heard a noise.

I froze.

What was that?

I listened but didn't hear anything else. Had that been movement inside the house? But no one was home, despite the eerie feeling I'd had earlier.

Besides, if someone else was here, they would have come out by now. In the very least, they would have called the police.

My heart pounded in my ears.

Bad idea, bad idea, bad idea. The phrase kept repeating in my head.

This *was* a bad idea, no matter how I tried to paint the harebrained plan in a positive light.

I had to clean this bathroom, and then I was getting out of here.

I gulped in one last breath and pushed the light switch up.

I blinked at what I saw there.

It was a man. Lying on the floor. Blood pooled around his chest.

He was dead.

No doubt about it — dead.

CHAPTER 2

I backed away, a scream catching in my throat.

Oh my lands . . . that man was dead. Lifeless. Gone.

Based on the wounds across his chest, his death hadn't been a peaceful one. There was too much blood, too many wounds, and a frozen expression of horror on his face.

"Retro Girl, are you okay? I thought I heard a gasp."

"I . . . I—"

I pulled my eyes away, panic racing through me. Without thinking, I darted toward the front door, threw it open, and sprinted outside to the van.

I jumped inside, slammed the door, and turned to my friend Jamie. "Go!"

She stared at me like I'd lost my mind. "What happened?"

I pointed down the road. "There's no time to talk! We've got to get out of here. Now!"

Jamie threw the beat-up minivan into drive and squealed down the road. She charged out of the neighborhood and across the interstate, and she didn't say a word.

That was a good thing because, if I opened my mouth, I feared I might throw up. My stomach twisted in knots, and the dizzy fairy danced in my head.

Oh my goodness, oh my goodness, oh my goodness . . .

I rocked back and forth, trying to settle my

thoughts, trying to keep myself from passing out.

Finally, Jamie pulled to a stop in front of our favorite coffeehouse. She put the van in park, and we sat there for several minutes in silence. I ignored the college kids barhopping around us. I ignored the drunken frat boy who made kissing faces outside the van window. I even ignored my friend who sat beside me, staring at me like I'd lost my mind.

She turned down the jazzy gospel music crooning through the speakers. The necklace with the carved wooden figure of a girl, one she'd gotten on a mission trip to Jamaica, finally stopped swinging back and forth from the rearview mirror. A jar of coconut oil — my friend's answer for every ailment — slid onto its side on the floor in front of me.

"You want to tell me what just happened?" Jamie finally said. Her black, curly hair usually sprang out from around her mocha-colored face like rays of sunshine. Right now, the forecast of her expression pointed to a partially cloudy day with a good chance of storms. "Did you realize what a bad idea this was? Did you get spooked?"

I knew the only reason she'd agreed to be my getaway driver was in case anything went wrong. Thank goodness she'd been there. I didn't think I could have driven out of the neighborhood without hitting everything in my path.

Which would only add more things to my rap sheet.

"It was awful, Jamie . . . she said as the understatement of the year." My mind still raced, still replayed what had happened. As the bathroom scene flashed into my mind, nausea rose in me. One glance at the old banana peel on the floor of her van, followed by inhaling the rotten scent, and I was done.

I opened the van door and hurled.

"Girl, are you okay?" Jamie's hand went to my back. "What happened in there? Should I take you to the hospital?"

I grabbed a napkin from the glove compartment and wiped my mouth. A winter wind that whipped into the van nearly froze my vomit to my lips — not a pretty sight. Or feeling, for that matter.

As soon as I closed the door, I jerked it open again. More contents of my stomach emptied from me.

My thoughts collided with each other. What had happened to that man? Why had I ever thought it was a good idea to go to Katrina's house? What was I going to do now?

Panic gripped every part of me, from my trembling limbs to my queasy stomach to my unsettled spirit.

"Should you call your doctor?" Worry tinged Jamie's voice.

I held the napkin over my mouth as I closed the door again. I didn't trust my body, didn't know what would happen next. My physical being had already betrayed me big-time. Despite that, I shook my head. "No, I'll be fine."

I wished I could say the same for that man I'd seen.

"What happened, Holly?"

I closed my eyes, wishing I could erase my thoughts. "It was awful, Jamie. Just awful."

"Was her house that dirty?" Skepticism laced her urban-drenched voice.

My friend had no idea. No idea. If she knew what I'd seen, she wouldn't make light of it, not even in an effort to cheer me up.

I finally pulled my eyes open and turned to my friend. "Jamie, there was a dead man in the bathroom."

Her eyes widened and her mouth sagged open. "Say what?"

I nodded. "I think he'd been shot. He was . . . he was dead. Murdered. Violently." I opened the van door again as more vomit arose.

I pulled my head back inside and rested it against the dashboard. I felt awful . . . but, as I remembered the dead man, I was thankful just to be alive.

"We've got to call the police."

"No!" I said a little too quickly. "I mean, if we call the police, how am I going to explain how I found the body? How I was in the house?"

Jamie pursed her lips, a cheeky expression on her face. "That's a great question."

I rocked back and forth. "I know. I know. It was a terrible idea. I don't know what I was thinking. While I was lying in my safe little bed at night, my plan seemed brilliant, like something bold, that would make a statement. But I have no idea what to do now. What am I going to do, Jamie?"

"Girlfriend, this isn't good. It isn't good at all. You were at a crime scene. A crime scene. You fled." Her voice lilted with a brassiness that usually got me fired up. Right now, it only tightened the imaginary noose around my neck.

"I know! You don't have to remind me." I rubbed my cheek. "What am I going to do?"

She let out a breath and leaned back in her seat. "Let's brainstorm. Maybe you could tell the police you stopped by Katrina's house for work."

"At midnight with no one home?"

"You noticed the door was ajar and stepped inside. That's when you found the body."

I shook my head. "No one will believe that. Besides, I can't lie."

"You're worrying about lying? Do I need to remind you that you broke into someone's home?"

Without looking, I could feel her stare on me. I squeezed my eyes shut and leaned my forehead against the cool glass of the window. "It sounds so awful that way."

"It is awful."

"You're not helping," I moaned.

"Okay, let me help. If you sit on this information, you could be charged with being an accessory to a crime. You have a moral duty to report this."

I sprang up, my stomach still roiling. "Think about it, Jamie. If I call the police and they find out I broke into the house, then they'll arrest me. Then my sister — an assistant district attorney — will have to prosecute me —"

"They wouldn't actually let her do that, since you're related and all."

"It doesn't matter! That's what it will feel like. Then, my brother — who's running for state senate, need I remind you — will lose the election because his sister was arrested. You know the pundits, namely Rex Harrison and his crew, will use this against him. Don't deny it."

She raised her hands. "No denial here. You're the overly optimistic one. Not me."

"Then, my mom will have to explain herself at every board meeting she attends. She'll be known as the woman with a daft for a daughter!" I wanted to

15

disappear. Simply disappear. In the very least, to rewind time.

"These are the things I wanted you to think about before you got all impulsive and idealistic and decided to do this."

"I knew it was coming. The 'I told you so.'" I couldn't even hold it against her. She'd been right. And I'd been so, so wrong.

"So, what are you going to do?" The overhead light in the parking lot illuminated the compassionate look in her eyes.

"I have no idea . . . she said like someone who was hopelessly lost and dim-witted." *And self-loathing.* I didn't say that part out loud, though.

"First of all, take your forehead off of the dash."

I hadn't even realized I'd put it back there. I sat up and let my head drop behind me instead.

"Now, you've got to make a decision. What are you going to do? Doing nothing isn't an option. You've got to get a handle on this."

A handle . . . handles made me think of buckets, and buckets made me realize—

"I left my cleaning supplies at the house. Oh my lands, Jamie. All of my stuff is still at the house!"

CHAPTER 3

Jamie slowly rolled toward the street where Katrina's house was located.

I could do this. I could run inside the house, grab my stuff, and leave. Then I'd figure out the next plan of action. I'd figure out how to let the police know what had happened.

I'd repent, vow to never do this again, and beg God to somehow allow things to work out.

I let out a long breath, praying I wouldn't throw up again. My hands—all of my bones, for that matter—shook so badly that I nearly jiggled out of my seat.

I'd messed up big-time. I'd been in my little idealist daze, thinking I could float in, do a good deed, and never be found out. This was the very thing my family always rode my case about. They told me I needed to come back down to earth, that I needed to think things through using my head instead of my heart. My diagnosis had stirred something in me, though—a new kind of boldness, fearlessness.

"Check this out, girlfriend." Jamie pressed on the brakes.

I held my breath, unsure how to read her voice. Check out good? Check out bad?

I had my answer quickly. Flashing lights lit the sky at the end of the street.

The police were at Katrina's house.

They'd somehow discovered the dead body in the hour since we'd driven away.

How had they done that? Had someone seen the van there and called the police? I had no idea.

I only knew that a bad situation had just gotten ten thousand times worse.

"Keep going," I whispered. "Moral obligation done."

"Yeah, the moral obligation of reporting a dead body has been covered. But how are you going to handle it when the police find your supplies, and you're their first suspect?"

***

The next morning I glanced into my rearview mirror. I ignored the fluffy pink dice dangling there, beckoning for carefree days of driving through the countryside with the windows down and Peggy Lee's version of "Fever" blaring through the speakers.

Instead, I focused on the circles under my eyes. Were they from the fact that I hadn't slept a wink last night due to my increasing worry over what had happened? Or were they from the disease that was slowly ravaging my body?

It didn't matter. All that mattered right now was that I did my job as a social worker; I had to concentrate on that and forget about the dead body.

All evening I'd waited for the police to knock on my door and take me down to the station. I thought about what I'd tell my family. I imagined the unflattering headlines, splashed across every newspaper in Cincinnati. Maybe all of Ohio.

Dim-witted social worker breaks into client's home in moment of lunacy.

Idiotic nonprofit employee spends her final days on earth rotting in jail.

Daughter of prominent family ruins the reputation of relatives and makes them the laughingstock of community.

I let out a sigh and tried to put it out of my mind. People and their children were depending on me to do my job today, and I had no intention of letting them down, especially not the children.

I'd recently started working for a private foster care agency called Caring Hands. I did home visits and tried to make sure I wasn't taking children from one dangerous situation and putting them into a new one. Sometimes all they needed was one voice, crying out for justice on their behalf. I wanted to be that voice.

I ran my hand under my eyes one more time. My skin was getting paler; I was sure of it. But I wouldn't waste time tanning, even if I'd be dead by the time skin cancer could do any damage. I had too much to do in the little time I had left. Things that would make a difference after I was dead.

Looking on the bright side kept despair from claiming me and swallowing me whole. I wasn't going to let that happen. After all, I had been voted "Most Optimistic" by my high school class. Some had called me perky; others had said annoying. I supposed it was all in how you looked at it. Of course, I was an optimist, so I stuck with the positive definitions.

I'd pulled curbside to an old shanty of a house located in the Price Hill area of Cincinnati. The place, skinny and tall, was three levels and looked like it could fall over if a strong wind hit the burgundy shingles hard enough.

I stepped out of the car and into the sunshine. Price Hill stood in its glory all around me. I'd grown up on the outskirts of this Cincinnati neighborhood, and, despite its reputation, I loved it here. Parts of the community were nicer than others, but the area, with all of its steep hills and skinny houses, bordered downtown Cincinnati. The view from some of the hilltops was simply breathtaking. One could see the Ohio River, the stadium — including fireworks on certain nights — and Union Station, a place that looked like something straight out of Gotham City.

Folks from Appalachia had moved into Price Hill to get jobs several decades back. Some of them had spread out to the suburbs in recent years, and the inner-city poor as well as Mexican immigrants had moved into the area, creating a strange mix of people all sharing the same community.

Most of the homes in the area wouldn't win any awards for "Best-Kept Yard." Far from it, truth be told. But the neighborhood had character. It had gone downhill further in recent years. At least, that's what some people said. To me, the area was like family. It was imperfect and sometimes messy, but it was home.

I straightened my snow-white sundress. I tried to appease my supervisor by wearing a tailored brown blazer over my dress to make it look more professional and less I-should-be-dancing-through-a-field-of-flowers, as Doris liked to say. I always said I should have been born in the fifties, when women were applauded for looking feminine and soft and ladylike.

I reached into the backseat and grabbed my briefcase. As I started to stand, I heard footfalls behind me. Before I could look back, someone said, "You're supposed to wait in the car."

I jumped, hitting my head on the roof. I kept my head lowered, rubbing what was sure to become a knot. Before I could straighten, I saw the shiny black shoes on the grass beside me and recognized the standard-issue footwear.

A police officer.

Was he coming to arrest me? Had my fingerprints already been run through the system? I mean, sure, I'd worn gloves. But my prints could still be on my bucket or the mop. I could have left a hair, a shoe print, or a drop of sweat! I'd seen those crime shows on TV; I knew how it worked. Investigators would find anything they could to frame me and lock me up for the rest of my short life.

I glanced up, trepidation coursing through me. But I froze when I saw the officer's face. I knew this man.

Oh. My. Sweet. Goodness.

I knew this man.

And I didn't want to. I was never, ever supposed to see him again. That humiliating time of my life was supposed to be far, far behind me.

He was even taller than before—if that was possible. Even broader than before—if that was fathomable. And he was even more handsome than I remembered—and I was pretty sure that *was* impossible.

"Chase Dexter," I muttered, a hand going to my hip.

Recognition spread across his perfect face, and a satisfied grin curled half of his lips. "If it isn't Holly Anna Paladin." His grin widened. "Long time no see."

I scowled, forgetting all about trying to be ladylike. "What are you doing here?" My voice came out with a little more hiss than I intended.

One of his eyebrows casually flickered upward. "I'm supposed to escort you on this visit as a safety precaution. I heard you had some trouble with the children's birth father. The director wanted an officer to be here with you."

I straightened my jacket again and raised my chin, totally forgetting — or was it not caring? — about being professional and the epitome of well mannered. "I don't need you to escort me."

He raised his eyebrows in that arrogant manner that was exactly how I remembered. I'd seen it many, many times in our encounters during high school. "Do I need to remind you about the situation regarding these children's father? Weapons charges? Domestic disputes?"

I bit back a sigh and finally nodded. The whole custody situation with this family was rather scary. I'd worked as a CPS investigator until a couple of months ago. I'd determined that the three children needed to be taken away from their mom and dad for safety reasons.

"What are you still doing in this area? I thought you left?" I finally asked.

"Been back a couple of months now. Got a knee injury and had to give up football. Worked in Louisville a few years in the police department, and now I'm here."

How lucky for Cincinnati . . . and for me. He'd fooled everyone else in the community into thinking he was some kind of saint. I knew the truth. He was stuck on himself and the master of disguising his true nature, a nature that lent itself to belittling people who didn't meet his superficial standards. "Well, isn't that . . .

splendid."

I started climbing the cracked cement steps that stretched up the front lawn of the house and toward the front door. It would be safer to climb up cinder blocks randomly placed on a hillside than these crumbling stairs that wiggled and teetered with each step.

Chase's long strides quickly caught up with me. He tugged at one of my wavy curls. "You look nice, Holly Anna."

I tried not to be vain, but I did love my hair. I spent too much time smoothing and then curling it. The look took me back in time, and if I was honest with myself, I'd give anything to go back. I wanted to be a little girl again, so full of hope about the future. I wanted to sit in my daddy's lap and listen to his stories and feel safe.

Most days, I felt alone, like no one understood me and like I'd drawn the short straw. Sometimes I felt like I needed to just give up my job and start traveling across Europe or something. But my mom needed me now that Dad had died. My brother was running for office, and my sister was getting married. Besides, these kids needed me to be their voice.

I felt Chase's gaze on me, and I scowled.

"I still get under your skin, don't I?" He laughed, deep and bellowing and sure of himself, just like the brute he was. "Even after all of this time."

"Why would you get under my skin?" I could list a million reasons and still keep going.

He shifted his weight at the doorway. The action reminded me of a giant about to go to war. "Look, high school was . . . it was high school. A different lifetime ago."

"You can say that again. I've practically forgotten all about high school. What was our mascot again? What was that class they insisted we'd use later on in life? Calculus or some other nonsense?"

He chuckled and tugged at one of my curls again. "You're funny."

I swatted his hand away. "There's a difference between being funny and being made fun of." I swallowed the lump in my throat. "Of course, you wouldn't realize that."

Chase had been Mr. Cool, and I'd been the pathetic geek who'd had a crush on him. He'd found out about it and made me miserable.

"I never made fun of you, Holly Anna." His voice sounded smooth and serious. But he'd just called me Holly Anna again, so any points he'd won with his supposed sincerity immediately disappeared . . . and then some.

"Please stop calling me that."

"It's your name."

"A very ill-fated name. My parents had a twisted sense of humor."

"I've always thought it fit you."

I gripped my briefcase with one hand and knocked at the door with the other. "I don't view life through rose-colored glasses, thank you very little."

"A little testy today, aren't we?"

"I don't want to talk to you anymore." So much for going the mature route. I banged on the door again, a little harder than I intended, which was especially noticeable since my knuckles throbbed. "Why aren't they answering? I told them I was coming today. You'd think—"

Before I had the chance to finish my statement, a loud pop sounded.

"Get down!" Chase threw me on the rough cement slab of the porch.

I looked up just in time to see a gun peeking through the window of an old Cadillac on the street in front of us. The gun was aimed . . . at me.

CHAPTER 4

Once the drive-by shooter emptied four bullets and squealed away, Chase and I both pulled ourselves back to our feet and faced each other on the lopsided porch. Reality hadn't quite sunk in yet. What had just happened?

"Are you okay?" Chase asked, concern filling his eyes.

I nodded, although I wasn't nearly that certain. "Yes."

"You have a cut on your forehead."

I reached into my purse and pulled out a handkerchief with an *H* embroidered on the corner. I tried to find my injury when Chase reached out to help. I flinched when his fingers touched mine.

"Hold that there a moment," he instructed, pressing the handkerchief into my temple.

He radioed the incident in before turning back to me.

Chase's steely gaze latched onto mine. "Why in the world would someone shoot at you?"

I shook my head, erasing the fog in my head like a picture from an Etch A Sketch. I pictured Katrina's house. I remembered what I'd done. Was this somehow connected? "I don't know. Coincidence?"

"Is there anyone who might want to hurt you?"

"My sister is an assistant district attorney who's put

countless criminals behind bars. My brother is running for state senate, where his viewpoints have angered about half of the people in the state. And in my former job as a CPS investigator, I routinely took children away from homes where their parents were violent. You narrow it down."

He shifted his weight and sighed. "Is there anyone specifically that you can think of?"

I shook my head and took a deep breath, willing myself to calm down and act like the lady I knew I was. "No. I haven't been threatened directly, if that's what you're asking."

A couple of forensic techs arrived on the scene. Chase patted my arm and excused himself to go talk to them. I watched him interact and realized something seemed different about him. Had he grown up? It was doubtful.

He wrapped up the conversation, and the techs began collecting and documenting evidence—evidence like bullets, shell casings, and skid marks. A couple more officers showed up, as well as a detective who got a statement from me before questioning neighbors. In the meantime, the homeowners still weren't here, and if they'd merely told me in the first place they weren't available, all of this mayhem could have been avoided.

Mainly, *Chase* could have been avoided.

I wiped the dirt from my dress again, an exercise in futility if there ever was one. The clothing was ruined, and I just needed to accept that. I needed to accept a lot of things, for that matter, but sometimes issues should just be ignored for sanity's sake.

"Can I go now?"

He stared at me like the big brooding beast that he

was. "How will you get home?"

I stared at my windshield. He was right. Sally was in no position to cruise down the road right now. Apparently, the shooter had also pierced one of my tires with his bullets. I'd need to call a tow truck.

I looked back at Chase. Part of his lip looked like it wanted to tug upward in a smile. He knew I was running out of options, which meant that I'd need to depend on him.

I crossed my arms. "I'll call a cab."

"Don't be ridiculous. I'll give you a ride." He flicked his hand toward his police cruiser, which was parked behind Sally.

I considered my options and came up short. Sure, I could call a cab. I could call someone in my family. I really didn't want to do either of those things, however. I knew my family. They'd worry. They'd call me naïve. They'd tell me to give up this job and do something more reliable and advantageous. You know, something more like what they did, a job where my name could make the papers or I could be named Woman of the Year.

Chase was waiting for my response. I let out a very unladylike sigh. "I'm sure you have other things to do."

"We've done all we can do here." He put his hand on my back. I mentally cursed the shivers that raced through me at his touch. My body just seemed to be working against me lately — in more than one way. "Come on. Let's get you out of here."

Somehow, I found myself being led down those cement stairs again, over the cracked sidewalk, and into his police car. Chase climbed in a moment later, his form filling the space with more than his fair share. I guess that's what happened when you were six foot five and built like a gladiator.

Not that I'd noticed.

I expected him to start the car, make some snide remarks about my name, and then pull away to begin his obligatory duty. Instead, he turned toward me. "That was probably more excitement than you're used to. I'm glad you're okay, Holly."

I sent some mental telepathy down to my cheeks, begging them not to redden. They did anyway. Again, everything about my body was revolting.

I cleared my throat. "Thanks."

"Where to, ma'am?" He turned the keys in the ignition.

I swallowed, anticipating how the rest of this conversation would play out. "Elwood Street."

His head jerked toward me, his blue eyes widening. "Elwood Street? Isn't that where you grew up?"

My cheeks reddened again. Why did that embarrass me? It shouldn't. I should be proud of my heritage — even if I was still living at home at twenty-eight. "Yes, it is."

That grin began curling his lips again. "So you bought your parents' place?"

My eyes narrowed. I knew exactly what he was doing. He knew the truth; he just wanted to make me say it. "No. I live with my mom. There. Are you happy now? I said it, so now you can go ahead and gloat."

"Just your mom?" He glanced over before his steady gaze went back to the busy, slanted streets the neighborhood was known for.

"My dad died two years ago." My throat burned as I said the words. I still couldn't believe he wasn't here anymore, that he'd left me alone with . . . well, alone with the rest of my family.

Chase's grin disappeared. "I'm sorry to hear that. He was a nice man." Sincerity stretched across his voice, softening my heart for a moment.

"He was the best."

"What happened?"

"Pancreatic cancer." Tears still stung my eyes whenever I thought about it. I had so many plans for my dad and me, starting with him walking me down the aisle one day. Life really stunk sometimes. Thank goodness for the hope of heaven. "He fought it, long and hard. Tried every treatment out there. None of them did any good."

"How's your family doing?"

I shrugged. "We miss Dad. But otherwise, everyone is great. As always. My sister's getting married. I think I told you my brother's running for office. My mom's involved with all of those boards still. She's always running around doing something. She's still a real estate agent and does some interior decorating."

"All in this area?"

"Yep. We're all here."

"And you're living at home still . . . why?"

I kept my head high and my shoulders back. "Social work really is a labor of love. The monetary rewards aren't that great. I'm trying to save some money, have a little more financial freedom, and keep my mom company in the process."

"That's it." He jammed a finger into the air, stealing another glance my way. "There you go. That's the real reason. You're there for your mom."

"You don't know what you're talking about."

"That's very sweet, Holly."

I kept my chin raised high. He thought he was so smart. I guessed that he was, because he'd nailed it even though he hadn't seen me in years. "And you?"

"I live over in Clifton."

Clifton was the neighborhood near the University of Cincinnati, where there would be plenty of parties and young college girls. That fit my opinion of Chase perfectly.

"I got a great deal on this fixer-upper there. My problem is I just haven't had time to fix anything up."

So maybe parties and girls weren't the *only* reason he'd moved there. Still.

I sucked in a breath, trying to think of the proper way to respond. "Demanding job, huh?"

"I've been working some extra gigs to earn some more money. You know, security at ball games or special events. Such is life."

Such is life. Could be my motto lately.

I pointed to my street. "Right there."

He pulled to a stop in front of a Tudor-style home. It was on the outskirts of the neighborhood, in a section where the city's rich had once lived. Each house on my street had an expansive yard—expansive for Price Hill, at least—and a unique design. The surrounding streets were run down and crime ridden, but these houses never failed to make people pause and relive the area's glory days.

Chase stared up at the house now. "That place is a beauty. It really is. Your parents did a great job fixing it up."

A grin wanted to emerge, but I fought it. "Thanks."

The next thing I knew, he was turning off the car

and running around to my door to open it for me. He stood there in the driveway, offering a hand, and appearing like the perfect gentleman. And, for some reason, I found myself reaching for his hand and letting him help me out.

I wasn't sure who was more dazed—Chase or me.

I immediately let go of his hand.

"You didn't really have to get out," I muttered.

"Don't be ridiculous. I don't mind. I need to make sure you get safely inside, with your head injury and all."

"It's just a little cut on my forehead. I'm fine." My pulsating headache could be knocked out with a couple of Tylenols.

But Chase's hand was on my elbow, and he swept me past the lush green grass that my mom paid someone to maintain, past the *Better Homes and Gardens* flowerbeds, and toward the front door. If luck had been on my side, there would have been no cars in the driveway, signaling that no one was home. But luck was hardly ever on my side, especially not today.

Before we even reached the door, it flew open and my mom stood there. She was tiny and blonde and wore expensive business suits and handed out her business card with all the ease of a little kid spreading the flu. She was what most people would consider a "mover and a shaker."

She grinned and clapped her hands. "If it isn't Chase Dexter! How are you?"

I was convinced that my mother had been southern in a previous life. She even made sweet tea with the best of them. But no, she was a Cincinnati original, born and raised here and proud of it. She'd fought to preserve historic houses, and worked on the committee to organize "Price Hill Pride Days," and served on uncountable boards and clubs. Every time I turned around, she was doing a fund-raiser for some cause. It was a wonder—and a shame—she was even home now.

"Mrs. Paladin! You look beautiful, like you haven't aged a day." Chase gave her a friendly hug.

My mom fluttered her hand in the air, her entire face beaming. She may have been almost sixty years old, but her skin looked flawless and her hair was still glossy and youthful. "Oh, you. What a sweetheart. Come on in." She hooked her arm through his and ushered him inside.

Only then did she glance back at me. When she saw my face, she squinted. "Holly, are you okay?" She dropped her arm from Chase's.

"It's nothing. Just a little accident."

"It was more than a little and more than an accident," Chase interjected.

"Oh, sweetie." She reached for me. "Can I do anything?"

I shook my head. "Just let me get cleaned up. I can explain later."

"Call me if you need me," she insisted, before continuing to lead Chase inside.

I came from a family of overachievers. They were all type A success hounds. They'd climb one mountain, and instead of enjoying that victory, they'd search for the next challenge, so they could climb higher and higher.

I'd been more like my dad. I was laid back, a dreamer who enjoyed evenings alone or with a close circle of friends who liked having deep conversations over warm tea. I liked baking using old recipe books from the bygone eras and dancing alone in the living room when no one else was there. I liked sending handwritten notes to people and taking long baths where I could reflect on life.

I hated fund-raisers and election campaigns and being fake with people just so they'd give you their money or their vote. I hated rubbing elbows with people, only on the premise of what they could do for you. Most of all, I hated hurrying through life so quickly that you didn't take time to appreciate every moment.

Now that Dad was gone, I didn't feel like there was one single person in the world who really understood me. I sighed, pulling back the tears that threatened to emerge. I stepped onto the glossy hardwood floors of my home and shut the door behind me. The comforting scent of orange, rosemary, and vanilla filled my senses.

Chase and my mom were already gone, though I could hear their voices floating through the air, probably from the sunroom, if I had to guess. My mom laughed as if Chase were hysterical. Chase's voice rose, like he was telling a great story.

Too bad Chase wasn't born into this family.

I sighed. Maybe that title of "Most Optimistic" didn't fit me at all. At least when it came to my family and Chase Dexter.

I dropped my purse by the front door and kicked off my shoes.

My etiquette guide—one I'd found at a thrift store that was copyright 1955, a real treasure that had made me smile for weeks—would instruct me to go and be social. I just didn't feel up to it, though. Instead, I went upstairs and changed into a clean dress, another one that I'd found at the thrift store. I loved searching there for finds from eras past.

After I cleaned up, I made a quick stop in my favorite room in the house — the study. Ceiling-to-floor bookcases and cozy chairs just beckoned someone to sit in them and relax. Which is exactly what I did. This had been Dad's favorite room also.

I reached over and pulled out my favorite Ella Fitzgerald album, stuck it on the antique record player, and let the soft strands of "You'd Be So Easy to Love" float through the room.

I laid my head against the back of the chair and closed my eyes, trying to block out today. Crazy, crazy today.

Crazy, crazy last night.

And now my mom and Chase were catching up. Wasn't that just peachy?

My mom had gotten to know Chase when she chaired the prestigious Newhart Family Scholarship Fund. The fund offered a full-ride scholarship to someone in the community who'd risen above a hard upbringing and overcome challenges to excel in both academics and community service.

The committee had weeded out applicants from all over the city before choosing Chase Dexter as their man. My mom had nothing but good things to say about him after reading his application and sitting through an interview with him. "This boy," she would insist, totally oblivious to the fact that he'd made my high school years miserable. "He's someone to watch for. He's taken life by the horns."

Chase's mom had passed away when he was six. As soon as my mom found out about that, she began inviting Chase over for dinner. As in, all the time. I always tried to disappear, however. Chase and I went to high school together and—

"That is so awesome." Chase's voice rang through the room. "I've always loved this about your house."

I pulled one eye open. This could not be happening. But it was. My mom and Chase stepped into the room from behind a swiveling bookcase that offered a secret passageway from this room into the living room.

My dad had been a regular handyman, and when he redid the house, he added all kinds of quirky features, including a couple of secret passageways. One of the bookcases in this room could turn and become the bookcase in the family room.

My mother gawked when she spotted me in the chair. "Holly! I didn't realize you were in here. Especially since we have a guest over." Her voice subtly rose in pitch, her polite way of reprimanding me.

My mom still thought I was eight. Some things would never change. Nor would anything ever change how disappointed she was that I was . . . well, me.

"She had a long day. We had a run-in with a shooter, and she hit her head," Chase said.

"I just needed a minute," I told her.

"A shooter?" My mom gasped.

"It's a long story," I insisted. "But the good news is that I'm okay. No harm done, unless you count my dress."

Chase looked at me and then back at my mom. Why did it seem like he had some insight into our relationship that most people didn't?

Finally, he nodded toward my mom. "Well, I need to get to work. It was a pleasure seeing you, Mrs. Paladin. You too, Holly."

I fluttered my fingers in the air. "Bye, Chase." *Good riddance.*

Man, I was not in a good mood, was I? I had to be more gracious. It was what God would want me to do. To be forgiving and loving and accepting.

Besides, I was limited on time. So why live out my final days with a grudge?

I reminded myself that this was probably the last time I would see Chase Dexter in a long time. Sure, I might run into him on the job once in a while, but I would just keep it professional. Now that I knew he was back in town, I could prepare myself to deal with him more effectively.

"Thanks for everything, Chase," I muttered, glad to put this encounter behind me.

"Don't forget about your car," he called over his shoulder. "You don't want to leave it on the street overnight."

"I'll call the repair shop now."

Then I'd borrow my dad's old Ford F-150, grab a bite to eat, get back to work, and hopefully see what kind of information I could find out about the dead man at Katrina's house.

So much for staying home for the rest of the day.

CHAPTER 5

I met Jamie at some gluten-free pizza joint after I finished up work for the day. The place was located in an area of town appropriately called Mount Healthy. Jamie knew where all of the local organic restaurants were, but they were scattered all over the city. It didn't matter to her; she'd traverse deserts and climb mountains to get good food that fit her diet.

I wasn't going to eat there—no, my mom had cooked something, and I'd promised her I'd be home. I tried to honor her nightly ritual of eating together whenever possible. That was when there wasn't a fund-raising dinner or some other philanthropic activity going on. The scent of bubbly cheese and roasting vegetables from the wood-fire oven against the back wall made me question my commitment to eat at home, though.

"The police knocked down your door yet?" Jamie asked, taking a bite of her veggie pizza. She'd turned her life around two years ago and lost a hundred pounds. Ever since then, she was a health food nut.

The two of us had met in English class on our first day at the University of Cincinnati. We'd been inseparable since then. Her family had moved to the area only a few years ago from Pittsburgh, much to Jamie's dismay. She claimed they'd followed her here, afraid their only baby girl would get in trouble. They claimed that her father, a musician, had been offered a gig he just couldn't refuse.

I shook my head. "Not yet, but I've been watching over my shoulder all day."

"I thought you'd like to know that I did hear something over the police scanner this morning. Then I used my contacts at the newspaper to find out some more information."

I leaned closer, pressing my arms into the thick wooden tabletop. "Okay. You're leaving me in suspense here. I tried to find out stuff all day on my job, and everyone was tight lipped. I couldn't press too hard or people would get suspicious."

She put her pizza back on the plate and leaned closer, as well. "The guy was apparently shot three times. He had traces of some kind of drug in his system — not surprising. So many crimes in this area are, in some way, because of drugs."

"Was he related to Katrina?"

She shrugged and leaned back, picking a mushroom from the gooey cheese. "That, I haven't been able to find out. I did hear that a neighbor called the police. He saw the front door was open and got suspicious."

Oops. That would have been my fault. At least my mistake had meant I hadn't had to report the crime myself. It had also meant that the police now had my cleaning supplies.

How long did it take to run fingerprints and DNA through the system? My sister probably knew. I just had to think of a creative way to ask her.

Jamie raised her pizza again. "The bad news is that there was a suspicious van reported fleeing the scene."

The blood drained from my face as "Jailhouse

Rock" began blaring through the overhead. "Are you serious?"

She nodded. "Dead."

"Oh, Jamie. I had no idea." I bit back a frown.

"I willingly went with you, so the blame's on me. Still, I really don't want to have to explain all of this to the police."

"I'm going to make this all better, Jamie. I promise."

"It's going to be hard to do that from jail."

My jaw dropped open.

She waved her hand in the air in that sassy, sarcastic manner I should have been accustomed to by now. "I'm just kidding, girl. You keep quiet. They'll never discover you."

"You are not making me feel better."

"I'm giving you a dose of reality." She pulled out a bottle of vinegar from her purse and put a squirt in her water.

I tried not to turn my nose up. She insisted that vinegar in her water helped to keep her thin. I'd just keep drinking my lemon water, thank you very much.

I closed my eyes, fixating again on my problems instead of Jamie's vinegar water. "What am I going to do?"

"You can't do anything except wait . . . or turn yourself in." She took a long sip of her drink.

Guilt pounded harder. I struggled with guilt over small things, like bugs that flew into my windshield or the snake that accidentally got caught under the lawn mower. Those moments of guilt seemed gnat sized compared to the mountains of culpability I faced now. "If the police show up at your door, I'll explain everything, Jamie. I'll take the blame and make it clear that you had nothing to do with this."

She cocked her head to the side. "And if they don't believe you that you didn't murder anyone, why would they believe you when you say I had nothing to do with it?"

"Good point." I buried my face in the table. "I've made a huge mess, Jamie."

She patted my hand. "Yes, you have."

I sighed and pulled my head up. "I guess it's not your job to make me feel better."

"Most of the time, I'd say yes. But this one is all over my head, girlfriend. I don't even know what to tell you." She shook her head. "Why don't we change the subject? Anything else new?"

I frowned. The only other "thing" new that I could think of wasn't a happy thing. It was . . . "Chase Dexter is back in town."

My friend raised her skinny little eyebrow. "Who is Chase Dexter?"

"The guy I had a major crush on in high school."

Her eyebrow crept higher. "The one who looks like that actor who plays Thor?"

I frowned again. "Yeah, he's the one. He's on the police force here. I hope I don't end up working with him anymore."

"Would it be that awful?"

I shrugged. "Yes. Why would I want to work with someone who rejected me publicly?"

"Define 'rejected you publicly.'"

"He started dating this girl named Darcy Fitzgerald. Darcy announced to everyone in our calculus class that poor, pitiful little Holly Anna actually thought she had a chance with Chase."

"It doesn't sound like he publicly rejected you. It sounds like his girlfriend did."

"He had to tell her. Otherwise, how would she have known?"

"Not necessarily. Girls pick up on stuff like that."

"Well, he just laughed when she said it and looked at me with pure pity in his eyes. Either way, I don't want to work with him. He's always been arrogant and sure of himself and cocky—"

"After all of these years, he still gets to you." She shook her head, an amused look in her eyes.

"I just don't have any pleasant memories. That's all."

Her amused expression only strengthened. "Well, there's always Brian."

Brian Bieber . . . the guy everyone wanted me to date. Everyone in my family, at least. I supposed he was responsible with a steady job and a good reputation. Despite his unfortunate last name, there could be worse people to date. The only thing was that I didn't feel that spark with him. I wanted a spark. I wanted what I called a "Great Love," not just a mediocre imitation.

Despite that, I thought we could probably be happy together. We were most likely compatible. And, my impression was that Brian was interested. Okay, it was more than an impression. He often asked me to go with him as a date to various events around town. Whenever he tried to turn the conversation to something more serious, I quickly changed the subject.

Just as I would now. "Moving on . . ."

Jamie took a long sip of her drink just as the waitress walked by with some garlic knots. My stomach grumbled. I was getting hungry now. Great. I had to be home in an hour to eat. I hoped I could wait that long.

"How are you feeling lately?"

As if possibly being arrested for murder, running into my arch nemesis, and talking about rejection wasn't enough, the question of how I was feeling sobered me even more. I shrugged. "Mostly I'm doing okay."

Jamie raised her pizza and glanced over the top of it. "When are you going to tell your family?"

"The special election is only a couple of weeks away, and my sister's wedding is eight weeks away. When both of those are over, I'll tell them my news."

Three months ago, I'd been diagnosed with a very rare cancer called subcutaneous panniculitis-like T-cell lymphoma. It was an aggressive, fast-moving disease that meant I only had around a year to live. I could have treatments, but they'd only extend my life for a few months, plus they'd make me extremely sick in the process. I decided I wanted quality over quantity.

"I really think you should tell your family sooner."

We'd had this conversation before. "I know. But I'm waiting, and I feel okay about it. It's what I should do."

"Okay, you should get a second opinion, then."

"Two different labs looked at my blood work. Plus, my doctor said that so little is known about this disease that there are no specialists. I don't want to live in denial or fighting the inevitable."

"But the CT scan didn't show anything!"

"The doctor said this was normal with this type of cancer. The good news is that I feel great."

"Which is suspicious in itself." Jamie frowned.

43

I squeezed my friend's hand. "You worry too much."

"You don't worry enough."

"I'm not going to add any amount of quality to my life by worrying. Nor am I going to add anything to the life of my family by making them worry. What will be will be." And that was a great segue for me to leave. "Speaking of family, I've got to run."

I stood and grabbed my purse.

"Uh-huh," Jamie muttered. "No more random acts of kindness. Not without my approval. Do you understand?"

I smiled over my shoulder. "I hear you."

***

I pulled up at home and saw a truck in the driveway. Great. Who had my mom invited over for dinner now? She was always having some board member or city council representative over.

As I walked toward the front door, Mrs. Signet waved to me from her porch. She was a small woman with faded blonde hair that formed a poof around her face. It seemed like she'd been old for as long as I'd known her, but she hadn't slowed down any. Right now, she swept her porch.

"Did you hear about that skunkball?"

I paused, bracing myself for another urban legend. "Skunkball?"

She nodded, totally serious. "I got two emails about it. I forwarded one to you. Make sure you read it. These teens today. They're taking rags soaked in gasoline, lighting them up, and throwing them into cars stopped at red lights. Keep your eyes open."

One of the worst decisions I'd ever made was giving her my email address. She sent me virus-filled emails daily. "Yes, Mrs. Signet. Thanks for the warning."

She had a new urban legend every day, and in case I missed her email, she always made sure to mention them to me, as well. I tried to explain to her that most weren't real. I showed her websites that verified the inaccuracies of the emails. It didn't matter. She believed each one as if it were the Bible.

I pulled a hair behind my ear, ready to put on my presentable self and not embarrass my mother. I walked inside, inhaling a savory scent that only intensified my hunger, and plastered a grin across my face. As soon as I walked into the kitchen, my grin disappeared. Quickly.

Chase Dexter. What was he doing here?

He grinned, standing from his seat at the breakfast table. "Holly! Good to see you again." His voice rolled through the air, just as smoothly as ever.

"I'm glad you could make it." My mom worked at the kitchen counter, scraping the mashed potatoes into a cheerful bowl. "I'm just about to slice up some of that roast beef you love so much."

I dropped my bag on the bookshelf and resigned myself to sitting at the breakfast nook beside Chase. If I left, it would only look suspicious, and I'd end up making a bigger deal of things. Besides, my rules of etiquette instructed me to stay.

I looked at Chase. "This is quite the surprise."

"Your mom insisted I come over and catch up."

"Isn't it wonderful that he's back in town?" my mom called over her shoulder.

"Wonderful." I should have tried to muster more enthusiasm, but I just couldn't do it. Instead, I nodded forcefully.

"Before I forget, some woman called for you today, Holly," my mom said. "She didn't leave a message, just said she'd call back. Pleasant woman."

"Thanks." It was probably the nurse at my oncologist's office. They wanted me to keep having checkups, but why? I already knew the outcome.

Chase leaned back in his chair, picking up on the conversation he'd probably been having with my mom before I came. "And in other news . . . it looks like I'm being promoted to detective."

"You'll make a great detective," my mom crowed, pride beaming from her face.

I sure did wish she'd look at me like that. My dad had been the only one who'd understood me, and now he was gone.

"Didn't you just move here and start on the force?" I asked, hating to be the voice of reason here.

He grinned. Man, he *did* look like Thor. It was unfortunate—for my heart, anyway. At least he didn't have the killer Australian accent. "I did, but I accepted the job understanding that I'd be moved up to detective. They wanted me to start with patrol, so I could become more accustomed to the area first."

My mom set the roast beef on the table. "Now we really have a reason to celebrate."

I helped her with the rest of the food, trying desperately to think of an excuse to get out of this. Nothing acceptable came to mind. Finally, we all sat around the table, prayed, and dished out the food.

"So Chase, have you been assigned your first case

yet?" My mom adjusted a piece of parsley atop the corn.

Yes, she even garnished on nonspecial occasions.

Chase nodded. "I have. You'll never believe me if I tell you what it's about."

"Tell, tell." My mom raised her eyebrows.

I took a long sip of my sweet tea in an effort to bite my tongue. How did Chase always manage to cast a spell on my mom . . . and everyone else, for that matter?

"Someone cleaned this lady's house before killing her cousin."

I coughed, nearly spitting my tea out all over the table.

"Holly, are you okay?" My mom paused for long enough to eye me with disapproval.

I nodded. "I'm fine. I . . . I just thought maybe I was in the middle of a sitcom or something. Someone cleaning the house before a murder. What a calling card."

Chase nodded, taking a hearty serving of mashed potatoes. "Crazy, isn't it? Kind of a lame case, but I'm the new guy, so I'm stuck with it, I guess."

"I don't know. At least the killer has manners. Holly, you remember when your father was in the hospital, those ladies from church came over and cleaned our house and brought us food for a week?"

Boy, did I ever remember. They were the ones who'd inspired me to break into Katrina's. I bet they'd never anticipated I'd pay it forward as I had, though. I nodded.

"I'll never forget their kindness," my mom continued. "Sometimes a clean house and warm food is all you need to brighten your day. Too bad whoever did this couldn't have stopped there."

"It's a strange case. But we're trying to extract some evidence from the cleaning supplies now. The results should be back in a couple of days, and we hope to close in on this guy."

CHAPTER 6

I dropped my fork, and it clattered on the table.

"Holly? What has gotten into you?" my mom reprimanded.

I shook my head. "Just feeling a little clumsy today. I mean, the thought of a killer being that calm — calm enough to clean your home before murdering someone. It's disturbing. Are you sure the cleaning isn't unrelated to the crime?"

"You think someone else broke in and cleaned on the night there just happened to be a murder there?" Chase chuckled, a slab of roast beef poised to be eaten on his fork. "What kind of crazy coincidence would that be?"

I let out a feeble laugh. "Good point. That would just be crazy. Insane. Totally unbelievable."

I heard myself rambling, saw the strange look Chase sent my way, and stopped myself.

"Any good leads?" I asked instead. I pushed my food away, my appetite suddenly gone.

I tried to control the tremble that threatened to claim my entire body as I waited for his response. He had to finish chewing his dinner first, and he seemed to be savoring every bite.

"I can tell you what we've released to the press." He put his fork down and wiped his mouth with a napkin. "Right now our best lead, other than the cleaning supplies, is an old van that was sitting outside. One of the neighbors saw it. An old blue Toyota, probably an early 2000s model."

"Sounds like your friend Jamie's," my mom added, totally clueless.

"Yeah, it was Jamie's. She's a reporter by day, and serial cleaner by night," I muttered.

Everyone laughed, which should have helped my nausea. It didn't. This was awful.

How much time did I have until I was discovered? Maybe crossing off things on my bucket list should be kicked into hyperdrive.

"Enough of this talk about murder," Chase said. "What's new with you, Holly?"

Both my mom and Chase turned toward me, waiting for my response.

Oh, nothing. Just terminally ill. Possibly going to be framed for murder. On the verge of disgracing everyone in my life.

I shook my head. "Nothing. Absolutely nothing."

"Come now, there's got to be something new," Chase continued to prod.

"My life is pretty boring. I like it that way. Except for the skunkball."

Chase's eyebrows knit together in confusion. He opened his mouth as if to ask, when my mom rushed in. Thank goodness.

"If you're ever hiring more detectives, maybe you should consider Holly. She helped her friend solve that cold case involving the Mercer family." My mom raised her thin eyebrows and grinned, casting me a knowing glance.

Chase tilted his head. My mom just had to bring

that up. It was one of her most recent favorite stories to tell.

"The Mercer family, huh? I remember that case quite well. It wrapped up right about the time I came into town. Tell me more."

At least this beat talking about the other case I was currently involved with. I chased a piece of corn around my plate, trying to look hungry. "My friend, who was hired as a PI, actually solved it. I just helped her." More like, I just drove her around town while she was here. It had actually been fun, something off my bucket list: pretend to be Nancy Drew and solve a mystery. Done. I didn't need any more investigations in my life.

"That's amazing, Holly." Chase nodded, something close to admiration in his eyes.

"Isn't it?" My words didn't sound quite sincere.

Chase eyeballed me, a twinkle in his eyes. "I'm not so sure she'd make it through the police academy with the hair and nails, though."

I touched my curly locks. "No prissy police officers allowed? No problem, because I'm not interested."

"Oh, stop, Holly. She's being so humble." My mother let out a brittle laugh. "She's doing quite well for herself in social work. She's dating a nice guy—"

"Brian and I are not dating, Mom."

My mom laughed. "She's in denial. We all know they're dating."

I stabbed a piece of roast beef with no intention of eating it. "No, really, Mom. We're not dating."

"Okay. You're not dating." She said it unconvincingly—and unconvincingly on purpose. "She's also been volunteering down at the youth center once a week."

Chase smiled. "Sounds like a full, happy life."

I raised my tea glass. "Full and happy."

Chase's phone beeped. He glanced down at it, saw the number, and frowned. "Excuse me a minute."

When he stepped back a few minutes later, disquiet stained his features. "I think we have a lead on that minivan. I've gotta run."

"You'll come back again sometime, won't you?" my mom called.

"Anytime, Mrs. Paladin. Anytime." He leaned down and kissed her cheek before waving to me. "Good to see you, Holly."

I pushed my plate away as I forced my smile. "You, too."

But all I was thinking was: I was in a heap of trouble.

Jamie, too.

***

Five minutes later — a respectable amount of time, I thought — I excused myself from the dinner table, feigning a headache and hurrying to my room. My mom thankfully didn't ask any questions.

As soon as I was in my room with the door locked, I called Jamie. "Where are you?"

"I'm doing some research at the library. Why?"

"The police have a lead on the van at the scene last night," I whispered.

"What do you mean?" Her voice rose in pitch.

I did a quick rundown of dinner.

"You think the police are coming here?" A touch of

fear reached her voice.

"I don't know, Jamie. I have no idea. I'm going to ruin your life. I can't let that happen." I fell back on my bed and stared at the ceiling as tears pressed at my eyes.

"You're not going to ruin my life. It's like I said—I went along with your plan willingly."

At that, I had a moment of sudden clarity and sat back up. "I'm going to go tell the police what happened, Jamie. That's all there is to it. None of this was ever my intention."

Jamie softened her voice. "I know I was all encouraging you to talk to the police, Holly. Now I'm not so sure it's a good idea."

"Why?" Because she might be implicated?

"This is a murder investigation, Holly. You were there. No one's going to believe you're innocent."

"I don't even own a gun." My voice squeaked higher than I'd like to admit.

"It was Katrina's gun that was used at the scene."

"How do you know that?"

"I'm a reporter. I have my ways."

"So they'll think I took Katrina's gun and shot the man." I squeezed my eyes shut again.

"They could even believe your original story. Maybe you went there to do a random act of kindness. But what if you ran into the cousin, didn't recognize him—thought he was a threat, for that matter—and you grabbed Katrina's gun and shot him."

"You've got this all worked out, don't you?" I felt like I might pass out and began fanning my face.

"I just want you to think this through."

Another thought hit me with the force of a Mack

truck. "You don't think I did it . . . do you?" Her theory seemed pretty well thought out.

"No, of course not. I know you're innocent. I still remember you crying when we found that dead goose at the park that time. No way could you kill someone."

"No way am I going to let you take the fall, either."

I made up my mind. I was going to the police station. I had to own up to my part in all of this before I buried myself — or anyone else — any deeper.

CHAPTER 7

I stood at the reception area of the police station. I'd asked to talk to a detective, and the officer behind the desk had told me just one minute.

I began pacing, smoothing the folds of my dress. At least I'd look cute in my arrest photos.

A million thoughts rushed through my mind, and none of them were good. Well, the only good one was that I was doing the right thing, no matter how much the consequences would stink.

I'd probably be locked in jail, I realized. Maybe I should have told my family first? It was too late for that.

I shuddered to think about the process of being booked. As a social worker, I'd heard some horror stories.

I imagined spending my final days not with my family but with a cellmate named Big Annie who had gold teeth and a mean case of acid reflux.

When news spread, I was going to ruin my family's lives.

My brother had once told me that my optimism would be the death of me. He was right.

Chase burst through the door, a phone to his ear. He paused when he saw me and raised a finger, indicating I should wait.

"I see," Chase muttered into the phone. "I'll head

out there now. Thanks for the update."

He hung up and looked at me. His eyes were bright with curiosity. "Holly. What brings you here?"

I wiped my sweaty hands on my lavender dress. "I was going to talk to someone about—"

"Dexter, you hear about that van?" Another officer burst through the door, not slowing down.

"Justin just gave me the update. A convicted drug dealer sounds like a good lead to me."

Chase inched toward the exit, casting an apologetic glance my way. "Unfortunately, I don't have a lot of time. Is there anything I can do for you, Holly?"

My thoughts raced at such a dizzying pace that I nearly lost my balance. "Convicted drug dealer?"

He shrugged. "The van's owner. We think we have enough to bring him in for questioning."

My heart stuttered and time seemed to freeze.

They weren't going to arrest Jamie? Me?

Chase pointed toward the door. "I really do need to get going."

"I just wanted to . . ." To what? "You know what? I think I was overthinking something. I'm good."

Chase nodded and pointed toward the door. "All right, then. I've got to run."

***

An annoying chirp pulled me from a restless sleep the next morning. I popped one eye open and scowled at my cell phone. Who was calling at . . . I checked my alarm clock . . . 5:30 a.m.? Could there have been an emergency at work?

I checked the ID and saw that it was Jamie. My

friend never called me this early. I put the phone to my ear, making sure that my voice sounded especially pathetic so my friend could know she woke me.

"Hello?" I croaked.

"Turn on the news."

I sat up a little straighter when I heard the serious tone of her voice. "What?"

"No time for questions, just turn on the news."

I shrugged my sleep off, grabbed the remote from beside my bed, and flipped on the TV that sat on my dresser. The early morning news blared across the screen, and I came in halfway through the story.

". . . the Good Deeds Killer has struck again. Another man was found dead inside a home in Price Hill, three gunshot wounds to the chest. At both this scene and an earlier one, a mop and bucket were found and part of the house had been cleaned. The victim's name hasn't been released yet, pending notification of next of kin. The police are looking for any information on this crime. If you know anything, call . . ."

"Oh. My. Goodness," I whispered. So many thoughts raced through my mind that I could hardly make sense of any of them.

I listened as the news anchor offered some information on the first victim. His name was Dewayne Harding, he was twenty years old, and he'd grown up in the area. Friends said he was bright and always up for a good time, and that he wouldn't hurt a flea.

I blanched when I saw his face. Sure enough, he was the same man I'd seen on Katrina's bathroom floor.

"What's going on, girl? This is crazy."

"*Crazy* is an understatement . . . she said feeling dumbfounded." I stared at the TV, something close to shock numbing my body and mind.

I was still sleeping, and this was a nightmare. That had to be it. No way was this actually happening.

I'd just settled on that thought when Jamie said, "Someone is copying what happened at the last murder. They know about the fact that you came and cleaned, and they want to keep that as a pattern."

My heart thudded in my chest. "Why would someone do that?"

"To frame you?"

"Why would someone do *that*?"

"Why would someone want to frame you? Girlfriend, do I really need to answer that? To get the attention off of themselves, of course."

The familiar feeling of nausea gurgled in my stomach. What had I done? The even bigger question— how was I going to fix it?

I had no idea. But just when I thought things couldn't get worse, they had. Big-time.

The killer knew about me. And as soon as the evidence was processed at the lab, there was a good chance my fingerprints or DNA would be found.

"Are you still there?" Jamie asked.

"Yeah, I'm still here." I wished I weren't, though. I really wished I weren't.

CHAPTER 8

By the time I showered and got downstairs, my brother and sister were there. They came over once a month to have breakfast with Mom. I usually fixed my "famous" coffee cake, and my mom made freshly ground coffee. We'd all catch up for a few minutes before heading in different directions. It was a nice little ritual that ensured we all kept up with each other.

My sister and brother were older by quite a bit: Alex by ten years and my brother by eight. Alex was an assistant district attorney for the city and was getting married in a couple of months. My brother Ralph had been married, but his wife had died in a car accident only six months after they said, "I do."

That had happened twelve years ago when Ralphie was twenty-four, and I was only sixteen. It all seemed surreal. Ralph said he was never going to get married again and instead threw everything into his career. He'd been a high school principal before running for the school board. That had lasted five years, just enough time to give him a real hunger for politics.

"Did you hear?" my sister asked, downing a sip of coffee.

My sister was what most people called "The Total Package." She was blonde, thin, smart, savvy, confident, and successful. Pretty much, she was perfect. She'd been homecoming queen, been listed on more

"Who's Who" lists than I could count, had graduated from Harvard, and owned a gorgeous house in the suburbs.

I lowered myself into a chair. I'd normally help my mom serve the food, but today my brain spun at a dizzying pace. I just needed to sit for a moment.

"Hear what?" Ralph grabbed a banana from the center of the table.

My brother was tall and thin and wore plastic-framed glasses. He had a love for sweater-vests and was kind of nerdy cute, I supposed. I mean, he wasn't cute to me, of course.

"About that Good Deeds Killer they're talking about on the news?" Alex continued. "There are sick people in this world. That's all I'm saying."

"You see the worst of them," my mom added, thrusting some coffee into my hands.

I hoped my gaze said the appropriate amount of "thank you."

"You're right." Alex slid a bite of cake into her mouth, leaving not as much as a crumb on her perfectly plum lipstick. "I do see the worst offenders. So the fact that I even think this killer is messed up should tell you a lot."

"This guy has a calling card — cleaning supplies. I really don't get that. Is he cleaning up the crime scenes before the police get there?" Ralph asked.

Alex shook her head. "From what I heard, no. The crime was executed in a different part of the house. It's like the killer wants to be nice to make up for their evil. *Sorry about killing your loved one. Let me clean part of your house so you can more easily accept visitors who come to offer their condolences in the aftermath of what I've done.*"

"This might be the time to think about getting an alarm system." My mom sat at the table.

Ralph prayed for the food, and then we all dug in. The time frame we had was limited, so everyone ate fast and talked even faster.

"The house where the first crime took place was actually the home of someone on my caseload," I offered. It would seem weird if they found out later and I hadn't shared.

Everyone in my family seemed both impressed and horrified.

I still felt like I was living in an alternate reality. I'd dug a hole for myself and fallen in, and now I had no idea how to get out without pulling other people in with me.

"Let's talk about something happy," Alex suggested.

"I have good news," Ralph announced. "I'm up by six percentage points. If no skeletons from my past come out, I think I'm going to be able to take this election."

My hole got deeper.

My mom laughed. "Skeletons? In your closet? I don't see that happening. You have a squeaky-clean past."

"It's amazing the things the media can dig up." Ralph frowned.

More of the imaginary dirt in my hole was thrown to the surface. I felt claustrophobic even thinking about it.

The media liked to talk about Melinda—Ralph's wife. The whole story of her death had been a gut-wrenching human-interest story that made people instantly like my brother Ralph.

"I thought I'd also add that Rex Harrison is a scumbag," Ralph said. "He's going to dig up whatever dirt he can. I have no doubt about that. He'll make up dirt if he has to."

"Dirty is as dirty does," Alex agreed. "I don't care if everyone else in the city thinks it's great that he used to be a cop, a public servant. Some people are cops to serve people; others because they want power. I know what category I'd put Rex into."

"Maybe it doesn't matter," Ralph said. "I heard his campaign is in serious financial trouble. At least, that's what Brian said a couple of weeks ago."

"All right, enough about this. Holly, name one new thing with you," my mom encouraged.

I shook my head, running a napkin over my lips. "Nothing new here. Same old, same old."

"Did you all hear that Chase Dexter is back in town?" My mom's eyes sparkled as she glanced at Alex and Ralph.

"Good old Chase," Ralph said. "I haven't seen him in years."

"I did hear that he was working for the police department, on the fast track to becoming a detective," Alex said. "He looks like one of those made-for-TV detectives, doesn't he?"

"Don't let William hear you say that," my mom laughed.

William was Alex's fiancé. He was a general surgeon at a nearby hospital. My sister, also known as "Alex the Great," lived what I called a charmed life.

"He's always reminded me of that guy who plays Thor," Ralph added.

Why did everyone always say that? Chase wasn't *that* handsome. I mentally snorted.

That's when I realized everyone was staring at me. Maybe that snort hadn't been mental.

"You don't think he's handsome?" Alex grinned, a sparkle in her eyes.

I shrugged. "I think he's arrogant."

"Don't tell Brian that Holly has a crush on Chase Dexter. He'll be mopey for weeks," Ralph said.

"First of all, I don't have a crush on Chase. Second of all, Brian and I are just friends. There's nothing to be mopey over. Third of all—"

"Keep telling yourself that. All of it. All of your dozens of reasons. We all know the truth." Ralph stood, chugging another sip of coffee. "Okay, I've got to run. I've got a meeting with Brian." He threw me a smile.

"We're just friends," I repeated in a singsong tone that I often used to hide my annoyance.

"Keep telling yourself that. You're going with him to the fund-raising gala, right?" Ralph slipped his coat on.

I nodded. I'd forgotten about that. Brian had asked me a few weeks ago. We both needed a date, so I'd said yes. Going together just made sense, since Brian had to be there anyway. He was Ralph's campaign manager.

My family liked to give me a hard time for a multitude of reasons. But one thing they really liked to tease me about was the fact that I'd had this crazy idea in high school to save my first kiss for the man I married. And that didn't mean the man I was engaged to, even. It meant that on my wedding, after I said, "I do," I'd kiss the man I'd spend the rest of my life with. So, it was true that I'd never been kissed.

I'd been engaged once, but my fiancé had broken it off. So, one of the things on my bucket list was to fall in love. To experience my first kiss.

I was up in the air about it all, truth be told. I'd realized when I'd almost gotten married that having not kissed my fiancé led my thoughts to dwelling more on my kiss than I did on my future marriage. While I could still see good aspects of dating that way, I couldn't say it was definitely for me. It did seem like a shame to die without ever experiencing my first kiss.

"That's great that you're going together." Ralph smoothed the front of his argyle sweater. "Someone from the newspaper asked if we could get a family photo for a feature they're running. You guys all good with that?"

We all nodded.

Alex stood, downing one last bite of coffee cake. "I've got to go prep for a court date. I'll see everyone at the gala."

"I've got a board meeting so we can raise money for that new children's hospital," my mom added.

I felt like I needed to contribute something. "I've got mounds of paperwork that I need to do, even though I really need to do home visits."

Everyone — except me — rushed out the door. I sat there a moment, dumbfounded.

If I admitted the fact that I was at the first crime scene, I might single-handedly ruin Ralph's campaign. Maybe I'd come forward *after* the election. If the police didn't catch onto me by then, I'd go to them myself. That was all there was to it.

I collected the plates, put them in the sink, and then got to work.

It was time to face my boss, Doris Blankenship, a.k.a. the Devil.

As if my life couldn't get worse.

***

I'd finished up my paperwork — piles of bureaucracy, if you asked me — in the morning, and right now I sat on the couch of Edna Edmond's house. I'd been doing home visits with her for the past six months. She had custody of her four grandchildren, and she'd have liked to have permanent guardianship.

"Are you okay, child? You seem distracted today." The grandmotherly lady had puffy wrinkles under her eyes and painfully unnatural red hair. She was thin, spoke in a gravelly voice, and always had cookies around.

I jerked my head toward her. "I'm so sorry, Mrs. Edna. I guess I just had a long day yesterday."

"You make sure you get enough rest now, you hear me? Enough sleep is my secret to a long life. That's what I always say."

I smiled. If she only knew my situation. "I'll keep that in mind."

"You stay safe out there, too. This world is getting crazy." She shook her head back and forth in long, heavy swings.

I stiffened. "I guess you heard about the murder a couple of streets over."

"Murders aren't unusual in this area. I know that — I've been around the block a couple of times. But this guy just sounds creepy. He cleaned that woman's house before shooting her cousin." Her voice rose along with her thin eyebrows.

I swallowed hard. "I know. That's crazy, isn't it?"

"You were her social worker, weren't you?"

I licked my lips. "I can't discuss that."

"I know you are." She waved a hand in the air and grunted. "I've talked to Katrina before. One of her boys is in school with one of my granddaughters. We both think you're the bee's knees. We have the best social worker in the area. Some of the people who work for your agency—you can tell they don't really care. You're the real deal, though."

Great, another person I'd disappoint if I were found out. I croaked out a "Thank you."

"I've also heard that Frank Jenkins has been talking trash about you all over town."

I shifted in surprise. There was a name I hadn't heard in a while.

Frank Jenkins was a man I'd always suspected of hitting his children. He had a nasty temper and a drinking problem, and was oblivious to it all. His kids had been taken away from him and placed in a foster home where they were now thriving. He desperately wanted them back.

He'd turned all of his rage toward me. He'd made threats, called me names, told me I'd get my payback.

As scary as it sounded, the whole scenario had slipped my mind.

Could he be the one behind the bullets that had flown my way while I stood on the porch with Chase?

I called in sick from work for the rest of the day. Partially because I was making myself mentally sick with anxiety. The other part was the disease ravaging my body.

Really, the best medicine I could get right now was talking to Jamie. I just hoped she was available.

***

"You're going to have a mental breakdown if you don't do something," Jamie said.

I stared at my friend as she sat on the couch across from me at my mom's place. "If I go down, my family's going down with me. Look, I've been thinking about it, and telling the police that I was there won't help anyone. I have no idea who the killer is. I saw nothing. I know nothing."

"But the bucket and mop . . ."

"Originally, I worried that by me leaving it there, I'd be wasting the police's time. That they'd be investigating something that wasn't integral. But now that the killer left his own mop and bucket, that's not really the case."

Jamie sat cross-legged on the couch wearing utility-style khakis and a long-sleeved black T-shirt. "The guilt is eating you alive, Holly. I can see it on your face."

I shook my head, knowing I was spiraling down into a pit I might not get out of. For a moment, this had all made me forget about my terminal illness, and that was a feat within itself.

I sighed and flipped on the TV. The news should be on, and I wanted to hear if there were any updates on the investigation.

As I expected, this story was front and center. A possible serial killer in the city grabbed headlines.

"The victim has been identified as twenty-one-year-old Anthony Stevens, who lived in the 2800th block of

Hawthorn Avenue."

I froze. Again. I didn't know why I didn't think anything could shock me, but life continued to do just that.

"That's one of my clients' houses," I mumbled. "I was a caseworker for that family."

Jamie put her hand on my knee. "Girlfriend, are you serious?"

I nodded.

Why did I suddenly feel like I was being framed? I'd walked into the middle of a murder, and now my life was inevitably woven with the real killer's.

Just then, the doorbell rang. Who would be coming over now?

I pulled the door open. When I saw Chase standing there, I knew I'd been discovered.

CHAPTER 9

"Holly." He nodded stiffly. "Sorry for stopping by unannounced. You mind if I come in for a minute?"

He was being awfully kind, especially considering he was about to arrest me. I glanced beyond him. I didn't see the flashing lights of any police cars. At least he hadn't brought the entire squad with him.

I pulled the door open. "Of course. Come in. Can I get you coffee?"

I wasn't sure why I sounded so calm. I'd fallen back into my old habits of being a polite and proper hostess without even trying. My etiquette book would be proud, but my conscience . . . not so much.

"I will take some coffee, if you don't mind. I've been up all night working this case."

A lump formed in my throat. "It sounds like a real doozy."

I closed the door and directed him to the couch, introducing him to Jamie and letting the two of them chat for a moment while I both cleared my head and started a pot of java.

Everything would be okay, I told myself. Despite what felt like the impossible, I'd get through this. Eventually my family might forgive me. I might even forgive myself. I'd been praying every day, over and over, that God would forgive me.

Maybe it was simply time to face the music, so to

speak.

I poured a mug of steaming liquid and carefully set it on the table beside Chase. He and Jamie were talking merrily, as if they'd known each other for years. Of course, Jamie was like that. She could talk to anyone, which really came in handy as a reporter.

I lowered myself into a chair across from Chase, trying to accept my fate. Maybe owning up to all of this would really be the best thing for me. Jamie was right—I was on the brink of a breakdown.

I wiped my hands on my dress, disguising the action as smoothing the wrinkles of my skirt. "So, to what do I owe the honor of this visit?"

He looked very stiff and proper in his seat—like he wasn't comfortable. And Chase Dexter always looked comfortable.

This wasn't a good sign.

"You've heard about who the media is dubbing as the 'Good Deeds Killer'?"

I nodded, willing myself to breathe so I wouldn't pass out. "I have."

"In the course of my investigation today, I discovered that you were a social worker for both families who were affected by the crime."

I nodded slowly. "I just saw that on TV and realized I was connected with the second family as well."

"When I realized that—"

I braced myself, imagining putting my wrists together so the handcuffs could go on.

"I wondered if you might be able to offer any insight."

What? Was this a trap? Was he for real?

"Holly? Did you hear me?"

I snapped out of my stupor. "What?"

"I wondered if you might know something that connects the families, since you were working with both of them."

"How . . . how'd you know I was working with them both?"

"We found your business card, for one thing. We called your former boss at CPS, and she approved us talking to you. Is that a problem?"

I shook my head, stealing a quick glance at Jamie. "No, no problem. I'll do whatever I can to help."

"I figured you would." He leaned toward me, elbows on his knees. "Is there anything you can think of, Holly, that would link those two families—besides you?"

I sighed and looked off in the distance. What would connect those families, other than me? The police had to know most of what I knew already, though.

"I can only speak about Katrina and Bernice. Both of the women had spouses who abandoned them. Then again, most of the kids growing up in lower-class homes don't have male role models. Many of them have been abandoned by their fathers."

Chase nodded. "Anything else?"

"Dewayne was just visiting Katrina, so I never met him before. There's not a lot I can say."

"Does the Praetorian Guard mean anything to you?" Chase asked. "And I'm not talking about the one from ancient Roman times."

I stared at him a moment. "I've heard of them. I mean, everyone around here has." They were a violent street gang that the police had been trying to bring down for years. Instead of them disbanding under the threat of arrest, that possibility seemed to bring them closer. "You think this is because of the gang?"

Chase nodded. "There are rumors that both were involved in the gang. No one's owning up to it, though."

"Most parents don't want to admit that, I suppose. Although, to find their kids' killer they might."

"Unless they're being threatened."

I let my head drop back slightly. "Unless they're being threatened."

Chase tilted his head. "I wondered if you might be willing to talk to your former clients."

"They're not going to tell me anything, Chase. Even though I'm not a CPS investigator anymore, they're afraid I'll take their kids away from them."

"Maybe if they thought their safety was at risk, you could convince them to talk—for the sake of their kids. You know they don't trust the police. As soon as they spotted me coming their way, they clammed up. But you have a way with people."

"A way with people?" Had he just given me a compliment? That was strange because I had the impression he thought I was a total loser.

"Yeah, you're sweet and kind. People take to that. They know you're a good listener." He shifted, but his eyes never left me. "So, what do you say?"

I nodded, hoping my cheeks didn't heat. "Of course. I'll do whatever I can to help with this investigation."

A grin spread across his face. "Thank you. Whatever you do, don't put yourself in any danger. I think I know you well enough to know that you're not the risk-taker type. You always think things through."

I had been that type—up until the point in time

when I'd been given a year to live. Apparently, I thought that gave me a year to make stupid decisions. I'd learned my lesson, but I feared I might be too late.

"Of course. I'm Holly I-always-think-twice Paladin." And I usually was thought out, responsible, the one everyone depended on. My timing just happened to be lousy.

He stood. "Nice to meet you, Jamie."

She grinned a little too widely. "You too, Chase."

He turned toward me and offered a curt nod. "I'll be in touch, Holly."

As soon as he was gone, I turned to Jamie. Neither of us needed to say anything to know the other's thoughts. This was horrible. Just horrible.

I plopped down and stared at my friend, knowing her emotions mirrored mine. We'd known each other long enough to not have to say anything sometimes.

I raised my palms in shock. "I know, right?"

Jamie fanned her face before nodding in agreement. "Absolutely. He's totally hot."

My mouth sagged open. "Jamie! That's not what I was talking about!"

She shrugged dramatically. "What? He wasn't what I expected. Seriously, the way you described him, I thought he was a Neanderthal whose knuckles drug the ground and who spoke in grunts."

I hated to describe myself as stupefied again, but . . . "Did you hear a word he said? Do you realize what's going on?"

The smile disappeared from her face as she nodded. "Yeah, unfortunately, I did."

I stared into space, my thoughts churning. Jamie moved over to sit beside me and patted my knee.

"Look, you're one of the best secret keepers I know. Someone who can keep the fact that she has cancer from her family definitely knows how to stay quiet. I'll trust your judgment if you think you need to keep your mouth shut on this, too. I just don't want you to get into bigger trouble later."

"Thanks, Jamie. I appreciate that."

"That's what friends are for."

CHAPTER 10

"How are you, Katrina?" I leaned toward my former client, a weird range of emotions circling inside of me. There was some guilt, compassion, anxiety, and concern, all rolled into one super storm.

I'd stopped by to visit her, partly because Chase had asked and partly because I was genuinely concerned about her well-being. I had to admit that being in this house after what had happened last time I was here left me unbalanced. Every time I closed my eyes, I felt the surge of worry I'd felt when I'd broken in. I felt the satisfaction of cleaning and trying to help a sister out. I felt the horror of finding the dead body.

But right now wasn't about me. It was about Katrina. I had to stay focused.

She wiped her eyes. "I guess I'm okay, Ms. Paladin. I don't know. I don't know nothing anymore."

Her voice held an odd mix of urban hip and Appalachian. She was one of the people in this area who had moved up to find jobs after everything dried up in the mountains of Kentucky and West Virginia. Sometimes, it felt like this neighborhood was a subculture in and of itself.

I leaned toward her and squeezed her hand. The woman was young, and she looked young—too young to have four children. She'd worked as a stripper to pay bills at one point, only giving it up so she could keep her kids. But working in a grocery store didn't pay nearly as well as baring her skin.

"Were you close to your cousin?"

She shook her head, running a blue-tipped fingernail under her eyes. "He was only staying with me for the week. His mom kicked him out. Said he'd been up to no good and she'd had enough of him. She would've changed her mind. She always does."

I handed her a tissue. "Tell me about your cousin. Dewayne."

She wiped under her eyes again with the tissue I'd given her. "Underneath everything, he was a good guy. He just got mixed up with the wrong crowd. You know how that can be."

"What do you mean by *wrong crowd*?" I asked.

She shrugged. "Just kids who weren't trying to stay on the straight and narrow. Not bad kids, necessarily. Just kids who seemed to like trouble."

"It wasn't a gang, was it?"

Her eyes widened, and she hung her head toward the floor a moment. "I feared he might be involved in one. He'd been gone a lot lately, you know? I asked him what he was up to, and he'd always give me the same answer. 'Same old, same old.' He was working at the fast food place down the street, but he was bringing in some big money. He'd bought a new phone, a new watch, expensive sunglasses."

"And you have no idea where he got the money for it?"

"No idea. He wouldn't tell me." She suddenly straightened, looking startled. "You're not going to take my kids away from me, are you? Just because I let him stay here?"

I shook my head. "That's not why I'm here. I'm just trying to figure out how you are."

The first hint of a smile tugged at her lips. She ran a hand through her bleached-blonde hair, exposing dark roots underneath. "You're always so nice, Ms. Paladin. You've been a real lifesaver. I know you were the one who paid for Reggie to be able to play basketball at the rec center. The receptionist didn't want to tell me, but I finally got it out of her that the person who'd paid was wearing a frilly dress. I knew it was you."

I contemplated whether or not I should own up to it, but I finally nodded. "I'm not really supposed to get involved with things like that. But I know you're trying hard to do right by your kids. I just wanted to give you a helping hand."

"Reggie's having a great time playing ball. It keeps him off the streets."

"Exactly." That had been my thought behind it. If you kept some of these kids occupied, they stayed out of trouble. It was when they had too much time on their hands that they connected with the wrong people. They needed to find positive peer groups.

"Dewayne did like to play basketball, also. He always went to that new court down on Eighth."

"I heard about it. Orion Enterprises donated the money to build it." I only knew that fact because Jamie had covered opening day for the newspaper. Orion Vanderslice had made quite the impression on her—in a bad way. She'd thought he was rich, arrogant, and stuck up. Yet, when the cameras came on, he became a different person.

Katrina let out an uneven sigh. "I just can't imagine who would do this. What really scares me is that this person has struck again. Another young man with his whole life ahead of him has gone to meet his maker too soon."

"Did your cousin ever hang out with that other boy? Anthony?"

"You mean, the other boy who was killed?" Katrina shrugged. "I wish I could tell you, but I have no idea. He didn't exactly bring his friends over here to meet the family."

"Did he say anything to indicate someone was angry with him?"

Katrina raised one eyebrow. "You're not working for the police or something, are you?"

My cheeks heated. "I just want to make sure you and your kids are safe."

"No, he didn't say anything to me. But you could talk to his mom, Desiree. She might have some names for you."

***

That evening after work, my mom dropped me off so I could pick up my Mustang—the girl looked as good as new—and then I went to the youth center where I volunteered once a week. As a June Cleaver wannabe, I stood out like the proverbial sore thumb, but that didn't stop me from coming here and usually bringing homemade cookies, to boot.

The center was located in an old strip of shops that time hadn't treated well. A small convenience store stood on the corner, if your idea of convenience was alcohol and cigarettes, the main staples here. There was also a bar—the dark, seedy kind with no windows—

across the street and a diner-style restaurant a few doors down.

The location wasn't great, but it was right in the heart of where the kids lived. Plus, the rent was cheap and part of the parking lot had been turned into a basketball court.

Abraham Willis ran the center. He'd gone to a local Christian college, seen the need for something like this in the area, and felt God leading him to open the place. That was six years ago.

Abraham was here almost every day, and he worked tirelessly for little pay. Whenever I could, I tried to anonymously send him and his wife gift cards for restaurants or even groceries, in an effort to make their lives a little easier. His wife, Hannah, stayed home with their little one-year-old boy, Levi, and I knew money was really tight.

While Abraham played basketball with some of the guys, I usually stayed inside and helped the girls with their homework. When I wasn't tutoring, I helped them make cookies or we talked about boys or we did our nails. I liked it when I could get the girls apart from the guys because when they were together, all they wanted to do was flirt.

The relationships I'd developed here seemed unlikely, but I was appreciative of each of the girls I'd gotten to know. I wanted to see them succeed and not fall into the cycle of poverty and crime, as I'd seen it happen so many times. I wanted them to know that there was more to the future than drugs and violence and gangs. Most of all, I didn't want them to be on my caseload one day.

Of course, now that wouldn't be a problem. But

when I'd started here, that had been my primary thought.

"Ms. Holly," someone yelled in the distance.

I looked over and spotted the teen affectionately known as Little T. Little T was anything but little. At sixteen, he already stood well over six feet and was built like a linebacker. He had a deep, booming voice and an infectious personality. He was the type that seemed ripe for trouble, like someone with a wandering eye who always looked for new opportunities.

For some reason, he was particularly fond of me and always went out of his way to talk. He put his phone down for long enough to give me his little handshake, high five, one-handed patty-cake, give-the-dog-a-bone routine.

"What's going on, Little T?"

"Did you bring cookies?"

I held out the plate. "Of course."

He grinned and snitched one. His eyes closed in delight when he took the first bite. "Can I marry you?"

"I'm too old for you, Little T." We'd had the playful discussion before.

"But I want to eat these cookies forever."

"You just worry about keeping yourself out of trouble. Then you'll meet a good woman and settle down. When you do that, I'll teach your wife how to bake cookies like these. How does that sound?"

He grinned. "It's a deal."

"Wait. Don't hurry away yet. I heard about those two boys who were shot. Did you know them?"

He nodded. "We had some mutual friends, you could say."

"So, Dewayne and Anthony were friends?"

"Yeah, I guess they ran in the same circles."

"Man, losing two friends in a week. That's rough. How are you holding up?"

He glanced out the window. "Hard to say. Lot of people is scared, wondering if someone's going after people in our group. Maybe they're targeting us."

"Why would you think that?"

His gaze swung back toward me. "Isn't it obvious? Two of them dead."

I tried to choose my words carefully. "You have any idea who's behind it, Little T? I don't want to see you get hurt."

He shrugged. "Everyone has their theories."

"What's yours?"

He shrugged again. "There's this guy."

I leaned closer. "Okay."

"I don't know who he is. They call him Caligula. I guess he calls a lot of shots."

"Caligula? You mean, like the Roman emperor?" If my memory served me correctly, he was not only an emperor, but he was evil, causing a lot of suffering among his people. One thing I knew for sure: he wasn't known for bringing anything good.

"Beats me."

I needed to refresh my memory on Roman history. This wasn't the time, though. "So, this Caligula is a gang leader, essentially?"

He glanced from side to side. "I could get into trouble for telling you this."

"No one's listening, Little T, except for me."

He swallowed hard, and I feared he'd clam up. Instead, he blurted, "All the drugs go through him.

He's loaded, and he's got a whole army of dealers who do his bidding for him. He's the one who came up with Cena. He created it, he makes it, he sells it."

"Wow. And you don't know who he is? If you know, maybe the police can—"

"You're on the popo's side?"

I raised my hands. "I didn't say I was on anyone's side. I'm on the side of justice. If someone is killing people, he needs to be behind bars."

"I only started talking to you because I thought I could trust you."

"You can trust me, Little T. I don't want anyone getting hurt."

"Well, no one knows who he is. He has people that do his bidding for him. All I know is that I need to stay away. And, if you're smart, you will, too."

***

After the kids had cleared out, I stuck around for a few minutes to talk to Abraham, the director. I found him in the game area putting away the Ping-Pong paddles and balls. He was in his midthirties with thin, dark brown hair and a pudgy stomach. He'd been a high school basketball player at one time, but middle age had apparently gotten the best of him. Still, the kids here liked him and trusted him.

He looked up when I trudged into the room. "Holly. What are you still doing here?"

I paused by the foosball table and propped my hip there. "Just wanted to check in. How are things going here?"

He smiled wearily, latching the box where he kept

the sports equipment. "You doing the social worker thing?"

I shook my head. "Just the friend thing."

He sighed and straightened, exhaustion showing in the circles under his eyes. "Overall, we're doing fine. I wish I could concentrate just on running the center and not on trying to raise funds for it and doing all the paperwork. I guess that comes with the territory, though."

He began straightening chairs against the wall as we spoke. I knew I should help, but he wasn't the only one feeling exhausted. I needed to up my vitamin intake or something. I hoped my weariness wasn't a sign of the cancer's progress.

I crossed my arms, hoping to sound more casual than I felt. "I know this might sound kind of strange, but have you noticed anything unusual about the kids lately?"

He threw me a curious look. "Not especially. Why do you ask?"

I shook my head again. "I'm just curious. You know, with everything that's been happening around town lately and all."

"I know. Those murders are pretty crazy, aren't they? I mean, what kind of freak cleans up before murdering someone?"

I nodded, hoping my cheeks didn't heat and that I didn't give any other telltale sign of my involvement. "Exactly. Have you ever heard of Caligula?"

He shook his head. "The Roman emperor?"

"No, a gang leader who goes by the same name."

"I can't say I have. Why?"

I shrugged it off. "Just wondering. I like to keep my

pulse on things going on in the community. What affects one person affects us all."

"It's true. If I hear anything, I'll let you know. I want to keep these kids away from stuff like that. But if the DEA hasn't been able to stop America's drug problem, I have my doubts that I'm going to be able to either."

"Even if you just help one person make wise decisions, it's worth it."

I turned to walk away when Abraham called my name. I paused.

"By the way, Hannah and I may be taking a trip out of town. If we do, I was wondering if you might cover for us here?"

I nodded. "Sure, I'd be happy to help. When's the trip?"

"Maybe in a couple of weeks. We'll have to see how it all works out."

"Going anywhere exciting?"

He grinned. "The Bahamas, I hope."

I tried to keep any judgment out of my mind. But I couldn't believe that Abraham could afford a trip to the Bahamas. He and Hannah lived in a run-down apartment, drove a fifteen-year-old car, and never ate out because of the cost.

Where did he get the money for that? Unless . . .

I mentally shook off the thoughts. No way was Abraham in some way involved with this whole drug thing. I mean, sure, he had access to a lot of the kids around here, but he would never do something like that. I felt ashamed for even thinking the thought.

"Sounds nice," I finally said.

"Yeah, I think it will be good for us."

"Just let me know the dates."

Then I slipped outside, trying to put my thoughts to rest. Too bad that was easier said than done.

CHAPTER 11

I desperately wanted to stop by and visit Katrina's cousin, Desiree, the mother of the first young man who'd died and whose image I couldn't get out of my mind. But my schedule was more hectic than I'd like to admit.

I'd already taken off work the next morning for a meeting with my oncologist. However, I canceled the appointment at the last minute. I didn't want to hear what he had to tell me. Was I living in a bubble? Was I too comfortable with my ignorant bliss?

Or what if Jamie was right? What if I was just in denial? I very well could be. But who wanted to truly own up to the facts of dying? I certainly didn't.

Life was easier if I just pushed ahead, kept going, and made the most of my days.

I had my own little end-of-life plan worked out in my mind. I didn't want to be poked and prodded and scrutinized. If the pain ever became too unbearable, I'd request some medication to help with it. I didn't want my final days to be filled with unbearable suffering.

No, I wanted to be surrounded by friends and loved ones.

Instead of going to work, I'd stopped by the post office to mail a vintage surfing record I'd found at a thrift store to my cousin Chad, and when I stepped out onto the sidewalk, I paused.

A chill washed over me as I felt someone watching me. I looked over in time to see a man in a suit. He stood on the corner, his cell phone to his ear, but his eyes were on me. A strange smile curled his lips before he nodded at me and walked away.

My chill deepened.

Who was that? Why was he watching me? Coincidence? I didn't think so.

I hiked my purse higher and fell into step behind him. I wanted to see where he was going. If Jamie were with me, she'd know exactly what I needed to do to trail someone. I had no idea, though.

I paused at the corner and peered around it just in time to see an old Cadillac pull out.

Just like the one I'd seen the day I was shot at.

Had the man gotten inside it? I glanced toward my Mustang. It was parked two blocks away. There was no way I'd get to it in time to follow the car.

I squinted, trying to see the license plate. It was no good.

Just then, something hit the ground by my feet.

A bullet.

I was being shot at, I realized.

Again.

CHAPTER 12

I ducked around the corner, using the edge of the brick building for cover as more bullets flew through the air.

Around me, people screamed and ran. A mom and her teenage son hid behind the car in front of me. Two other people threw themselves into the space beside me. Panic pushed others down the street, scattering them like autumn leaves in a savage wind.

A car squealed away in the distance.

I waited a moment. My heart raced as I realized what had just happened.

With trepidation, I peered around the brick wall, trying to get a fleeting glimpse of the driver.

I couldn't see anything. The windows were too dark, too tinted.

Why was someone after me? What sense did that make?

Maybe that shooting the day Chase had been with me wasn't a coincidence.

I remembered what Edna had said about Frank Jenkins. Could he be behind this? The man I'd seen on the corner wasn't Frank, but could he be a cohort?

Once the car disappeared from sight, I stepped out. I rushed toward the mom across from me. "Are you okay?"

She nodded. "I think so."

"He's gone," I told her. "I'm going to call the police."

Less than five minutes later, two cruisers showed up, as well as an ambulance and a fire truck. Ten minutes later, four more police cars were on the scene. Twenty minutes after the shooting, Chase arrived.

It was my lucky day.

"Holly, you're here?" Chase said, squinting in thought.

I nodded. "Gun-wielding crazies seem especially fond of me lately."

Another man stood beside Chase, his hands on his hips and his chest puffed out. I soaked him in.

The man wasn't necessarily tall, but he carried himself like a giant. I couldn't decide if he was black or Latino, which made me think that possibly he was both. He had dark curly hair, cut close to his scalp, and a certain sense of street toughness about him.

"Holly, this is my partner, T.J. T.J., this is Holly."

I smiled, but T.J. didn't return the courtesy. He only nodded with an icy, aloof glare.

Two alpha males as partners? I could only imagine how well that worked.

"Why don't you tell us what happened?" Chase started.

I gave Chase and T.J. a rundown. Chase grunted and took notes while crime scene techs collected the bullets and measured trajectories and took photos.

T.J. finally said he was going to check out any security video feeds from the surrounding area. When he disappeared, Chase turned to me.

"You have a minute to grab some coffee, Holly?" Chase asked.

I wanted to refuse. To say I had to get back to work. Before I could voice my excuses, Chase spoke up again.

"You have to eat," he insisted.

"You said coffee."

He smiled. "Well, it is lunchtime."

Finally, I nodded. "Yeah, I have a few minutes."

He kept a hand on my elbow and led me down the street to a little coffeehouse that sold sandwiches and soups. I ordered some lobster bisque and a decaf coffee, while Chase got a club sandwich with sweet potato chips.

As soon as the waitress disappeared, I waited for awkwardness to slip between us. If not awkwardness, then I waited for Chase to say something accusatory. Had he put everything together? Did he know what I'd done?

"How are you, Holly?" he asked.

His question startled me, and I flinched. "How am I?"

He nodded, no hint of a grin on his face. "That's right. I want to know how you're doing."

His question threw me off guard enough that I floundered for an answer. How was I? I wasn't even sure anymore. Finally, I shrugged. "I'm . . . okay, I guess."

"You've gotten shot at twice in a week. That's enough to shake anyone up."

I swallowed hard. "It's crazy, isn't it?"

"More than crazy. Any idea why someone would want to shoot at you? Beyond the answers you've already given me. I know you've taken children away from their parents. I know your sister has put bad people behind bars. I know there are people who hate your brother and everything he stands for. But what aren't you telling me?"

My throat tightened. "What makes you think I'm not telling you something?"

"Nothing." He shifted and looked at the table a moment, as if trying to find the right words. "The first time you were shot at, I might have been able to rationalize was random. But twice? The same car? It's obvious you're being targeted by someone."

"I really don't know, Chase." My words came out as a squeak.

The waitress was a welcome relief as she set two mugs in front of us. I grabbed mine, hoping it would form some kind of barrier between Chase and me, and that I wouldn't feel so exposed.

"I want you to know you can trust me, Holly," Chase murmured.

His words nearly made me choke. He sounded so honorable, not like the man I remembered in high school. "I, uh . . . I appreciate that."

I rubbed my throat, hating how off kilter this conversation was making me feel.

He shifted, his fingers hugging the mug of coffee in front of him. "I know that in the past things were strange between us. I want you to know that I'm not who I used to be."

This seemed like a great opportunity to turn the tables and talk about Chase instead of me. Plus, I wanted some answers. I wanted to know why he seemed different.

"Why the change?" There was no need to beat around the bush. I didn't quite believe him, and I needed to know why I should.

His expression sobered. "Life happened."

I didn't say anything, and instead waited to see if he wanted to add anything more. It was one of the techniques I'd learned when I'd studied counseling: Don't always fill the silence. In the silence, sometimes people said the things lingering deep in their souls.

He stared at his coffee, the muscles at his throat appearing tight and strained. "My brother was murdered."

"What happened?"

"He was bludgeoned to death. Found dead in his apartment."

"That's horrible. I'm so sorry, Chase. Did they ever find the person who did it?"

He shook his head. "No, they still haven't. It's been five years."

"I can't even imagine. It was hard enough to lose my dad to natural causes, but the senseless taking of a life . . . " I shook my head.

"It can consume you." Chase's words sounded dull, yet I heard the big emotions that lurked beneath his tone. "I took his death pretty hard, to say the least. It made me realize how short life is. It rearranged my priorities."

"I'm sure it did. I'm really sorry, Chase."

He nodded slowly. "Me, too. I don't want to pretend to be someone I'm not, Holly. The truth is that, after my brother died, I didn't exactly turn my life around. Quite the opposite, to be honest. I started drinking. A lot. I guess I was trying to numb the pain. It's not something I'm proud of. I lost a lot of things as a result, one of them being my job with the police in Kentucky."

His words caused my heart to slow to a thud. Compassion and understanding collided inside me. "Alcohol can do that to people."

He shook his head. "Don't I know it? I ruined relationships, friendships. People who were depending on me saw an ugly side of my personality. It took me two years to get my life back on track."

"You're sober now?"

A hint of a smile curled at his lips. It wasn't a self-satisfied smile but a victorious one. "Fourteen months without even a sip."

"Good for you, Chase. That's a huge accomplishment."

"I have to admit that every day is a struggle. Literally. And I hate myself for feeling so weak at times."

"What you call weakness, many would call strength."

His eyes locked on mine. "Those were the things I didn't want to say to your mom, Holly. She's always seemed so proud of me, and I hate to let her down. She believed in me when no one else did, and I couldn't bear to see the disappointment in her eyes."

"Overcoming an addiction to alcohol is something to be proud of, Chase. No matter what anyone says." I'd worked with enough people with addictions to see how drugs and alcohol could destroy lives. It wasn't pretty, and it wasn't something I'd wish on anyone.

He tilted his head, his gaze observing me. "How do you do that, Holly?"

I raised an eyebrow. "Do what?"

"It's like you have the ability to see through facades, right into the heart of a person. You've always been like that. In high school, it was a little bit intimidating, to be honest."

"I don't know what to say. I've always liked to listen and observe." That was just how God had made me. It had seemed like a curse at times during my younger years, but I'd learned to accept it as a gift.

He stared at me a moment. "You're different. That's a good thing. And I'm not just talking about your affinity for vintage dresses and old music and trying to do things the way they were done sixty years ago. I'm talking about you and who you are."

My cheeks heated. Those cheeks of mine. They betrayed me at the most inopportune times. I cleared my throat. "I still don't know what to say."

He leaned back, looking away for a minute as if he realized how uncomfortable I was. "I didn't mean to get off track. The one thing I learned through beating this addiction was the importance of righting wrongs. I know you don't think—"

"I've got one soup and a sandwich with chips," the waitress interrupted.

My heart played a funny little rhythm in my chest. I wasn't sure if I was grateful or grumpy the waitress had appeared when she did. What was Chase about to say? Even more, why did I care?

CHAPTER 13

I hated to admit it, but I was beginning to see Chase more as a person and less as a Neanderthal. I'd thought of him as a jerk for so long that I had no idea what to do with these newer, kinder realizations. Hating him came a lot more easily.

We settled back to eat. I knew I had to get to work, but I'd called Doris earlier and explained what had happened outside of the post office. And, officially, I was still talking to the police. This particular officer just happened to look like a muscle-bound superhero . . . and maybe act like him, too. In a good way.

It was true. I'd been in denial, preferring to remember Chase as a monster. But now all of those reasons why I'd had a crush on the man came rushing back, and I felt like a high schooler again. Feeling like a high schooler was the last thing I wanted.

Whatever he'd been about to say was apparently forgotten. He straightened, focusing on his food, a professional aura coming over him.

He grabbed a chip and popped it in his mouth. "Did you find out anything from your former clients like I suggested?"

I cleared my throat again, grateful for the subject change, despite the curiosity that now burned inside me. It was best if Chase and I just kept things professional. "I did hear something. It's about a drug lord named Caligula. You heard of him?"

Chase's eyes narrowed, his lips tightened, his shoulders tensed. "Unfortunately, I've heard of him. Every cop within sixty miles of the area has."

"Who is he?" I took a sip of my soup, waiting in anticipation.

I'd done some research last night and confirmed that Caligula was a Roman emperor. Though historical accounts varied, most agreed that he'd done some heinous things with his power. He'd tortured those under him and sought power, as well as pleasure.

"If we could tell you that, we'd have the man behind bars. No one knows who he is. He has a layer of management that protects him as part of his supply chain. Those guys are the ones who take the supply to the street army. They're not telling."

"You mean, they'd face jail time to protect him? They must be pretty loyal."

"Not exactly. All of them say that he wears a mask and disguises his voice."

I tore off a piece of my bread, trying to digest what Chase said. "Is that weird?"

"Lots of things are weird. Obviously the guy doesn't want to be discovered, for reasons like we just talked about. If his dealers can't identify him, that puts him in a better position." He popped a sweet potato chip in his mouth.

"I'm not naïve. I know all drug lords are dangerous. But what sets this guy apart?"

He drew in a deep breath. "He's good, for starters. Between you and me, this guy is manufacturing a synthetic drug that's lethal. We're trying to take it off the streets or to even find where it's being manufactured so we can shut the place down. But we've got nothing. Somebody somewhere knows something. It's just a matter of finding that person."

"Basic profile? Is this some kid running the operations?"

Chase shook his head. "No, it's way more complex than what a kid could do. This person has connections. He's smart and deceptive. Maybe he even has another job that allows him a cover for what he's really doing. Maybe his job puts him in contact with likely distributors."

My first thought was Abraham. Could Abraham be Caligula? Was that how he'd gotten his money? His job would definitely put him in a good position to recruit impressionable young people who might be anxious to make a buck. Besides, Abraham was college educated. He'd probably studied rulers like Caligula, who reigned during biblical times, while he was in college.

But I just couldn't see Abraham stooping that low. He was a stand-up guy . . . wasn't he?

"So, you think this Caligula guy is connected with the murders?" My stomach roiled whenever I thought about the two men who'd died and my connection with the crime scene. I wasn't sure that feeling would ever go away until I came clean about everything.

"I can confirm that there was evidence of Cena in the systems of the guys who were murdered. That seems to be a pretty good indication."

Cena was the newest synthetic drug to hit the market, and it was all the rage in the area because it was cheap and people liked its effects. I remembered enough from my classes to know that Cena meant "the main meal of the day" back in Roman times. That meant our local gang, the Praetorian Guard, had a leader named Caligula and that Cena was their main recreational drug. Whoever was behind all of this wasn't your run-of-the-mill gangbanger. They had been educated.

"So, is this a serial killer or a drug lord offing his underlings?"

Chase shook his head. "Nothing is ever certain. For all I know, this could be some kind of vigilante thinking he's doing the city a favor by killing people hooked on drugs. Maybe the cleaning supplies he left were his way of saying he's cleaning up crime in the area."

I shivered. "That would be . . . morbid."

"I've seen worse. And, of course, I'm just speculating right now. I can't share details of the case."

I broke it down in my mind. A serial killer who just happened to focus on young men involved in drugs? A drug lord killing to either punish those under him or teach them a lesson? A vigilante thinking he was doing a good deed?

None of those options were comforting.

"None of that, however, explains why I'm being shot at." Even if the gunman was someone who'd seen me enter Katrina's house that night, why would he be trying to shoot me?

Then I remembered the noise I'd heard when I'd been at the house. Was it the killer escaping? Hiding?

What if that person thought I'd seen them? What if someone was trying to kill me to keep me quiet? And, just in case that didn't work, they were setting up the crime scenes to make me look guilty. They were doing whatever it took to take the attention off of them.

"What are you thinking? I can see your wheels spinning."

I shook my head and took a sip of my soup to buy myself some more time. "Maybe whoever is shooting at me thinks I know something," I offered. I had to be selective in how much information I presented. But that amount seemed safe enough. Certainly Chase had probably put that much together in his mind.

"Could be. That is, if this is connected." He leaned closer. "I just feel like there's something you're not telling me, something that could break open this case."

I froze. Couldn't breathe. Didn't dare move.

He knew, didn't he?

I had no idea what to say. How to handle it.

A smile cracked on his ultraserious face. "Just kidding. Like you, of all people, would have unlawful connections with the underworld."

I released my breath and let out a shaky laugh. Joking. He'd been joking.

And I'd almost gone and owned up to everything.

His eyes became serious again. "I do wonder what's going on behind those blue eyes of yours, though. You're a hard one to read sometimes."

"A girl can't tell all of her secrets."

"That in one of the etiquette books your mom mentioned you loved to read?"

I'd have to thank my mom for that later. I half shrugged. "That and other groundbreaking tips like, 'Never sit next to someone prettier than you are.'"

"That's not a problem for you, is it?"

My throat tightened. "What do you mean?"

"Girls don't get much prettier than you, Holly Anna."

His stare sent blood rushing to my cheeks and my ears and probably any other visible surface of skin. I opened my mouth to retort, to sound clever and coy — two things I actually wasn't that great at being. Before something humiliating left my lips, his cell phone beeped.

He excused himself and put his phone to his ear. "I've got to go."

"A new lead?" I asked, wishing the question was as innocent as it sounded.

He pulled some money from his wallet and dropped it on the table, then slid a piece of paper to me. "Yep. Here's my number in case you need anything or have any more trouble. Please be careful, Holly."

I nodded and watched him walk away.

Maybe I was wrong about Chase.

Not likely. But maybe.

CHAPTER 14

I still had a little time before I was supposed to be back at work. I was going to swing by Katrina's cousin's house and ask about her son. I needed some answers.

I had a year left on this earth, give or take a week. No one was going to cut into that time. I still had a whole bucket list of items I wanted to do. Some things, I knew would never happen. I wouldn't make it to Italy and meet a handsome man. I wouldn't get married and have a houseful of kids. Nor would I even fall in love, most likely.

But I was going to live with purpose, and my purpose right now was figuring out what was going on.

Katrina had given me the woman's address. Her name was Desiree Harding, and that was pretty much all I knew about her. Katrina had promised me she'd let her cousin know that I might be stopping by. Hopefully, she'd done that, since a lot of people in this area were hesitant to trust outsiders.

I pulled up to a house that mirrored most in the neighborhood: tall, skinny, and run down. This one was painted turquoise, the yard was littered with broken toys, maybe a shirt and a couple of unmatching shoes, and two tires were stand-ins for shrubs in the flowerbeds.

With thoughts of that Cadillac still heavy on my mind, I glanced up and down the street as I climbed from my Mustang. I didn't see the car anywhere, nor did I see anything else suspicious.

That didn't ease the tension in my shoulders as I climbed the steps snaking through the yard and toward the front door. I skirted past a "Rex Harrison for State Senate" sign. I moved more quickly than I would have liked—a sure sign that I was nervous—and rang the bell.

There was a car in the driveway, so I hoped that meant someone was home. A woman answered a few minutes later, blinking rapidly and running her hands through tousled hair. Apparently, I'd woken her up.

I'd seen grief before; I'd experienced grief before. I knew it could consume you. This woman was consumed.

She was in her early thirties with dirty blonde hair that slouched to the side in a head-top ponytail. She didn't bother to pull her oversized, floppy sweatshirt over her shoulders, which were nearly bare because of the spaghetti straps of her low-cut white tank top.

"Can I help you?"

"Desiree? My name is Holly Paladin, and I'm a friend of Katrina's. She said she would mention me to you."

The woman stared at me a moment, her eyes glazed, before nodding. "She may have said something. What can I do you for?"

"I know this is an awful time, but could I come in for a minute?"

Seconds passed until finally she opened the door farther. "Just for a minute. I'm . . . busy. Got lots of stuff

I should be getting done."

I stepped into the battered entryway and went to the kitchen table, where remnants of some oriental noodles were stuck to the top of the wooden tabletop. Desiree sat across from me.

My heart went out to the woman, and I prayed that I'd have the right words. "First of all, I'd like to say that I'm really sorry for your loss."

She nodded and stared off into the distance. "Thank you."

I licked my lips. "I'm guessing that Katrina may have told you I'm a social worker?"

"You here to take the rest of my kids away?"

"No, not at all. I'm here just to check on you."

"I feel like I've lived through a nightmare. Worse. It's like I can't wake up, no matter how many times I pinch myself."

"It's going to take some time. Grieving is a process." I shifted. "Desiree, I know the police have talked to you. But I'm worried about the crimes in this neighborhood. More than one of my clients have been affected by these acts of violence."

Her eyes sparked. "The whole neighborhood's going downhill. What's the world coming to? Why are people so senseless?"

"Many reasons. But drugs are one of them. They seem to turn off people's consciences."

Her finger sliced through the air like a vigilante with a sword. "Drugs. You're right. They're destroying people. But not my son. He didn't mess with stuff like that."

I shifted again, hoping my words sounded compassionate. "Desiree, did your son hang out with

RANDOM ACTS OF MURDER

people who may have done drugs?"

"Everyone around here knows someone who does drugs. It's a way of life here in the Hill. Why are you asking all of these questions?"

"I'm just concerned."

"Why don't you talk to your brother about it?"

I blinked as her words set in. "My brother?"

The woman glared at me. "I know who your brother is. Ralph Paladin. He's running for senate."

I remembered the sign in her front yard. "I guess he's not the candidate of your choice."

"He doesn't care about us. But Rex Harrison? He's going to end this drug war around here, once and for all. Mark my words."

"The election will be interesting for sure." I leaned toward her, ready to change the subject. "So, Desiree, I know of this great group of people who meet once a week to talk about losing loved ones . . ."

CHAPTER 15

Four days had passed since the murder at Katrina Dawson's house.

Every day, I waited for the police to knock on my door and arrest me.

Every day, I waited for a phone call from Jamie saying she was being investigated.

Every day, I anticipated my family's disappointment in me.

Every day, so far, I'd been wrong.

I hadn't run into Chase Dexter again.

It was eleven days until the election, and my brother was ahead by four percentage points.

My sister's wedding plans were coming along nicely. I'd even tried on my bridesmaid dress Thursday night and was pleased with how it looked. The fact that I'd lost about five pounds from the stress of this week alone helped.

Life continued on.

I'd revised my whole random-acts-of-kindness plan. I had left some groceries on the doorsteps of a couple of my clients. That was safe enough. I'd sent the pastor at my church a gift certificate so he could take his wife out to eat.

I'd hoped this whole cleaning thing would get swept under the rug, and maybe I would actually get my wish.

Right now, I was on my way to a conference that Helen insisted I had to attend. It was some leadership thing that she felt would be beneficial for the Caring Hands employees. I didn't ask any questions, although I'd much rather be keeping up with my workload.

I parked in a garage in downtown, and, of course, I was running late. I ran down the sidewalks. The day was briskly cold but sunny — but not briskly cold enough that I wasn't wearing a cute dress that Jamie had found last week at the thrift store. I liked to take old dresses and make them my own by adding belts and jewelry. Sometimes I hemmed them or added a sweater or leggings. It worked well for my style, as well as my budget.

I ran into the lobby, breezed past the people standing by the entrance, and ran toward the large, dark conference room. I stopped in my tracks, nearly stumbling, when I saw the head honcho boss, Helen Weatherly, standing there.

"Holly, I thought you may not make it."

"I'm sorry. I didn't realize you'd be waiting for me." I straightened my turquoise cardigan, wishing I'd planned a little better.

"It's no problem. I just wanted to make sure we sat together. We just started a few minutes ago."

Helen was married to the city's police chief. They'd both lost their spouses, Helen's to cancer and Walter's to a heart attack. They'd gotten married three years ago and seemed like a match made in heaven. I'd met Helen when I worked for CPS, and we got along fabulously. When she'd started Caring Hands, she'd persuaded me to come work for her, and I'd agreed.

We rushed inside. I stayed low and took a seat

between Helen and Doris.

I turned my attention to the stage where the mayor was giving a speech.

"So, on behalf of Orion Enterprises and the city of Cincinnati, it is with great honor that I'd like to announce the winner of this year's Volunteer of the Year," he said. "This person has worked tirelessly for the city, giving of herself day in and day out."

What? I thought this was a leadership conference. What was going on?

Helen smiled beside me and patted my hand.

"Holly Paladin, for her work with the teens in our area!"

I blinked, uncertain about what was going on. Then Helen shoved me, and somehow I ended up onstage behind the microphone, and a plaque was thrust into my hands.

"Would you like to say a few words?" Mayor Hollinsworth asked.

"A few words?" I questioned.

The audience laughed. I laughed back, only to make it seem like I was in control and totally knew what was going on. In truth, I had no idea.

He nodded toward the microphone.

I cleared my throat and looked out over the audience. There had to be five hundred people here. I thought—but I wasn't sure—that I'd just received an award for volunteering. For the entire city.

I could only make out the faces of the people at the tables closest to the front. I spotted my mom, my sister, my brother, my sister's fiancé, Jamie, and Abraham.

They all grinned at me.

Walter, the police chief, was onstage. He smiled

encouragingly. I think he liked me by default since Helen had taken me under her wing. There were several other city bigwigs seated around him, though I couldn't place their names.

I cleared my throat again and adjusted the microphone, mostly so I could buy time.

"Wow, I just don't know what to say. Usually when I'm in this position, I say something a little hokey. Forgive me because I'm not great with speeches when I plan them, and I'm especially not great when I'm surprised."

Another ripple of laughter filled the room.

That's when I froze again. Not because of stage fright, but because my skin started to crawl.

The killer was in this room.

I don't know why I knew with such certainty, but I did. He was watching me from the darkness, one of many unseen faces within the crowd.

I had to get myself together.

"There's one thing I know for certain, and that's that in life there are very few certainties. We must live each day as if it were our last. We must hold to and treasure every moment. We must cling to the hope we know and not let our minds be clouded by despair, whatever our circumstances." I raised my plaque. "Thank you again for this award. I'm truly honored."

Before I could scoot off the stage—and run for my life—the mayor caught my elbow. I glanced over on the other side and saw Orion Vanderslice himself. He had dark hair on top that was silvering at the temples. His face was square with pleasant features—if it weren't for his scowl. He may have been brilliant in business, but he was horrible when it came to social graces.

The man wasn't especially looking at me with fondness. I knew he'd sponsored this award for years and that community organizations in the area voted on the winner.

"The press would like a moment before you go," the mayor whispered.

I nodded and, like a good girl, stayed onstage beside him for the remainder of his speech. Finally, I was able to sit down in an empty seat on the stage while other award recipients were called out—Teen of the Year, Senior Citizen of the Year, Officer of the Year, etc.

Two hours later, I made my way offstage and was greeted by hugs from my family and friends.

"You guys knew about this?" I squealed.

"Of course we did! We couldn't wait to surprise you," my mom said. "But did you know how hard it was to keep this quiet?"

"Especially for me," Jamie quipped.

In the middle of all the congratulations, a new voice piped in. "Good job, Ms. Paladin."

I looked over and saw Rex Harrison standing there. The man stood at about six feet tall. He had close-cropped black hair and a smile that could make a nun want to give up her vows.

Charisma. There was no doubt the man had it. When he spoke, people listened.

He was a former cop who'd given up his job in order to run for office. Many in the community called him the People's Choice. He'd vowed to keep the area safe and had taken a stand against the drug problem rampant in the area by starting a mentoring program. He'd been spurred on by the fact that his brother had been a drug addict.

If my brother were running against anyone else, he'd win. But Rex would give him a run for his money.

My mom nudged me until I broke away from my thoughts. "Thank you."

"I have to admit, your record for selflessly volunteering in our community is impressive, even if you are the competition's sister."

"I appreciate that," I offered.

My brother cast a disparaging glance at Rex before pulling me back. "We want to take you to lunch to celebrate, so don't go anywhere, okay?"

I nodded. "Got it."

I reached into my purse to grab my lipstick and freshen up when my fingers encountered a piece of paper. Curiously, I pulled it out and opened the neatly folded square. I didn't remember seeing this in there before.

"I know who you are," it read.

My blood went cold as I glanced around the room. Whoever had left this had been close enough to touch me.

That thought was anything but comforting.

CHAPTER 16

As my family and friends whisked me to my favorite Japanese steak house for lunch, one realization had remained in my mind: whoever was behind the murders knew me. I didn't mean he'd *seen* me — that much was clear. It went deeper than that. This person had *recognized* me at that first crime scene.

My blood froze every time I thought about it. It could be someone I talked to on a regular basis who was behind these crimes. There was no other reason for them to identify me. The thought wasn't comforting.

By the time all of that was over, I had to head back home to get ready for the big fund-raising gala for my brother tonight. Brian was going with me. Or I was going with him. I wasn't sure.

I didn't want to wear just any little black dress, so I'd opted for a little green number instead. The rest of my family had already gone, and I was waiting for Brian to pick me up when I noticed the door to my father's detached garage/woodshop was open.

I hurried toward it and started to shut it when I paused. The scent of sawdust and varnish lingered in the room, even two years after the death of my father. Inhaling the odor took me back in time.

Even though everyone thought I was a girly girl, I used to love sitting out here and watching my dad work. He'd been a locksmith by trade, but in his free time he liked to make birdhouses and shelves and wooden toys. He'd always make extras of things and give them to families in the church. Once in a while, he'd let me help with sanding or picking out a design.

I missed those days. I missed the security and unconditional love I felt when I was with my dad. I'd give anything to have him here now.

Closing my eyes, I could picture him working out here. I envisioned me sitting on the stool not too far away, talking about my day. I could hear me asking his advice. He'd keep working, casting me glances every now and then as he spouted his wisdom about life.

My smile felt bittersweet. I went to close the door when something inside caught my eye. I stepped inside and let the fading sunlight fill the room.

What I saw made me catch my breath.

There were four yellow buckets, four blue mops, and four purple scrub brushes, just like the ones I'd taken to Katrina's house.

***

Brian arrived promptly, as always. My heart was still racing, though. The killer knew who I was. He knew what I'd done. And now he wanted to scare me.

His plan had worked.

"Holly. You look fabulous." Brian twirled me around before planting a friendly kiss on my cheek. Brian was thirty-two years old. He was only two inches taller than me (I was five foot six), and his trim build was offset by his heavy jawline. As a go-getter, he fit in well with my family. He worked as my brother's campaign manager and was perhaps one of the biggest schmoozers I'd ever met.

"You ready to go?" he asked.

I nodded, trying to cast my thoughts aside, but the buckets in the garage kept haunting me. I'd started to throw them away. Then I'd realized the police might find them in the trash can. I'd almost hidden them in my bedroom closet. But then I realized they could look there, also. Finally, I'd taken them upstairs to the garage attic. My dad had a little cubbyhole that most people didn't know about. The door blended right in with the wall, and there was no handle. Only my family knew about the space.

No one would find the cleaning supplies there.

At least, that's what I was counting on. Especially since my fingerprints were now on everything.

I closed my eyes.

Could this get any worse?

"You've got a little smudge of dust right . . ." Brian reached for my cheek and used his thumb to wipe something away. ". . . there. All gone now."

I forced a smile. "Thank you."

Brian walked me to his car and opened my door for me, and when I was safely inside, he took his place behind the wheel and started down the road.

I wished I liked Brian. I really did. But I just didn't feel that spark that I'd always dreamed about.

Then again, maybe romance and happily ever after were about more than a spark. Maybe they should be based on a friendship like the one Brian and I had. I just had to convince my heart of it.

"Did I hear you were shot at? Twice?" Brian asked.

I bit back a frown. "Crazy, isn't it?"

"More than crazy. It's insane. Maybe I need to hire

you a bodyguard."

Chase Dexter's face flashed into my mind. I quickly erased it. "I think I'll be fine."

"So, what do you think about those two guys who were killed around here recently? Makes you want to stay inside and lock your doors, doesn't it?"

I nodded. "For sure."

"To think there could be a serial killer in Price Hill. It's spooky stuff."

He wasn't making me feel better. "It's more than scary. *Scary* defines how you feel when watching a movie. This is more like terrifying."

"Did you know any of those kids?" He glanced over at me.

I shook my head. "I didn't know them. But I knew people connected with them."

"Speaking of which, would you be interested in doing some campaigning out—"

"I can't campaign to my clients, Brian. You know that. That would be an ethical breach." *Much like breaking into one of their homes had been.*

"I know, I know. It's just that we're down by twenty whole percentage points in that area."

I remembered my conversation with Desiree. I remembered running into Rex at the award ceremony and the charisma that had emanated from him. "People are calling Rex the People's Choice."

Brian frowned. "Sounds like something Rex would plant in people's minds. I don't trust the man as far as I can throw him, personally. And it's not just because your brother is running against him."

"Do you think my brother is going to win, Brian?"

He nodded slowly—slowly enough that I wasn't

convinced. "Yeah, he's got this. It's all going to come together. Numbers like this are normal for this stage in the election. You know how the media is — they claim they're not biased, but they're giving Rex a lot more airtime and a lot less criticism. We're going to take this, though."

Brian was the spin master, which was in reality what made him so good at his job.

"After he's elected, you're going to come work for him, right?"

I laughed. "Me? A social worker? I'm not sure there's anything I can do for him."

"He needs good people on his team, people he can depend on to help on his staff."

"I'm not sure I'd be the right person."

"You should think about it."

"I'll wait until he's elected first."

"You sound skeptical."

"I'm not skeptical. I really do believe in my brother, and I think he'd make a great senator." *If I don't blow his whole campaign to smithereens, that is.*

Brian pulled to a stop in front of a hotel in downtown Cincinnati, and a valet appeared. I stepped from the car, and Brian met me on the sidewalk. He took my hand and led me inside. "Here we go. You ready for this?"

"Ready as I'll ever be."

We mingled for all of ten minutes before Brian was whisked off to talk to some city commissioner. It was fine with me. I could use a break from his incessant talking. I grabbed some punch and took a sip before finding a spot against the wall.

"Hello, there," a deep voice rumbled.

I looked up and saw Chase.

At once, I pictured being arrested here at the gala in front of all my family and their supporters. That would be the ultimate disappointment to them if that happened. That familiar panic started in me.

Until I realized that Chase was wearing a tux. And drinking punch. And smiling.

"Chase? What are you doing here?" At once, my shoulders went back, I held my head higher, and my pulse spiked. Man, was he ever handsome in that formalwear. More handsome than anyone should have the right to claim.

"After everything your mother did for me during my teen years, I wanted to support you guys. Coming to this was the least I could do."

My heart rate slowed some. "I'm sure Ralph appreciates it."

He tugged at his tie. "It's not really my kind of thing. I'd much rather watch a football game. But I try to be flexible."

"I'm surprised you could take any time off the case."

"You've got to step back sometimes in order to think clearly. I've been working nonstop, other than grabbing a few hours of sleep and eating a meal here and there. I figured it would be good to get away from the investigation for a moment."

"Makes sense to me. You've got to take care of yourself."

His gaze caught mine, and he grinned, stepping closer. "Holly, it was really great to chat with you for a few minutes over lunch the other—"

"Hi, there," someone interrupted.

I turned and saw Brian. He extended one hand toward Chase and put the other around my waist, a huge politician smile on his face. "I'm Brian."

Chase's smile dimmed some. "Chase."

The two shook hands, Brian jovial, as always. He had a way of making people feel like they were worth a million bucks. *How to Win Friends and Influence People* was apparently his favorite book.

"You're Chase Dexter! I've heard about you. Mrs. Paladin can't say enough good things."

"She's very kind." Humility saturated his voice.

"It's great that you can be with us tonight," Brian continued. "We're appreciative of everyone who comes out and supports Ralph. We think he'll make a great senator . . ."

I blocked Brian out. I wasn't really into politics.

I could tell that this wasn't Chase's favorite topic of conversation, either. As soon as there was a break, he pointed behind him, mumbled an excuse, and slipped away. I resisted the urge to look for him and forced myself to turn back to Brian.

"Shall we eat?" Brian asked.

I nodded. "We shall."

For some reason, my heart longed to keep talking to Chase, though.

***

The family was all ushered backstage so we could get a photo before my brother began his speech. Brian was meeting with a few members of the press in another room, and somehow Chase had ended up back here with my family.

"So, when are you going to stop beating around the bush with Brian?" my sister, Alex, asked. "Why don't you just date him?"

My throat burned. Of all the conversations we could have right here, right now, and in front of Chase Dexter of all people, did it have to be this one?

"We're just friends," I insisted. We'd had this conversation before.

"You have impossible standards for men," Alex said.

I squirmed when I noticed everyone listening, except for my brother, who fixed his bow tie in the mirror. "I do not."

"Oh, please. How about that one guy you broke up with because he had dirty elbows?" Alex's eyebrows shot up.

I shrugged. "He did have dirty elbows."

"Or that other guy? He was so nice. I think his name was Sonny," my mom added.

"His last name was Hooker. I couldn't possibly be taken seriously if my name was Holly Anna Hooker. I'd sound like someone from a 900 number."

Deep laughter rumbled in the background. Chase. He just *had* to be here to hear all of this, didn't he?

"Okay, then what about Allen Smith? He had a decent last name and clean elbows." My brother glanced at me from the reflection in the mirror.

"But he had no sense of adventure and terrible breath." I wanted to hide. Truly.

"It must be nice being so naïve and sweet," Alex muttered.

She was quite possibly my polar opposite. I was pretty sure she'd had a mental checklist of what she wanted in a guy and that her decision to marry William was based more on a series of cerebral check marks than love. I needed a balance.

I wasn't sure what it was about being the youngest that seemed to beckon people to pick on me, but I was the object of their teasing criticism yet again. Everyone stared at me now, waiting to see how I'd respond or what kind of excuses I'd make, or even for more evidence of just how rose colored my world was.

"I actually think it's refreshing," a new voice added.

I sucked in a deep breath when I saw Chase step forward. Was he actually defending me? Didn't he know he might get swallowed by the deceptively sweet sharks known as my family? Of course, Chase was the type who could stand on his own two feet.

"Not only is having standards good, so is making an effort to see the world in a more positive light. Life is about more than what you accomplish. It's about who you are. I don't think Holly should ever settle."

My family remained quiet. I could hardly breathe.

I wanted to hug Chase for stepping in and helping defend me. I wanted to cry because he actually sounded like he understood. Instead, I managed to keep my mouth shut, though it wanted to flop open.

Chase and I stared at each other a moment, something unspoken passing between us.

"All right, everyone! Let's go get that family photo!" Brian charged into the room. He paused and his eyebrows scrunched together. "What? Did I miss something?"

***

An hour later, I stepped outside, needing to get some air. Maybe being alone outside wasn't the smartest idea after being shot at twice, but I refused to live in total fear. Partial would have to do.

I pulled my shawl around my shoulders and shivered at the winter chill that hung in the air.

It was hard to imagine this being my last winter. Sometimes, I didn't feel like the implications of my disease had sunk in. Partly that was because I essentially felt healthy. Occasionally, I got tired, but that came from working and volunteering and staying busy. It was a good tired.

Or maybe it was my disease.

I let out a sigh, and my frosty breath fanned in front of me.

Life felt surprisingly unsimple at the moment. As a girl who always tried to keep things uncomplicated, I hated this. I just wanted the future to be clear.

I supposed it was. I was going to die. I didn't have much time to leave my mark on the world, and there was nothing I could do about it.

More timely than those thoughts, and nearly as pressing, was the fact that Brian had slow danced with me. He'd whispered, "You know, I think we could be really good together."

His statement was the first time he'd ever directly professed any interest. Before that, we'd just hung out casually and been fill-in dates when neither of us had anyone else. His statement left no questions as to what he thought about the two of us together.

I, of course, had stuttered. Stepped on his feet. Tried to find the right words.

Finally, I'd settled on "Do you?"

Thankfully, my brother had stepped up to the podium and we hadn't had time to finish our talk.

Now I was out on the street corner, staring at the valets and trying to get a grip.

"Holly! What are you doing out here?"

I looked up and saw Chase charging outside. He didn't stop walking, only slowed down when he spotted me.

"Just getting a breath." Something was going on, I realized with more than a little alarm zinging through me. "Where's the fire?"

He shook his head, not slowing down and nearing the curb now. "No fire. But we've got another murder."

CHAPTER 17

"Chase! Maybe I should go with you." I wasn't sure where the words had come from or if they were wise. But they'd slipped out. "You know, in case someone needs a shoulder to cry on. I am a social worker."

He paused for a millisecond before nodding. "Come on, then."

I temporarily forgot about Brian and about my brother's fund-raising gala and all the guests inside. All I could think about was the fact that the killer had struck again. I'd call someone later and explain where I'd gone. Maybe I'd do it in the car.

I hurried after Chase, my shorter legs working twice as hard as his long ones. He'd found a parking space three blocks away on the street, at a meter. Pretty smart thinking, since he was a cop and all. Valet service would have taken way too long.

We reached an unmarked sedan. He opened the door for me and waited while I quickly—but still like a lady—climbed into the passenger seat. He wasted no time slamming the door and hurrying to his side.

I'd had images of asking him questions, finding out more information. But he turned on his lights and siren and we were off. I held onto what Jamie called the "oh crap" bar above the window, trying not to be jostled into Chase.

Five minutes later, we pulled into the same

neighborhood where the other two crimes had occurred. I breathed an ever-so-slight sigh of relief when I didn't recognize the house.

As soon as we jerked to a stop, Chase turned to me. "You can't cross the police line. Got it?"

I nodded. "Got it."

I had no desire to see what was on the other side of that police line. The images of the dead body in Katrina's house still haunted me; I didn't think the pictures could ever be scrubbed from my memory. That was another tragedy in and of itself.

With more than a little hesitation, I opened the door and stepped onto the sidewalk. I pulled my shawl closer, trepidation surrounding me. There were probably six police cars already at the scene, along with an ambulance and fire truck—standard protocol, I supposed. A woman stood on the lawn, tears streaming down her face and a tissue balled in her hands. Two officers tried to calm her down.

I wanted to give her a hug and ask her if there was someone I could call.

But she was on the other side of the police line.

I'd been given boundaries, and I really needed to stick with them.

I stood there as minutes ticked past. I watched. I waited. I tried to keep my apprehension at bay.

I saw Chase come out and talk to the woman. He laid a hand on her arm, and the woman seemed to instantly calm down.

Then Chase's partner, T.J., charged onto the scene. Whatever he said obviously upset the woman because she began crying harder. Interesting dynamic, I mused. Good cop/bad cop? Or was this just a matter of compassionate versus jerky? I voted for the second option.

Just then, something vibrated under my arm.

My phone.

I quickly fished it out, realizing with panic that I hadn't told anyone where I was going. Even worse, I'd been gone probably an hour already.

I put the phone to my ear and rushed out, "Hello?"

"Holly? Where are you?" Brian's voice sounded across the line.

"I'm so sorry, Brian. I got called to . . . to an emergency, and I meant to let you guys know."

"We've all been worried sick. Your mom was about to make an announcement at the podium about you."

"Please! Tell her not to do that. Please."

"Are you sure everything is okay?" Brian repeated.

"I'm sorry. I'm doing something as a social worker right now. I'm not sure how long I'll be."

"How'd you get there? You don't even have a car."

"I got a ride from . . . from the police," I finally answered.

He paused for a moment. "I see. Well, if you need anything, let me know. I'd be happy to pick you up, if you needed me to."

"Thanks, Brian." As I hung up, Chase motioned me over. A uniformed officer let me under the police tape, and I met Chase halfway. He leaned close and lowered his voice.

"Could you stay with her? She could use someone right now. Says her nearest family is a few hours away still."

I nodded. "Of course. I'd be more than happy to."

"You're the best, Holly Anna." He took his coat off

and draped it over my shoulders.

Warmth surrounded me, as did the scent of leather aftershave. "Just Holly will do," I finally managed.

He squeezed my arm gently. "Thanks again."

I hoped he hadn't noticed the starstruck look in my gaze when he touched me. It was like my body had frozen as adrenaline zapped me. The clash left me feeling light-headed.

I really, really had to get a grip.

***

Three hours later, Chase escorted me back to his car. He didn't say anything until after the doors were shut and the engine hummed to life.

"Same MO, Holly. A young guy, shot in the chest, left for dead."

"So, you think this murder is connected with the earlier ones?" I tried to remain calm, to stay cool, to act collected even when everything inside me screamed: panic!

"There was a bucket and mop left there, and the kitchen had been cleaned."

Suddenly, my head started spinning. Someone *was* trying to frame this . . . on me! The real killer obviously knew I'd been to that other crime scene. Was there any better scapegoat? But why not just send an anonymous letter to the police? Why go through all of this trouble to make me out as the guilty party?

"Holly? Are you okay?"

I barely heard him. Wooziness threatened to overtake me, and I grabbed the "oh crap" bar again — for totally different reasons this time.

The next thing I knew, Chase had pulled over and put the car in park. He twisted in his seat until he faced me. "What's going on?"

Not now. My disease couldn't pick this moment to rear its ugly little head.

I raised my hand, trying to gain control of the situation. "I'm fine. I just need a moment."

"The crime scene was too much for you, wasn't it?"

Good. That's what he thought it was. He was going to be sorely disappointed if he found out the truth, though. Maybe I should just tell him. Right here, right now.

But the words wouldn't leave my lips. "It was a bit much, I suppose. This whole thing has left me feeling uneasy."

"It's left the whole city feeling uneasy." He reached out and rubbed a piece of hair back from my face. "I should have told you that you couldn't come. But you did work wonders with the victim's mother back there."

I forced a slight smile. "I'm glad I was a help."

His hand dropped. "I should get you home."

"Probably."

My entire body felt alive as we drove. There was something about being this close to Chase that made my senses more aware, made my heart pump harder, and made my mind feel more alert.

We pulled in front of my house. He parked on the street and ran around to open my door. I didn't object; I liked feeling like a lady, and there was no shame in that.

We started up the sidewalk, his hand on my back, and my brain being engulfed with fairy-tale-like endorphins. Feelings that I needed to get under control.

Chase glanced up. "You can actually see some stars tonight."

I paused and looked toward the nighttime sky. "There are a few out, aren't there?"

"That was the first time I ever remember talking to you, Holly." Chase looked at me. "It was about stars."

"You remember that?" I knew exactly what he was talking about. Which could mean that I still had a little high school crush on him all these years later.

He grinned. "Of course I do. We were assigned to be partners in our science class. Our project was on constellations."

My throat burned when I swallowed. That had been the start of my crush on Chase.

"That's when I realized that you weren't like the other girls."

A few days ago, I would have thought he meant that as an insult. But, right now, I wasn't sure.

"Was that a good thing or a bad thing?" I held my breath as I waited for his answer.

He stepped closer. "Definitely a good thing."

I raised my face toward him. Was it my imagination or was he leaning closer?

My heart raced, and my skin tingled as anticipation filled me.

He was going to kiss me.

And I wasn't going to stop him. The years weren't rolled out before me with endless possibilities. I didn't have gobs of time to contemplate true love. I only had the moment.

I closed my eyes.

"Now, that's true love if I've ever seen it!" A

horrible, scratchy yet nasal voice filled the air.

My eyes popped open. Not only had the moment been broken, but it was like the magnetism that drew Chase and me together suddenly reversed and propelled us away from each other.

Mrs. Signet.

She stood on her porch grinning.

In a not-so-ladylike moment, I wanted to throttle her.

Something in that instant changed on Chase's face. It hardened, and an unknown emotion — I wished I knew what — closed on him. He backed away, all traces of a smile gone.

"I should go."

I nodded and pulled his jacket off. I instantly missed it — but not as much as I missed the warmth in his eyes. "Here you go."

The lines on his face still looked tight. "I'll see you around, Holly."

CHAPTER 18

Normally I ate with my family after church on
Sunday, but today I decided to bypass lunch. I'd had
my fill of my family last night, and I wasn't in the
mood for their criticism and teasing today. I could
already hear them lecturing me about leaving the gala
without telling anyone, reminding me that I should
play it safe, warning me that I could be shot at again.

Instead, Jamie and I had gotten smoothies at one of
our favorite places downtown and then set out for a
walk down the Serpentine Wall, which ran along the
Ohio River, right in the shadow of downtown. I really
needed some girlfriend time now, as I tried to sort out
my jumbled emotions.

Jamie and I loved walking around the wall, and
we'd done it ever since our college days together. In the
summer, there were concerts here. At night, one could
marvel at the lights on the various bridges leading from
Kentucky to Ohio. It was our little oasis in the city.

"So, you really think Chase was going to kiss you?"
Jamie asked.

I pressed my lips together for a moment. "I don't
know that for sure. It felt like it, though."

"You really would have kissed him?"

I shrugged. "Maybe. I don't know. It's not like I
have forever. Before, I felt like I had my whole life
ahead of me. Now . . ."

Jamie raised a hand and nodded. "I get that. You're saving your first kiss for true love. Maybe it's Chase."

I laughed, quick and hard. "Chase? No. It was just the moment, you know? I mean, what's the use of waiting for true love for your first kiss if you're going to die before that happens?"

"I've always thought your plan sounded crazy. There I was, a hundred pounds overweight and wanting desperately for someone to want to kiss me. You had a line of guys, and you weren't interested in any of them."

I slowed my steps as I tried to sort my thoughts. "I thought the notion was romantic, and I still think that when I was younger, it was a really good plan of action. It helped to protect my heart. But I'm a big girl now, and I don't know. I don't want to be a hypocrite, but I'm twenty-eight and I've never been kissed. I'm going to be dead by next year at this time. It can change your perspective on things. I think I'm old enough to handle a kiss now."

"Even though I thought you were crazy, you actually managed to stick to it all these years, even when you were engaged to Rob. That couldn't have been easy—he was awfully good looking."

"He also ran away at the first sign of hardship. I'm so glad I didn't marry him. Things tend to work out the way they're supposed to."

She tossed her empty cup into a trash can and tucked her hands into the pockets of her black leather jacket. "So, your evening sounded like it was nearly perfect."

She obviously hadn't been listening all that well. "Aside from the murder and the bucket being found there."

"Exactly. Except for that. And Mrs. Signet."

I sighed and took a long sip of my mango-pineapple smoothie, thankful that there wasn't a biting wind sweeping through the downtown area. Otherwise, the cool drink would have me shivering all the way to my bones. "I just don't get it."

"If I ever understand men, I'll write a book about it and make millions. Men are confusing and complex and they get some kind of male version of PMS; I don't care what they say."

I chuckled. Jamie would know. She lived around enough guys. My mind quickly went back to last night, though. "It was like Mrs. Signet's words scared him. Terrified him, maybe."

"Talk of true love can be terrifying to some."

"I don't know. I can't help but think there was more to it." I shook my head. "Anyway, this isn't my biggest concern of the moment. My biggest concern is these murders. I mean, even if Chase did like me, as soon as he discovers I was at that first crime scene, he's going to resent me for lying to him."

"Maybe no one will ever find out. Isn't that what you're hoping?" The sun hit Jamie's wild curls, and her auburn highlights became illuminated.

"Someone seems desperate for the police to find out." I took another long sip of my smoothie.

"But why? What sense does it make?"

"You're the armchair detective. What do you make of it?"

Jamie slowed her steps for a moment. "It almost sounds like someone wants to frame everything on you. But why they just don't come out and give the police a bigger piece of evidence, I don't know. Why don't they just tell the police they saw you?"

"Coming forward would make them look guilty." I shrugged, never once having imagined that at any point in my life I'd be wandering through downtown Cincinnati having this conversation. "They've got to be more subtle."

"Subtle. Most criminals haven't mastered that art form yet."

My brain was going at nearly full speed now. "And how about the fact that someone's trying to shoot me? How does that tie in? This is all just crazy."

"That's a good question. The other question is: Are they missing on purpose or just a terrible shot?" She raised her eyebrows and cast a glance at me.

My head was beginning to pound.

"Well, I discovered something interesting as I was researching a story."

I looked over at my friend. "What's that?"

"You talked about a T.J.? You said he's Chase's new partner, right?"

I nodded.

"Well, Rex Harrison's former partner in the Cincinnati PD was none other than . . . drumroll please . . . T.J., Chase's current partner."

My mouth parted in surprise. "Really?"

She nodded like the cat that ate the canary. "That's right."

I absorbed that information. "That is interesting. It's a small world, isn't it? Are you doing an article on Rex?"

"For the newspaper, we have articles in queue for the election. So, we'll have a bunch of articles about Rex in case he wins, and a bunch on Ralphie in case he wins."

"You're not digging up dirt on my brother, are you?" I kept my voice light.

"Girlfriend, we'd publish that beforehand if we did. You've got to know us reporters better than that. We thrive on exposing hidden information."

I smiled. Jamie was loyal but tough. "Good to know."

"So, anyway, I've been doing some interviews about Rex and found out some information about his brother. He's the reason Rex is so adamant about cleaning up the drug problem in this area. Apparently, he was an addict."

I remembered Rex saying something about that when he spoke to the teens at the youth center. He'd mentioned how, on the surface, his brother had everything together. A good job, a nice house with lots of land, lots of money. But he had a secret drug problem that destroyed him. He ultimately took his life.

"We all have loss in our lives, don't we? There's no way to avoid it, no matter who you are. It's something we share as humans, despite the barriers of class, money, race, gender. And everyone's sad story comes out during election time. I guess it makes the candidates seem more human."

She swung her head toward me. "You talking about your brother?"

"Brian is more like it. Someone in the White House once said, 'Never waste a tragedy.' I guess that slithers all the way down to local politics as well."

"Nothing surprises me about Brian anymore."

I noticed a crowd of people ahead, gathered around

a platform set up in an open area. I'd seen protests here
before. Was that what was going on now?

We walked closer. My steps slowed when I saw the
campaign signs.

This was a rally for Rex Harrison.

Of course.

***

Twenty minutes later, I had to admit that the man
was charismatic. I'd give him that. And he made my
brother sound like the devil. Rex made all sorts of
promises that seemed impossible to carry through with.
Most politicians did. But did he actually believe his
own lies?

The crowd around him obviously did. They cheered
and clapped and chanted his name, even.

"I'm so tempted to vote for this guy," Jamie
muttered. She stood with her arms crossed, absorbing
the scene, maybe even with a touch of awe.

I gasped, partly in shock, partly in mock drama.
"Really? You'd vote against my brother."

"You see, that's the problem. If Rex were running
against anyone else, this man would totally have my
vote. But I like your family too much to not support
Ralph, even if I do trash-talk him sometimes."

I'd heard the debates between Jamie and Ralph
before. Jamie wasn't one to back down from an
argument. She let you know how she felt and when she
felt that way. But she was loyal, and I was thankful for
that.

"What is it about Rex that you like?" I watched
people gather around the man as if he were a celebrity.

"He doesn't seem all proper, like the Washington, D.C., type, you know? He grew up in a working-class family—"

"So did Ralph," I reminded her.

"But you guys are different. You might be working class, but you've got everything together, at least on the surface. Guys like Rex, they had to fight their way to the top. He knows what that's like."

To hear her talk, it was a wonder that Ralph was ahead in the polls. I think it had to do, in part, with my family's standing in the area. My mom served on a million different boards, and probably a lot of those people would vote for Ralph. Then there was my sister and the people who worked with her. All of those people I supposed encompassed the upper echelons of people in our community, however.

Rex's supporters came from the bad parts of town. They had very little, so Rex's promises had to tempt them, even if only a fraction of them were true. The man chose not to wear ties and nice suits. Instead, he wore shirts unbuttoned at the collar with nice jeans.

The man was no dummy, that was for sure.

The election was getting closer and closer. If something like what I'd done was discovered, it could cost my brother the win.

And his defeat would be on my shoulders.

I wondered if my brother would forgive me before I died.

"Come on. Let's get out of here," Jamie said, just as people began to disperse. "I want to swing by that organic bakery. They have the best almond-flour muffins ever."

***

Jamie had talked me into trying a muffin, and I had to admit, they weren't bad. We were walking back to her van when a group of people rounded the corner.

"If it isn't Holly Paladin," someone said.

That's when I recognized Rex Harrison and his posse.

Rex knew me. Not only had we spoken at the awards ceremony, but we'd also met at the youth center. He'd been there campaigning, even though I really thought it was more of a PR opportunity. In fact, Brian had given me a lecture because I hadn't insisted to Abraham that he reject Rex coming in favor of Ralph.

Just one more reason why I didn't like politics. They made things way too complicated.

"Hello, Rex," I managed.

His eyes sparkled with recognition a moment before he took my hand and kissed the top. "Hello, Holly Paladin."

Just then, I heard someone snap a picture. Lovely. The fact that I was cavorting with the enemy had been documented.

I quickly pulled my hand back and tucked it safely into the pocket of my gray wool petticoat.

"It was nice to see you at my rally." He looked a little too smug for my comfort.

"I just happened to be in the wrong place at the wrong time." I raised my chin.

He grinned, as if I'd paid him a compliment. "I don't believe in coincidences."

"Start believing, Rex. You need to start believing." His kind of charm might work on some people, but not on me. Sure, I'd been wrong about people before. Take Chase for example. But Rex just seemed too slick to me.

"And who is this vision with you?" He turned to Jamie, appearing all debonair and suave.

Jamie actually giggled. I'd never seen my friend giggle before, not in our ten years of friendship. "I'm Jamie."

He kissed her hand. "You're lovely."

"Thank you." She giggled again.

I scowled, and someone else snapped another picture. This was just great. I had a feeling these images were going to be all over social media.

"My day is brighter now that I've met you," he murmured, his gaze locked on Jamie.

I rolled my eyes. He was a charmer. I just couldn't believe Jamie was falling for it. Not my tough-as-nails friend. She was a better judge of people than this.

"I hope to see you both around," he finished, a smile tugging at his lips. "It was lovely running into you."

With a curt nod toward me, he and his entourage left. What kind of man used the word "lovely"?

I stood there, waiting until they were a decent distance away before turning my scowl on Jamie, who looked a bit starstuck with a dopey smile on her face, an almond-flour muffin crumb on her lip, and a dazed look in her eyes. My sunshine-inspired friend was glowing so much I needed sunglasses. "Really?"

Her smile slipped as she snapped back to reality. "What?"

"You fell for that?"

"Is it too much to believe that he thinks I'm great?" Her lips pursed as she waited for my answer. Every once in a while, her sass kicked in strong. She usually reserved that for people who weren't her friends and who really ticked her off.

I softened my voice. "No, you are great. I just think he's smarmy. You can do better than someone who just tells people what they want to hear."

Her eyebrow cocked up. "Do better than someone running for office? Than someone who has risen up from nothing? Someone who's managed to get half the city to back him?"

She had a point. But there was more to people than a list of their accomplishments. "I just don't trust him."

"You're the one who always turns heads. It's nice to know what that feels like."

I opened my mouth and then shut it again. My friend didn't very often admit to any insecurities. Sometimes it was just better not to have the last word.

CHAPTER 19

"So, you really think all of these murders boil down to some new synthetic drug?" Jamie asked as we drove back down the road to my house.

I shrugged, just happy to be on a different subject. "That's what it sounds like. I mean, who knows? It could be a twisted killer doing what he thinks is best for the city. It could be someone with a vendetta toward drug users. I have no idea. I was trained as a CPS investigator to see signs of abuse and to find solutions. I was never trained to figure out answers as to why people act the way they do."

"That's the great mystery."

"I also know that drugs and alcohol can make people act in unbelievable ways. It makes them do things they regret. If the killer is being influenced by drugs himself, then he may not even have a reason. He may just be acting on impulses that are exacerbated by the drugs."

We continued down the road, and I turned my thoughts over and over with each rotation of the tires. I wished I did have some answers.

"Did you recognize anyone at the scene of the third murder? They're not connected with you in any way, are they?"

I stared out the car window. "Not that I know of. I mean, I don't even know the guy's name who died. The police couldn't tell me much. I talked to his mom, but she just kept calling him 'her boy.' I'd never seen her before, though."

"Was that crime scene close to the other two?"

"A couple of blocks away."

"Where was the second scene?"

"The second scene was actually right down that road." I pointed at the street on my left.

"Here?" Jamie took a sudden turn, sending me smashing into my door.

"It's farther up the road, though." I rubbed my shoulder.

"My mom used to always tell me to stay away from this street at night," she muttered.

"There are probably a lot of places around here you should stay away from at night." As if to confirm the sentiment, two men talking on the sidewalk stopped and stared at Jamie's van as we passed.

People around here knew when an outsider was in the area; they didn't like it. They only trusted their own.

Even though I'd grown up on the outskirts of this neighborhood, I didn't count as a local in this area, mostly because I lived in a little section of houses that were five times as nice as the rest. My family refused to give up hope that this part of the city would one day be restored to its former glory.

I pointed to a house down the road. "Her place is down there. Why do you want to see it, anyway?"

"You just never know when something will trigger something somehow. That's a lot of 'somes,' I know, but you know?"

"Somewhat. Yes, I know. What do you know?"

We laughed, and the tension from earlier seemed to be broken. That was good, because there was no one else in the world who understood my goofy humor like Jamie.

"I don't know what I'm going to do without you, Holly."

Her words made me catch my breath, made my throat ache uncontrollably.

She braked and looked over at me. Tears pooled in her eyes. Jamie never cried. Like *never*, ever cried. Ever.

And I had no idea what to say.

It will be okay.

I'll always be there for you.

Nothing's ever going to change.

Those promises only worked if you were still alive.

Instead, a tear spilled down my cheek until we were both sobbing. It was the first time we'd ever addressed the fact that our friendship here on this earth wouldn't last until we were old and gray. I was going to die, and Jamie would be left here without a sidekick.

Life was going to go on without me. That thought was sobering, to say the least.

She grabbed a tissue. "Are you sure chemo won't help? Because I can't stand the thought of you not being here."

"It would only extend my life by a few months, if that. It's not worth it. Quality over quantity, right? That makes sense to me. I don't want my final days to be like my dad's final days. I want my life to be about living, not dying."

"It just doesn't seem real." She shook her head.

"Maybe I should start interviewing some candidates to take over for me as best friend." I tried to keep my voice light, knowing the idea was ludicrous.

"Interviewing candidates?" She sent me an incredulous look.

I nodded, trying to look serious despite the fact that my chest ached at the thought. "What about Sheila at the newspaper? She seems nice."

"She doesn't get my humor."

"Okay, how about your neighbor? What's her name—Nikki?"

"She thinks the fact that I'm an armchair detective is stupid."

Well, she wouldn't work, then. "I know! Tameka at church. She seems sweet."

"She is nice . . . but she's not you."

We both sniffled and hugged.

This conversation was making reality set in, and I didn't like it. I'd rather live in ignorant bliss. But, as time passed, that wasn't going to be an option.

She drew in a shaky breath and fanned her face. "Okay, I've got to get a grip."

She put the van back into drive and cruised down the road. The Rex Harrison sign in front of Desiree's house stared at me, even from a block away. Her house was the only one displaying his smiling mug, but a moment of foreshadowing clouded my mind. I wondered if my brother really would win this election.

Something else caught my eye. I grabbed Jamie's arm. "Slow down."

"What's going on?"

I pointed to Desiree's house and the man walking across the lawn there. "Please tell me I'm seeing things."

Jamie squinted. "Who is that?"

"That's Brian. And, for some reason, he's leaving Desiree's house."

CHAPTER 20

"Follow him." My voice sounded more authoritative than I'd expected, and I liked it.

"Yes, ma'am. I like how you think, my friend."

My smile faded. I tried to imagine Jamie doing this with Tameka one day. It wasn't jealousy that I felt, just a profound sense of loss. But I didn't have time to dwell on that now.

As Brian pulled away from the street in his plush Lexus, my mind raced. What in the world would he have been doing at Desiree's? It made no sense.

Brian wasn't the type of guy who liked to be hands-on like that. He was an expert at social media, and he could write a mean press release and even orchestrate an award-worthy press conference. But he hung out with people who were just like him—idealistic college graduates who drove foreign cars, liked drinking mimosas for breakfast, and worked twelve-hour days, rewarding themselves twice a year with a nice, very expensive vacation.

I expected him to travel back to his apartment downtown. Or maybe to his favorite restaurant, this tapas bar he talked about all the time. Maybe he'd even head over to Ralph's so they could talk more about the election and strategize about Twitter campaigns and how to keep every hair perfectly in place.

Instead, he headed down to the warehouse district,

an industrial area that had seen better days.

"Just what is he up to?" I whispered. "Make sure you stay a safe distance behind him. I don't want him to recognize us."

Thank goodness we had Jamie's van and not my Mustang.

"I've never thought Brian was the one for you," Jamie muttered. "Can I just say that this 100 percent confirms it?"

"Let's not jump to conclusions. Maybe he has a perfectly rational reason to be here." Not that I could think of a single one that seemed plausible.

Jamie's little grunt let me know she didn't believe that for a minute either.

We slowed down as Brian pulled over to the side of the road. He parked his car, stepped out, and looked both directions.

Which was suspicious within itself.

None of this was making any sense, and I was having a terrible time trying to wrap my mind around it.

He slipped inside the warehouse.

"I wonder what's going on inside there," Jamie whispered.

"Maybe they're stuffing campaign flyers into newspapers."

Jamie swerved her head toward me, and gave me what I called her "what the what?" look. "Sure they are."

"Or maybe they're manufacturing a synthetic drug that's killing teenagers and bringing a certain neighborhood to shambles," I mumbled. Saying the words out loud made me tremble with fear.

"Now you're thinking."

"And, just in case that second theory is correct, it wouldn't be wise to barge in and see what's happening, now would it?" I pictured it happening. The outcome wasn't pretty.

"Oh, no. Not wise at all. They'll take one look at you in that pretty little dress and eat you alive."

I stared at the building. There were no signs to indicate what it was or had been. There were no windows to peer in. All I saw was that heavy steel door at the front.

"What now?" Jamie asked.

"Now we wait and see how long Brian is inside. You have time?"

"I have an article due in the morning. I'll stay up all night doing it if I have to. I wouldn't miss this for the world."

***

We stayed for an hour. That's when Brian left. Of course, we'd followed him, but he'd only gone home.

I considered calling Chase. But I had nothing to go on. And, if I was wrong and this was some innocent operation on Brian's account, then I'd be setting up not only Brian, but my brother as well.

I didn't want to play the political game, but was that exactly what I was doing? If Brian weren't affiliated with my brother, would I have called the cops right away?

I'd like to think the answer was no. After all, I had no evidence. Everything here could be aboveboard. What would I say when I called the police?

I saw a friend of mine leave a bad neighborhood and stop at an unmarked warehouse? That excuse didn't seem very compelling.

At the moment, I was at Jamie's church. I knew that probably sounded weird, since I'd gone to my own church that morning. I always said that I went to my church to feed my brain. We were firm on doctrine and theology, and my pastor could deliver a great sermon that made me really think about the way I was living my life. We had more than six hundred members, a strong young career class—which ironically was where I'd met my fiancé, the one who'd broken up with me when my dad was ill—and there was some kind of activity going on there every night of the week, it seemed. I could spend all of my free time at the church and never have to step foot into the real world. They even had a gym!

But I went to Jamie's church because it fed my soul. I loved hearing the people worship there. I loved the heartfelt yet imperfect music. I loved how everyone got swept up in the Spirit.

True, I was the only white girl there. But I'd been going to the little church, which met in an old storefront and had around sixty members, for more than a year, and I loved it. Everyone there called me "sugar," and "sweetie," and one lady even called me "white chocolate."

I had no rhythm, but that didn't stop them from putting a tambourine in my hands on occasion. That didn't stop me from singing out. The pastor's sermons always got a lot of "amens" and "hallelujahs" and left me feeling fired up.

After the service, Jamie was talking with someone.

Tameka, actually. I pushed aside thoughts of her bonding with Tameka and pulling away from me in order to deal more effectively with my death. Instead, I sat beside Jamie's brother, John.

Jamie's parents, Louis and Val, had been determined to name their children after the twelve disciples. Not only that, they'd had a "feeling" they'd only have boys. Instead, they were only able to have three children, and one was a girl. Therefore, they had Peter, Jamie, and John. I got a chuckle out of it every time I thought about it.

Since then, they'd adopted three more boys from Haiti, and named them Andrew, Philip, and Matthew.

John was nineteen, and though I believed he was a good kid at heart, he'd gotten wrapped up in the same strongholds that a lot of people his age did. He'd played with drugs. Had some rough friends. Done some stupid things. He'd caused his family some grief throughout it all, but at least he was here at church now.

"Holly, my girl. What's going on?" He turned to face me, a wide smile stretching across his face. Though he was only nineteen, he looked like he was my age. He was well over six feet tall and as skinny as a pole.

"Same old, same old. How about you?"

"Staying busy. Got a job at the supermarket. I know the pay isn't great, but it's something."

"Good going, John. I think that's great."

An idea suddenly occurred to me. I wasn't sure if it was good or bad, but it was worth a shot. "John, I have a question for you."

"Anything for you, Ms. Holly."

"You ever heard of a drug called Cena?"

His smile slipped. "Yeah, everyone around here has. Why? You're not thinking about trying it, are you?"

"You know me better than that. I just want to know what you've heard about it."

He shrugged. "I don't know. People I know who've used it say it's good. Gives you a nice high."

"Where do you get it?"

He looked around as if the conversation was making him uncomfortable. That was a good thing; I didn't want him being comfortable talking about where to get drugs. Especially at church.

"I know some people."

I had a vision of me going undercover and buying some, but I quickly put the idea out of my mind. That would just be a bad, bad idea. I had to be realistic here.

"Why you asking about this, Ms. Holly?"

"You've heard about those people who died?" I asked him.

"Of course."

"I think it has to do with Cena."

He didn't look surprised, which seemed to confirm the theory. "Yeah, everyone's pretty shaken up about that."

"Any idea who's behind the production of it?"

He shook his head. "Nah, I hear he wears a mask. Whoever he is, he doesn't want to be discovered."

Would he kill to make sure that didn't happen?

CHAPTER 21

The next morning, as I was getting dressed for work while listening to Peggy Lee sing "It's a Good Day," someone knocked at my door. I had a Pavlovian reaction lately every time I heard someone on my doorstep. I tensed all over and prepared for the worst.

When I saw Chase standing there, I tried to mentally brace myself for what was to come. Really, living like this wasn't living at all. Fear sucked the joy out of life.

Much like chemo greatly diminished the body, fear ruined the spirit.

I'd created my own end to the quality of my final days, and I had no one to blame except me.

New item on my bucket list: figure out the best way to decorate my jail cell.

Item two: figure out a way to make the jail uniform look cute. Would they let me add a scarf? Could I bring my favorite Peggy Lee CD?

"Chase, what are you doing here?"

"Hey, Hollywood."

I readjusted my headband. "Not quite Hollywood."

His smile slipped. "Can I come inside?"

I opened the door wider. "By all means, yes. Come in."

I saw the apology in his eyes as soon as he stepped toward me, and my gut churned.

That's when I noticed the movement behind him. My stomach dropped.

T.J. walked up the sidewalk.

"Take everything he says with a grain of salt, okay?" Chase whispered.

I nodded, anxiety gripping me. I forced a smile as T.J. approached. "Good morning," I called cheerfully.

He scowled. "Something like that."

The lump in my throat grew larger as I shut the door and ushered them toward the breakfast nook. "Can I get either of you a cinnamon roll? I made them myself, all the way down to the icing. I even made the dough—"

"We're good," T.J. muttered.

I nodded, determined not to have my feathers ruffled. "Coffee?"

"I'd love some coffee," Chase said.

My hands trembled as I poured him a cup. They sat on opposite ends of the table. I set Chase's cup in front of him and then lowered myself between them, nervously smoothing my dress. "So, to what do I owe the pleasure of this visit?"

"I wish we were here with good news, Holly," Chase started.

"Look, let's just cut to the"—T.J. glanced at his partner—"chase, pardon the expression. Your fingerprints were found on the bucket at one of our crime scenes, Holly."

"Were they?" I knew somehow this would lead back to me.

Chase nodded. "We expected we might find it at this house, since you were the social worker. But we were surprised to find it on the bucket."

"Any idea how that happened?" T.J. asked.

"I, uh . . . It's strange. I — " My face heated.

"It's okay, Holly. No one is accusing you of anything," Chase said. His voice sounded even and compassionate. "We're just trying to put the pieces together."

I just needed to confess everything, own up to my part in this. I had to face the music. "Listen, I — "

"Holly, the chief wants us to pull you into this investigation," Chase said. "As a consultant. I guess his wife thinks you hung the moon and have amazing insight on people. Your time as a CPS investigator impressed her so much that she can't stop talking about you to Chief Weatherly."

I blinked, certain I hadn't heard correctly. "What?"

T.J. scowled. "It's true. He thinks you may be able to pinpoint the connections better than we can, especially given your history and relationships in this area."

I shook my head. "I'm not sure what I can do."

"The chief has talked to Helen, and she's agreed that you're free to do whatever you can to help us," Chase continued.

"I think it's a terrible idea, just for the record," T.J. said.

I twitched my head. "Do you?"

Chase's phone buzzed, and he excused himself for a moment.

I watched him walk away and then turned back to T.J., who glared at me.

"Why were your fingerprints on that bucket?" he demanded. "I know you've got Chase wrapped around your little finger, but I'm not falling for your innocent act so easily."

I raised my chin, pushing down the panic. "I don't know what you're talking about. Chase is not wrapped around my—"

"I'm talking about your involvement in this case, Holly. Your fingerprints didn't show up by chance."

"Then how did they show up?" I questioned, some of the fight—however foolish—returning to me. I needed to buy myself some time, even though everything in me wanted to confess. If I did own up to my part in this, it wouldn't be to T.J.

"That's what I'd like to know."

"You're the detective." *Dear Lord, please forgive me!*

He stared at me, his gaze icy cold. I held my gaze in some kind of silent standoff.

The moment shattered when Chase walked back into the room. He clipped his cell phone back to his belt. "So, what do you say, Holly? Will you lend your expertise?"

I nodded, pulling my eyes away from T.J. My heart still beat out of control. "Of course. Whatever I can do to bring this guy to justice." *Except owning up to my part.* My guilt pressed harder.

"Justice is what this is all about," T.J. muttered. "I want to nail this guy—or girl—too."

Was that a hint that he thought I could be guilty? Or was my own remorse just rearing its head, making me assume things that may not be true? I had no idea.

"Let me report into work this morning and see what I can delegate," I said.

Chase nodded. "We'll be in touch. We're questioning some people today."

As soon as they left, I leaned against the wall. My forehead was covered in sweat and my heart was racing.

T.J. was onto me. Would he find the evidence he needed to arrest me?

You didn't do anything, Holly. You weren't the one who killed those men. You just happened to illegally be in the wrong place at the wrong time.

My rationale did little to comfort me.

***

I'd talked to Doris and told her what was going on. I knew she hated the fact that Helen liked me. She also said something about my hours being loosey-goosey lately and to consider this a warning.

She was just my supervisor and she couldn't exactly fire me, not with Helen in my corner. What she could do was make my life miserable.

As I drove to meet Chase, my mind raced.

Maybe this was some kind of trap. Lure me in with visions of helping, then nail me for the crime. Play with me until I accidentally admitted something. Make me think I was doing a favor, all while trying to frame me.

I had to appear as cool as a cucumber, I reminded myself. One hint of guilt and T.J. would smell blood. This was going to be harder than I thought.

I forced a smile as I walked into the police station. Chase met me there, put a hand on my elbow, and led me down the hallway to another part of the building. We stopped at what appeared to be an interrogation room.

Uh-oh.

I'd seen this on TV. I knew how it would turn out.

T.J. waited there with his usual scowl. His sleeves

were rolled up to his elbows and the top button undone. Pictures and files were laid out on the table.

"Holly, so glad you could make it." T.J.'s voice sounded less than thrilled, and he didn't try to disguise it.

Chase seemed unfazed as he crossed to the other side of the table. "We're hoping you might be able to see a connection that we missed."

I stared at the photos on the table and blanched.

Three lives that had ended too soon.

"I know it's hard to look at, Holly," Chase murmured.

I shook my head, pulling my gaze away. "It is. It's just . . . it's sad."

"You knew both of the families. Is there anything you can tell us about them?" T.J. asked.

"As I suppose you know, I work with families in the foster care system. I do home studies, make sure the kids are adjusting well, make sure they haven't left one bad situation and gone into another."

Chase nodded. "Your boss loves you. Said you go above and beyond."

"Both of these families, however, were ones that I worked with before coming to Caring Hands. I worked with them as a CPS investigator. Katrina Dawson was reported by the school system because her kids were often dirty and didn't do their homework, and the youngest boy broke his arm. I did an investigation and worked with Katrina. I put her in a counseling program. She went through a parenting class. We helped her to find a new job. She turned things around."

"Sounds warm and fuzzy," T.J. muttered.

I ignored him. "Of course, the boy who was killed didn't live there. He was only staying temporarily. I never met him."

"What about the second family?"

"Similar situation. It was a family between a rock and a hard place. They just needed some resources. I was following up with them when I left my position."

"Why did you leave your old job, Ms. Paladin?" T.J. asked.

"There's a high rate of burnout with CPS workers. The job is very hard, very demanding, very emotionally exhausting. Helen offered me a position, and it sounded like a good change of pace." Plus, the doctor had said I needed to reduce my stress.

"I don't see what that has to do with anything." Chase gave T.J. a pointed glance.

I raised my chin. "Perhaps you have hard feelings toward me because your best friend is running against my brother."

He bristled. "I leave my personal biases out of things, and I resent your implications."

I held my gaze with his. "That makes two of us."

"Let's get back to business here," Chase interceded. "Did you see any connections between the two families that you've worked with? Besides you?"

"Too often with poverty there are other common issues. In this case, drugs and gangs. However, I have no proof that either of those boys was involved with either of those."

"The day we first ran into each other," Chase started.

"The day I was shot at?" I clarified.

Chase nodded. "That's the one. I was called to

156

escort you. Can you tell me why?"

I nodded. "Frank Jenkins's children were taken away from him. He was a mean drunk, and those kids didn't need to be there. In most cases, I do everything I can to keep the kids with their parents. But not in this case. Mr. Jenkins turned all of his anger toward me, blaming me for what happened."

"Was alcohol the only problem Mr. Jenkins had?"

I licked my lips. "I followed up with his former employers when I did my investigation. There were traces of Cena found in his urine. I knew he'd solicited some people in the neighborhood for the drug, as well."

"Anything else?" T.J. asked.

"I can say that I've heard from more than one person that Cena usually amplifies certain traits in people. The only trait I can see it amplifying in Mr. Jenkins is anger."

"I'm going to ask you this one more time," T.J said. "Is there anything you want to tell us?"

My throat felt dry and tight.

CHAPTER 22

I glanced over at T.J. Did he see the guilt written in my gaze, looming just beneath the surface?

"Do you have any idea how cleaning supplies with your fingerprints ended up at our first crime scene?" he asked.

I didn't say anything.

"Certainly you don't clean for your clients as well, do you?" T.J. asked sarcastically.

I shook my head. "I can't say it's my job requirement."

He plopped a picture down in front of me. "You ever seen these before?"

I stared at the picture and contemplated my answer. What if I was hampering their investigation? The last thing I wanted was for the killer to get away because of me. I had to somehow skirt around the truth. "As a matter of fact, I have."

I saw Chase's eyes widen.

I licked my lips before continuing. "I bought a bucket, mop, and scrub brush last week."

"Why didn't you mention this earlier?" T.J. demanded.

"I had no idea they'd turn up at a murder scene," I replied. "I have this thing with random acts of kindness. I like to help people whenever I can, and that's why I bought them. I surprised my brother by cleaning his house."

Chase leaned toward me. "Do you still have these cleaning supplies?"

I shook my head. "No, someone took them."

Please, forgive me, I silently prayed. I didn't want to lie. I didn't. But there was so much on the line.

"Took them from where?" T.J. stood beside me, towering over me.

An intimidation practice? I wondered.

"My garage."

T.J. narrowed his eyes. "When were they taken?"

"Just this week."

"You didn't report it?"

"Report missing cleaning items from my garage?" I shook my head. "No, I did not."

"You had to have heard that cleaning supplies were found at the scenes," T.J. continued.

"And I was supposed to assume they were my cleaning supplies?"

"I'm surprised the thought didn't cross your mind."

"Enough!" Chase's voice ended the argument. "Holly, if you hear anything else while you're out talking to your clients—both current and former— would you let us know?"

I nodded. "Of course."

"We're still searching for Frank Jenkins, as well. We want to bring him in for questioning. He's gone off the grid."

"I'd sleep better at night knowing he's behind bars." I looked up at T.J. "If there's nothing else, I've got a big caseload right now. Lots of work to do."

He scowled again. "We'll be in touch."

Chase stood just as I did. "I'll walk you down," he

offered.

I didn't refuse. We were silent until we stepped outside.

"Good job standing up to T.J. in there," Chase told me. "Not many people will."

A few months ago I probably wouldn't have. But now, in many ways, I just didn't care. "He's a jerk."

"I can't argue with that. He thinks his former partner walked on water. No one else will ever measure up, apparently. He's got a huge chip on his shoulder."

"God bless you for working with him every day, then."

Chase paused by my car. "Thanks again for coming in, Holly."

I nodded and gripped my purse. "No problem. I've got to finish work and then head to the youth center for a while."

"I'll see you around later, then," he said.

I nodded, something within me drawing me toward the man, making me not want to leave.

Which was purely ridiculous.

"Okeydokey. Bye, Chase," I forced myself to say.

Then I climbed in my car.

I nearly slapped my forehead when I realized I'd just said "okeydokey."

Based on the goofy smile on Chase's face, it hadn't gone unnoticed.

***

I was trying to wrap up a conversation with my mom during my lunch break when Helen popped her head into my office.

"Holly, can I talk to you a minute?"

"Of course." I gripped the phone. "Mom, I need to run."

"Two things real quick, honey. First of all, that lady called again, the one who never leaves a message. I think this is the third call from her. Do you know what's going on?"

The nurse from the oncologist's office, most likely. I bristled. "I'll see if I can figure it out, Mom."

"Second, don't forget to water my plants when I'm out of town."

She was going to some real estate conference in Chicago. "Of course."

"You're always such a big help to me, Holly. I don't know what I'd do without you."

My heart panged. My poor mom. First she'd lost her husband, and soon she'd be losing her youngest child. I knew those were some of the hardest things a person could go through, and I wished I could spare her.

"I love you, Mom."

We hung up, and I walked toward Helen's office. I tried to tell myself that this was just a chat, but I couldn't help but feel a touch of trepidation. Though Helen liked me, she was still my boss. Had Doris convinced her I was irresponsible?

I sat across from her and smoothed my dress. As I glanced at my boss, I noticed she looked tired and that her smile didn't come quite as quickly as usual.

"I know you've been under a great amount of stress lately, Holly. I know there were two separate incidents of being fired at. That two of the crimes happened at the homes of your former clients and that the police have called you in to help."

I waited to hear a "but . . ." or a reprimand.

I swallowed hard, trying to brace myself.

"I just wanted to check and see how you're doing."

I let out the breath I held. "I'm . . . hanging in."

"That's good to hear. I'm very proud of you, Holly. You do excellent work."

"I appreciate that, Helen."

"Walter is very concerned about what's going on in the city. I really think our work, along with the police, is what will be able to turn this city around. The police are starting some task forces, and I'd like you to consider serving on one. I think you'd be an excellent addition."

"You know I'm always willing to help."

She smiled weakly. "Thanks, Holly."

"How are you, Helen?"

She sighed and leaned back. "I'm doing okay. Just been busy. Walter has been working a lot. He's obsessed with this case. It's all he wants to talk about."

"Hopefully, we'll find this guy soon."

She nodded. "Hopefully. For all of our sakes."

***

I got to the youth center late. I planned on making cupcakes with the girls tonight, but when I walked in, there was no one in sight.

I'd replayed my conversation with Chase and T.J. a million times in my head. Had I said anything incriminating? Was my story believable? Would God ever forgive me for lying to save myself?

I didn't know. And worrying about all of those

things would only lead me to an even earlier death.

The bell at the front door jangled. I abandoned my flour and sugar and walked out to see who'd arrived.

Anger roiled through my veins when I recognized the figure there.

Rex Harrison.

His face lit up when he saw me. "Holly Paladin. Fancy seeing you here."

I crossed my arms. "You knew I worked here."

"So I did. Actually, I stopped by to see you."

I didn't like where this was going. "Did you?"

"I haven't been able to get your friend out of my mind."

"My friend? You mean Jamie?"

His grin widened. "That's the one. I was hoping you might give her this." He held out a piece of paper toward me.

I glanced down at it and saw some numbers there. A phone number? *His* phone number?

I shook my head. "Why would I be your go-between? You think I want my best friend dating you?"

"I don't think that's for you to decide. That's Jamie's decision."

I shook my head again in disbelief. "So you came here? Really?"

He glanced from side to side and then stepped closer. "Come on, Holly. Work with me."

"Never. Why would I?"

Something gleamed in his eyes. "Because I know your secret."

CHAPTER 23

All the blood drained from my face. "I don't know what you're talking about."

"I saw you, Holly."

Was he the one who'd sent me the note? Was he behind all of this? If he knew, why hadn't he leaked the information in order to help his campaign and ruin my brother?

"You have cancer."

I blinked. I almost wanted to laugh. Almost. Only cancer was no laughing matter.

"Why would you think that?" I finally asked.

"I was taking my friend to the oncologist. I saw you leaving. In tears."

My throat tightened. Was that possible? Had I passed him and not even noticed? It was entirely feasible. I'd been so wrapped up in the devastation of the moment that I'd hardly been able to drive home.

Of course, if he'd seen me leaving alone, he might have put things together. No, I hadn't been there with someone else. Since I was alone, he would have deduced that I was there for myself.

"You're not denying it."

"You're really going to threaten me with cancer?"

He shrugged. "I happen to know you haven't told your family."

"How would you know that?"

"I expressed my condolences to your brother, and he had no idea what I was talking about. I feigned ignorance, pretended I'd misspoke. Then I realized that you're the type who might keep news like that to yourself, especially during a high-stress time like an election."

"So, you're saying that if I don't give your phone number to my best friend, you'll tell my family that I might have cancer?" He was despicable and unlikable, and I really wanted to spit on him or, in the least, pluck him on the forehead. If only either of those were ladylike.

"That's exactly what I'm saying." His eyebrows twitched up in humor. "So what do you say?"

He had me, and he knew he did. I couldn't have my family find out through Rex. That would devastate them. And I wasn't ready to tell them myself. Not yet. I needed more time.

Aggravated, I snatched the paper from his hands. "You don't want to mess with me, Rex."

I didn't know where the bravado came from in my voice. I was usually the one to smooth things over, the one who hated conflict. But something about this man lit a fire in me—and not the good kind. I wanted to bust his chops.

He smiled again, his teeth flashing in that million-dollar smile. "I appreciate your help, Holly. I'll be seeing you around."

***

I was still scowling at the door when Abraham emerged from the back, a box of bulk chips in his arms.

"Did I hear someone come in?"

"No one important," I snapped.

"Wow. You seem a little wound up." He raised his eyebrows as he set the box on the table.

I softened the set of my shoulders. "I'm sorry. It's been one of those days."

"Don't apologize to me. I know how that can be. The kids today were hyped up. They nearly broke out into a fight on the basketball court. Speaking of which . . ." He rubbed his shoulder. "I think I'm getting too old to play. My body is killing me."

I smiled and pulled the chips out to restock the vending machine. "You still give them a run for their money."

He laughed airily. "Thanks, but that's not the way it feels. By the way, it looks like that trip is coming together for Hannah and me. Can you still help me out here at the center while I'm gone?"

Where had he gotten the money for something like that? This wasn't the time to start pointing fingers and alienating everyone in my life. So, instead, I nodded. "Of course. Just let me know the dates when you have them nailed down."

"Thanks, Holly. I appreciate that." He started unloading the snack-sized bags. He did look worn out, like each of his movements dragged.

"Listen, why don't you get out of here? I'll clean up. You look tired."

He rubbed his chin. "Really? You wouldn't mind?"

"Of course not. Go on." I nodded toward the door, indicating that he should get going.

"Thanks, Holly. I am a little tired, now that you mention it. You're the best." A few minutes later, the back door clicked shut, indicating Abraham had left.

I continued to restock the machine. Then I picked up some random wrappers and cups around the room, straightened some magazines and other literature, and made sure all the sports equipment was put back.

My mind raced as I worked. Rex was manipulating me. He was that kind of man.

But was he the kind of man who would kill?

I even shook my head at that. He was a former police officer. He was running for office. I certainly couldn't see him being that ignorant or stupid enough to put everything on the line. Besides, what reason would he have to kill people off?

Whoever this Caligula guy was, he was supposed to have influence. That would fit Rex.

But maybe this Caligula wasn't responsible for the murders. Just because he was behind some new drug didn't mean he was a cold-blooded killer. He might be a different kind of killer, the kind who didn't care who he trampled on in order to make a few bucks for himself. Who developed drugs at the expense of others' lives.

I finished and locked up, walking down the alley toward my car. This may not have been my best idea ever, but I had little choice now. It was too late to call anyone to escort me.

I quickened my steps, gripping my keys, my gaze surveying the area around me.

I didn't see anything. That was a good sign.

No dark, leering figures. No guns. No anyone.

I fumbled with my keys for a moment, trying to unlock my door and, for once in my life, wishing I had one of those key fobs that would allow me to hit a button and my door would be unlocked.

Finally, I slid my key into the lock, pulled my door open, and scrambled inside.

The first thing I did was to hit the locks. Something about being in my car made me feel safer, if only for a minute.

Once my heart slowed just a bit, I started my car. I crept toward the street, but stopped when I reached the edge of the building.

In the eave of a building two doors down, I saw Abraham whispering to someone. I stayed where I was. Neither seemed to see me. The conversation seemed heated, and it pricked my curiosity.

The guy Abraham was talking with stepped out into the streetlight for a moment.

I sucked in a quick breath.

It was Little T.

I shook my head. No, Abraham was not involved in this. There was no way he would do anything to put the lives of these kids in danger. He wasn't that type of person.

Then why did doubts continue to linger?

As the two walked out farther onto the sidewalk, I knew my chances of being spotted were increasing. I gently hit the accelerator and turned in the opposite direction.

Instead of heading home, I circled around the block. When I pulled back down the street, Abraham was gone.

But I spotted Little T. He was walking away from the youth center, in the opposite direction. I slowed, watching him.

Then I saw him approach a van parked in a corner

lot.

I blinked.

That was Jamie's van.

I squeezed out the thoughts that tried to invade my mind. It was no use. They attacked every usable cell in my brain until I couldn't ignore the facts.

That was definitely Jamie's van.

I continued to creep forward. As I passed the parking lot, I craned my neck for a better look.

It was just as I feared.

John was in the driver's seat, and Little T was climbing in beside him.

Just what was John mixed up in?

CHAPTER 24

I idled into the parking lot of a bank and cut my lights. I couldn't help but think I was a natural at this tailing-people thing. I'd managed fine so far. How hard could this be?

I waited until John pulled out. I counted to five and then followed behind him.

I wished it weren't so dark outside, so I could see better inside the van. I wanted to see John and Little T, try to ascertain if they were talking or arguing or on their cell phones. Instead, dark windows stared back at me, blocking my view.

Certainly John didn't have anything to do with this craziness that was happening around town. He couldn't. Not Jamie's brother.

But the facts remained in front of me, reminding me of an annoying little kid who wouldn't get out of your face. I couldn't escape the scrutiny. Not even remotely.

They eased out of the neighborhood, headed toward the interstate. I cruised along behind them, trying to stay a safe distance out of sight. I really didn't want to be spotted.

I stayed low in my seat, tried to keep at least two cars between them and me. If they saw me, I was done. I'd have no more answers than I had now.

That wasn't acceptable.

Once downtown Cincinnati came into view, John

accelerated. He headed downhill, toward a green light. If I didn't time this right, the light would change and I'd lose them.

I just prayed that my brakes didn't go out. It didn't happen very often, but it had happened before.

I gunned it, trying to stay on their tail.

As soon as they cleared the intersection, they swerved into the left lane.

Did they spot me? Had I been made?

I decided I didn't care. I merged to the left, leaving at least two cars honking at me.

There were now four cars between the van and me. I was okay with that, as long as I could keep them in sight.

Traffic thickened as we approached the area known for clubs and nightlife. Everyone seemed to be headed that way, ready to enjoy an evening of partying.

Maybe I *wasn't* that great at this covert thing, especially not while driving a 1964 1/2 powder-blue Mustang, I decided.

All of a sudden, the van veered back to the right and off an exit ramp.

I pulled my wheel toward the right when I saw a semi there.

I braked, trying to slow enough to merge after the truck passed.

Then I realized it was too late. I'd missed the exit. And I'd lost them.

***

I couldn't bring myself to meet Jamie the next day. I knew I'd be forced to consider giving her Rex's number and asking her about what her brother had been doing with her van last night. I wasn't sure I wanted to do either.

The stakes had risen. I needed to find out who this killer was for more than one reason. Not only to prove my innocence but also to preserve what was left of my life.

I pulled up to Katrina's house, surprised to see a new Mercedes in the driveway. Whose was that? I started to question my decision to come here. It looked like she had company.

But my curiosity burned inside.

I got out of my car, and before my hand ever connected with the door, it flew open. Katrina stood there, a new light dancing in her eyes. A light like I'd never seen before.

"Ms. Paladin, I didn't expect to see you here. Did we have an appointment?"

I took in the diamond necklace around her neck, her new hairdo, her smile. "No, we didn't. I'm sorry to stop by uninvited. I just wanted to check on you."

She stepped outside, hiking her purse up higher. Just then, a man stepped out behind her. He was short but wore a business suit—an expensive one, if I had to guess. I'd seen this man somewhere before; I just couldn't place where.

"This is Evan," Katrina said. "Evan, this is Holly, one of the nicest people you'll ever meet."

We nodded hello. It could have been my imagination, but I felt like the man's gaze lingered on me just a little too long.

Katrina walked toward her car, Evan staying close behind. "I wish I could talk, Holly. But I'm on my way to an appointment. Maybe another time? I have a lot to tell you."

"Sure." I fell into step behind her.

She pulled out her keys and hit a button. The Mercedes let out a beep.

She opened the door and offered a small wave. "Great. Later, then!"

As I watched them pull away, I realized he bore some similarities to the man I'd seen before I'd been shot at outside the bank.

***

Where in the world had Katrina gotten money for a car like that? She could barely pay her bills. I just couldn't fathom how she could afford that vehicle.

My mind went to the worst places.

Places where someone was paying her off to keep her mouth shut.

No, not Katrina. She loved her kids too much to do something like that. Of course, she probably loved her kids enough that she would do almost anything to keep them well fed and clothed and to keep a roof over their heads. Did that mean she would even resort to any illegal means to do so? I sure hoped not.

Of course, look what I'd been quiet about in order to protect both myself and my family. I'd certainly thought I was stronger than that.

The more I got to know about myself, the more I realized that maybe I wasn't as strong as I thought. It was a hard realization to swallow.

I closed my eyes. *Dad, I'm sorry. If you're up in heaven watching me, I know you're probably disappointed. You thought more of me.*

You taught me that I could do anything I set my mind to. You encouraged me that I should follow my heart and not listen to the naysayers.

What would you be telling me now?

I really hated letting the people I loved down. And everywhere I turned, that's what I seemed to be on the verge of doing.

I glanced at my watch. It was time for my lunch break.

I decided to swing by and see Ralph at his campaign headquarters.

Maybe I could make something in my life right.

***

The campaign headquarters was all aflutter, and not because anything big had happened. It just always seemed busy, a flurry of activity and excitement and hope.

That was a good thing.

People were excited about my brother. They believed in him, and I knew he could do great things for the state and for this district.

I knocked on his door. He looked up from his desk and smiled. "Holly! I didn't expect to see you here."

"I had a few extra minutes, so I decided to stop by and visit my big brother. I had to see what all of the hoopla was about."

He raised his hands, his face beaming. "This is my place, and these are my people, so to speak. I'm honored to have so many supporters behind me."

"I'm glad. You deserve it, Ralph."

Just then, someone breezed past me, coming to an abrupt stop just in front of me. "You'll never believe this."

Brian. He did a double take, and then a wide grin spread across his face. "Holly! You here to volunteer?"

"Not exactly. Although, if you need anything, you know you can count on me."

He squeezed my arm, his hand lingering a little too long for normal formalities. "One more thing to love about you." He turned toward Ralph. "You'll never believe what I just discovered."

Ralph sat up straighter. "What?"

"One of the major campaign donors to Rex Harrison is Orion Enterprises."

Ralph offered a half shrug. "Okay . . . they're based out of Cincinnati. Manufacturing and textiles, I believe."

Brian nodded. "That's right. The guy who owns it, Orion Vanderslice, is loaded. Absolutely loaded. There's also an investigation under way about his company."

"Why?" I couldn't resist jumping in. After my encounter last night with Rex, the last thing I wanted was for him to win.

"Apparently, some of his warehouses are practically sweatshops. On the outside, he acts like he's all about the little people. But if you dig deeper into his company, he doesn't put into practice any of the principles he professes."

"What does this have to do with Rex?" I questioned.

"He's accepting money from someone who's shady. That's going to reflect poorly on him. It might mean that he'd do anything to win."

Another thought rammed into my mind.

Brian seemed like the type who'd do anything to win.

Would he even sell drugs to lure people into votes?

CHAPTER 25

Brian jangled the change in his pocket, his excitement obvious. "We can use this if we have to. I'm going to do some more digging. We have to time the release of the information perfectly, and we've got to prove that Rex knows Orion Vanderslice is dirty. We let the media know about this a few days before the election, and this could seal the deal. You could win."

"I want to win, but fair and square," Ralph said.

"I don't know what's not fair and square about this. Deeds done in the darkness will be revealed. Isn't there a proverb about that somewhere?"

"The Bible," I mumbled. "It's from the Bible."

"That's right! Who wants to argue with the Bible? Well, a lot of people, truth be told, but I'm not one of them." He stepped back. "Okay, I've got to get back to work. I just wanted to let you know."

"Thanks, Brian."

Brian turned toward me as he took a step back. "You up for tapas yet?"

"Maybe after my brother wins the election."

He chuckled. "I like that. Just one more thing to motivate me to work extra hard." He patted my arm. "I love this girl. See you both around."

As soon as Brian disappeared, I turned to Ralph and shut the door. Ralph stared at me, a funny expression on his face. "Brian's not your type, is he?"

I shook my head. "No, he's not."

"I just don't want to see you with someone else like that Rob guy. He was a jerk."

I frowned. "He was a jerk. But really, the fact that he broke up with me was a blessing. It was hard to see in the moment. But now I'm so thankful I didn't marry him. And I would have married him. Sometimes we only see the things we want to see, don't you think?"

Ralph nodded. "You're becoming quite the woman, Holly. I know Dad would be proud of you."

I forced myself not to cry. Almost every time my dad was mentioned, tears wanted to well in my eyes. I missed him so much.

And while Ralph didn't act like my dad, there was no denying that he looked like a younger version of him.

"Thank you, Ralph. He would be proud of you, too, you know."

Ralph leaned back. "Sometimes I like to think that he's here, watching everything, and smiling."

"That sounds about right."

"Brian, he's a nice guy. But he's not for you. Sometimes I think he would do anything to get votes."

My throat squeezed. I'd been thinking that same thing yet trying to dismiss it.

I remembered Brian visiting Desiree. I remembered the unmarked warehouse he'd entered. What was Brian not telling Ralph?

Brian was worried that Orion Vanderslice could ruin Rex. What if Brian was doing something that could ruin Ralph's chances? It was a possibility I had to consider.

I cleared my throat. "Anything?"

Ralph's eyebrows shot up in surprise. "Not *anything* anything. I just mean he's determined and a little too intense for you. He's too rigid and looking for a trophy wife, if you ask me. There's nothing plastic about you. You've got a lot of depth to you, Holly."

Outwardly, I smiled. But inwardly, I remembered that I'd broken into someone's house. I remembered what the consequences could be if I were found out.

I wondered if my brother would say such nice things about me if I cost him this election.

***

As I left the campaign headquarters and climbed into my car, my phone rang. Again.

I knew without even looking that it was Jamie calling. We always checked in, usually once in the morning and once in the evening.

I hadn't called her last night, and I hadn't called her this morning either.

My friend was no dummy. She had to know something was up.

I frowned before putting the phone to my ear and starting up Sally. "Hey, girlfriend."

"Girl, I thought something had happened to you. I almost started calling hospitals in the area to make sure you were okay and that you hadn't been admitted. My goodness, I even almost called your mom!"

I swallowed hard. "I'm sorry. I've been busy."

"What's going on? And don't tell me 'nothing.'"

I started down the road. "How about if I come by after work? Is that okay?"

179

"I don't know if I can wait that long. You sure you're okay?"

"Yeah, I'm fine. There's just been a lot going on."

"Okay, I'll see you at my place. Whatever you do, don't make this a late work night. Please."

I swung by my house quickly before heading back to work. I'd been thinking nonstop about those buckets and mops. Maybe, I'd decided, I needed to take them somewhere and dump them. Literally. As in, take them to the dump and leave them somewhere no one would ever find them in my possession.

I didn't, after all, want to be framed for a crime I didn't commit.

I parked at my house, went into the garage, and climbed into the attic. I opened the door to the little hidden cubbyhole and squinted.

The space was empty.

That couldn't be right.

I knew I'd left them there.

My blood went cold at my next thought.

What if the killer had come back to retrieve them? He'd now have my fingerprints all over them.

I was trembling when I climbed back into my Mustang.

My trembles only deepened when I looked across the street and saw Frank Jenkins close his car door and pull away.

***

I knocked at Jamie's door at precisely 6:00 p.m. My nerves had been getting the best of me all day, ever since the cleaning supplies had disappeared and I'd seen Frank Jenkins watching me. Now I considered what to do if John answered the door.

Act clueless?

Look him in the eye and demand answers?

Be a friend and see if he'd confide in me?

None of those scenarios were necessary, because he didn't.

Jamie's mom answered instead. I adored Jamie's family. Her mom had a bum knee, which was why Jamie had moved back in after college. She complained about it often, but I knew she wanted to help out.

Her mom worked as a nurse's aide for a hospice agency, and her dad played trombone for a jazz band, teaching music lessons on the side. They weren't perfect, not by any means. But there was something very comforting about hanging out with people who knew their flaws and were okay with not always having it all together.

Louis Armstrong music floated in from the stereo in the background, only it wasn't a stereo, I realized. That was actually Jamie's dad practicing in the sunroom.

"Holly, girl," Mama Val said. "Good to see you. You're not coming around here much anymore. Everything okay?"

Jamie's mom weighed well over three hundred pounds, and she had a large personality to match. I also knew that I never, ever wanted to make her mad.

"I'm fine, Mama Val."

"That's good because God's been putting you on my mind lately, Holly girl. Every time I think about you, I pray, 'God, be with Holly Paladin. I don't know what's going on with her, but watch over her.' Can I get an amen?"

181

"Amen," I muttered.

"What was that? I didn't hear you?" She cupped her hand around her ear.

"Amen!" I said it with more enthusiasm this time.

"That's right. You know that Mama Val is there for you if you ever need it. Okay?"

"Thanks, Mama Val."

"All right, Jamie! Where are you? Can't you hear that your friend is here?"

I smiled. I always loved being around Mama Val. She was such a contrast to my own reserved, always socially correct mother. I loved my own mother, too. It was just nice to see people who weren't afraid to go against the grain.

"Come on in. Let me go find that girl."

I stepped inside. In the background, I saw the three little disciples running around in the living room. They stopped running for long enough to give me hugs—they called me Aunt Holly—and then they went right back to their swordplay.

I smiled as I watched them. I couldn't remember my brother, sister, and me ever playing like that. Of course, they'd been older. But my earliest memories, outside of hanging with my dad, were of taking piano lessons, and volunteering for community cleanup days, and redecorating our house every three years.

Jamie came downstairs and rolled her eyes at her mom. "I was doing my oil pull. Patience, Mother. Patience."

"Oil pulling? Makes no sense to me. You put coconut oil in your mouth, swish it around for fifteen minutes, and suddenly all of your health problems disappear? Sounds like voodoo to me."

She rolled her eyes again. "It's not voodoo, Mom. Several doctors back up the scientific study behind it. It works. And it makes my teeth feel smooth."

"I'm surprised it doesn't rot your teeth. I don't understand it. Do you, Holly?"

I stepped back. "I'm out of this one."

Mama Val raised her chin. "I see how you are. Okay, you two get along. Go play. I'll stay out of your way."

She lumbered off.

I turned to Jamie. "She has a point, you know. I really don't understand how oil pulling is supposed to be beneficial."

"I'm telling you, I haven't had one cold or sinus infection since I started doing it. Don't knock it until you try it."

I nodded and held up my hand. "Okay, maybe we should talk about something else."

"Let's. Come on up to my room."

I followed her upstairs. Her house was old and outdated, but clean and neat. It always smelled like cooked greens and fried foods, and there were gaudy remains of the art deco style that had once decorated the place: fake-marble-covered tables, shiny steel fixtures, faded pastel colors.

We went into Jamie's room and she closed the door. I plopped down on her daybed, just as I'd done so many times before.

"I'm surprised you didn't want to meet at that vegan pizza place," I told her.

"I would, but I have a flat tire."

I tried to keep my expression neutral. "Really? What happened?"

"Oh, I let John borrow the van last night, and he said he ran over a nail. Go figure. Now I have to wait until my paycheck comes in so I can buy a new tire."

"Ouch. What was he doing last night when he ran over a nail? Donuts in a construction parking lot?"

She snorted. "Sounds like something he'd do. I don't know about that boy. He said he was meeting some friends. I have no reason to doubt him."

"Of course."

"So, what's new? I need the inside scoop. You helped Chase yesterday, right?"

I frowned. "His partner is onto me. He thinks I have something to do with it."

Her eyes widened. "Are you sure?"

"Pretty sure. He's made it clear he's not a fan of mine."

"What does Chase say?"

"It's weird. It's like he's trying to protect me. He told me to take anything T.J. says with a grain of salt. That he probably doesn't like me because he's friends with Rex and knows my brother is running against him."

"Rex, huh?" Jamie smiled.

The weight on my chest pressed harder. Jamie was a big girl, I reminded myself. She needed the freedom to make her own choices.

And she was smart. She had a good head on her shoulders.

I was stressing out about nothing.

"Yeah, speaking of Rex." I reached into my purse and pulled out the paper he'd given me. "He stopped by the youth center last night."

She cocked her head. "The youth center? Why? I

thought he'd already been there."

I licked my lips, not wanting to let the words leave my mouth. I forced them out anyway. "He actually wanted to talk to me. About you."

Her eyes widened and she let out a soft squeal. "What?"

I nodded. "Yeah, he wanted me to give you his personal number. He wants you to call him."

"Why? Why in the world does he want me to call him? Is he trying to hire me? Does he need a reporter on his campaign staff? Not that I would ever accept the position. Not with your brother running and all." Her frown looked a little too forced.

"He wants to ask you out."

Her squeal was much louder this time. "Are you serious? Rex Harrison wants to ask me out? You're kidding? Girlfriend, if you're kidding, I'm going to give you the biggest wet Willie that you've ever had."

I raised my hands. Despite myself, a small laugh escaped. I loved seeing her so excited. I just wished it wasn't about Rex. "I'm not kidding. But, Jamie, you're not going to go, are you?"

Her smile disappeared faster than a feather on a windy day. "Why wouldn't I?"

"It's . . . Rex."

"Exactly." She nodded, her eyes scarily wide and adamant. "It's Rex." She fell back on her bed. "I never imagined in a million years that someone like him would give me the time of the day. Not only did he do that, but he went out of his way to find me. To track me down. That's what every girl dreams about."

I had to find the right words, but it was so hard. "Do you trust him, Jamie?"

"How can I trust him? I don't know him. He was a police officer, though. He started a nonprofit. If he wasn't running against your brother, you would like him. Admit it, Holly."

I shook my head. "I can't admit that. There's something about him that bugs me."

She sat up and narrowed her eyes. "For once, can't you just be happy for me?"

"I'm happy for you a lot, Jamie."

"No, you're not. You're not going to be here, Holly. You're leaving me. I need someone else in my life. Rex would be someone."

Her words felt like a slap in the face. I stood and stepped toward the door before my emotions got the best of me. "I see. Well, you should get on with your life."

"Holly, I didn't mean it like—"

"No, you're right. Life is too short to live for the approval of others. I just don't want to see you get hurt."

"Holly, please."

I stepped into the hallway and hurried down the stairs. I ran to my car and took off, fighting tears.

I'd been determined not to feel sorry for myself. But right now, all I felt was sorrow.

How did one come to terms with death? With the realization that life would go on without you?

I didn't know. But one way or another I had to figure it out.

Because reality was feeling realer and realer all the time.

CHAPTER 26

My phone rang as I cruised down the road. It was Chase.

"Hey, can we meet? I want to talk over a few things with you."

It beat going back to my house and feeling sorry for myself. "Sure thing."

He picked a café that overlooked downtown in the Mount Airy section of the city. I found him at a table by the window. The waitress was obviously flirting with him. He smiled back, saying something that made her giggle.

Why did my heart tighten at the sight? Chase and I could never be together. I knew that. Even if he was a changed man, there were still so many reasons to stay away. Disappointment still nibbled away at my spirit, though.

He looked over at me, something in his eyes shifting when he saw me. "Holly."

He stood and pulled out a chair. I willed my cheeks not to flush as I sat down. I loved being treated like a lady, though. It was almost like he knew the way to my heart.

Which was a shame, since he was just flirting with the waitress.

"She was just telling me that she's dropped two plates already today. She considered it fair warning,"

Chase offered. "I'm passing that info along to you now."

That released some of the tension I felt. Maybe he hadn't been flirting. Maybe he'd just been being friendly. "I see."

I let out a slow breath and smoothed the black tablecloth. "A Kiss to Build a Dream On" played on the overhead, and the comforting scents of bacon and eggs filled the air. I'd been here once before, and I knew the Cosmic Café prided itself in taking familiar foods and making them different. The whole café felt a little otherworldly with its brightly painted walls and open, airy design.

"I've been thinking about you all today," Chase started.

That lump — becoming all too familiar — appeared in my throat. I glanced over at Chase and tried to swallow. "Have you?"

"For the record, I thought T.J. was a jerk yesterday. I can't apologize for him enough."

I played with the water glass in front of me. "He has strong opinions."

"That's one way to say it. But he had no right to accuse you. I almost think he wants to nail you in this so his friend can win the election."

"People would do a lot of things to get into office, wouldn't they?"

He snorted and leaned back in his chair. "Being in office too many times means power. People would sell their souls to have that. I've seen it too often."

"I guess I just can't understand that."

He took a long sip of his tea. "It's because you're kind."

"If you'd heard the conversation I just had with Jamie, you wouldn't think I was so kind." I fought back a frown as my heart thudded into my chest. I hated fighting with people, but I especially hated fighting with Jamie.

"Oh, come on. It couldn't be that bad, could it?"

I nodded. "Yeah, it could. Rex Harrison asked her out, and I told her she should say no. She took it as an insult. It wasn't pretty."

"You're just looking out for your friend."

Exactly! "I wish she'd see it that way."

"She'll come around. She knows you well enough to know your heart." Chase offered a kind smile.

"The heart is easy to deceive Chase."

The waitress appeared again. "Here's a plate of nachos. Can I get you anything to drink? I promise not to spill it on you." She smiled.

I raised my condensation-covered glass. "The water is great. Thank you."

She nodded and left.

Chase nudged the nachos my way. "I hope you don't mind. I was in the mood for something spicy. These actually have shrimp and bacon on top, so there's something to offend everyone."

"You're surprising, Chase."

"As are you." He leaned back. "How's your mother doing?"

"I think she pours herself into her work because she misses Dad." I gulped, realizing I'd just way overshared. "Of course, that's not what you were asking. She's doing fine."

"The death of a loved one can leave a hole in people's lives, can't it?" His serious gaze held mine.

"It really can."

"How about in your life?"

I shrugged, already emotional and desperately needing some control at the moment. Despite that, I blurted, "No one in my family gets me, Chase. I feel like an outsider."

I wish I could say that life was too short to have superficial conversations and that's why I kept going to these deep, honest places with Chase. I really didn't know why I was pouring out so much, except that maybe I needed to talk and Chase just happened to be there.

"They love you."

"They make me feel incompetent because I don't react like they do." I shook my head, decidedly resolving to change the topic and get it off of me. "You know a thing or two about loss, too. I keep thinking about what happened with your brother. I'm really sorry, Chase."

"Me, too. Sometimes, in my line of work, I think I've accepted the uncertainty of life, of whether or not we'll see tomorrow. If we'll see our loved ones again. But there's really no accepting it. When it happens to someone you love, you can't prepare yourself for it. It hurts, no matter what."

I picked up a nacho and played with a chip for a moment. "I guess we should talk about the case, huh?"

"I'd rather we didn't." He let out a sigh. "But you're right."

"Anything new?"

"I'm still not sure how you tie in, though." He looked in the distance and shook his head. "Stealing your cleaning supplies? It's just strange."

"Maybe someone wants to frame me."

"But why?"

I shrugged. "To throw the election?"

He let out a slow breath and leaned closer. "I suppose that could be a possibility. But they'd be better off implicating your brother."

I couldn't argue.

He leaned closer. "Here's the other thing I don't understand. Shooting at you out in public is a very aggressive, in-your-face thing to do. Implicating you at a crime scene is a very subtle thing. I don't understand why someone's doing both."

"I've thought about that. I don't understand it either."

"It's almost like there are two people after you."

Alarm raced through me. "You really think so?"

He sighed again, long and slow. "I don't know. It just doesn't fit. Why try to take you out one minute and simply make your life miserable and complicated the next?"

Two people targeting me? Now that was something I hadn't considered. It was something I didn't want to consider because it was too scary, too unnerving.

"Is there anything else you can think of?"

I wiped my mouth, my mind racing. Abraham. Should I mention Abraham? How about John and everything that had gone down last night at the youth center? That had *potentially* gone down, at least. I had no proof. Only theories.

I shook my head. "I really don't know, Chase."

Chase leaned back and rubbed his chin.

I played with my straw a moment, considering my words. "What do you think of Rex Harrison?"

"Rex?" He shrugged. "I don't know. He's got the support of a lot of people, especially down at the station. T.J. thinks he walks on water. I've only met the guy once myself. Why do you ask?"

"There's something about him I don't like."

"Maybe it's the fact that he's running against your brother?"

"I don't know. I think it goes deeper than that. Have you heard of Orion Enterprises?"

"Everyone around here has."

"I guess Orion himself is a big supporter of Rex. His company has done some unscrupulous things."

"Most companies have, I'd imagine."

I obviously wasn't getting through to him. Maybe that's because there was nothing there. "I guess you're right."

He tilted his head. "Where's this going, Holly? Tell me what you're thinking. Please."

"I've heard that the leader of the Praetorian Guard is someone with power and money. I also know that Orion could fit that description."

"So you think he's killing people around town and implicating you?"

I sucked on my lip for a minute. "I just wonder if there's some kind of connection. I know it doesn't make much sense, but something in my gut is telling me that something is off."

"You've been under a lot of pressure lately. Maybe you should sleep on it."

I could tell when my idea had been dismissed. I couldn't even argue about it, though it was out there. And I hadn't connected all of the pieces.

"Trust your gut, Holly. There could be something

there. Maybe not that ties in with this case, but keep your eyes open."

Gratitude filled me. "Thank you. I appreciate that."

We finished eating, Chase paid, and we stepped outside. I soaked in the perfect evening for a moment. It had been freezing cold only a couple of weeks ago, and we'd gotten several inches of snow.

Today, it was in the sixties and almost felt like spring, only in February.

"Want to take a walk down to the park real quick?"

I glanced up in surprise. "I figured you had to get back to work."

He shrugged. "I do. But I still have a few minutes. I stand by my mantra that it's good to take a couple minutes to clear your head. Besides, I'm going to be working most of the night."

"Are you not sleeping?"

"Here and there. The mayor is putting pressure on us to figure out what's going on. Apparently, the national news picked up on this story."

I mentally paused. "Why? This doesn't seem like national story material. It seems like life in the inner city."

"I'm not sure how they caught wind of it. Maybe it's the whole 'Good Deeds Killer' designation."

I wrapped my arms over my chest and continued to walk toward the park in the distance. Silence fell between us, not necessarily uncomfortable, but I still felt the strange need to fill it.

"What's the killer doing right now, I wondered as I wandered. Plotting his next crime? Delighting in what he's already done?"

"What?" Chase jerked his head toward me.

I paused and shrugged. "What?"

If I acted like the words didn't come from my mouth, would that mean they didn't?

"Did you just say 'I wondered as I wandered'?"

"That would be weird if I said that." I slowed my steps.

"You're a piece of work."

"Artwork." I winked.

He chuckled, the sound deep and full. I loved hearing it.

"By the way, you've got something on your chinny chin chin." I pointed to a tiny feather that had probably been floating in the air.

"There you go again." He wiped the down away.

"What am I doing now?" I asked innocently.

"You're speaking as if you're in a fairy tale." We skirted toward the cars.

"Nonsense."

He cast me a sideways glance. "No one says *chinny chin chin*, and the other day, I caught you saying *oopsie daisy*."

"Well, they're missing out."

He laughed harder. "You're one of a kind." He paused by my car. "You know, tonight was good for me. Thanks for meeting. It was a nice tension breaker."

I smiled genuinely. I never expected to enjoy myself this much around Chase. But I had. He left me wanting more.

Not just more being around him.

More time on this earth.

His eyes held something deeper than before as he turned to me. "Good night, Holly."

"Good night, Chase."

CHAPTER 27

The next morning, first thing, I stopped by to talk to Anthony's mom. She was still distraught, but she seemed happy to see me. We'd always had a good relationship. She'd been a mess when I first met her, but the possibility that her kids could be taken away from her had been a huge wake-up call. The ongoing visits from her new CPS caseworker helped to keep her in line. Most importantly, those visits ensured that her kids' well-being was as it should be.

"How are you doing, Bernice?"

She shrugged. "I'm hanging in. This just should never happen. I prayed every day that my kids wouldn't be some of the ones I heard about on the news. Now look. That's exactly what happened."

I squeezed her hand. "I can't even imagine how difficult this must be for you."

"My other children are the only things that keep me going. I know they're all depending on me."

I nodded. "You're right. They do need you. That's very wise that you realize that. Are they handling this okay?"

"Mercedes cries herself to sleep. She was the closest to Anthony."

We talked for a few more minutes about the kids. I gave her some tips and encouragement, and I lifted up prayers for the family.

"Bernice, do the police have any leads as to who did this?"

She shook her head. "Not that I know of. Like they'd tell me."

"I know there are certain things they can't say, not until they know something for sure." I paused. "Did Anthony and Dewayne know each other?"

Bernice nodded. "I'd seen them together a few times."

I leaned closer. "What do you think's going on, Bernice?"

She shrugged again, her eyes looking vacant and grief stricken. "I'm not sure. Cena keeps coming up. I'm pretty sure the police think it's connected with these murders."

"What do you think?"

"I think that drugs can make people do crazy things." She shifted.

There was something she wasn't telling me, I realized.

"Bernice, what's going on? You have suspicions about something, don't you?"

She wiped under her eyes. "Holly, you've always been so kind to us."

"Let me help you now. You know you can trust me, right?"

She sniffled. "I found some things."

"What kind of things?"

"TVs, phones, other electronics. Some jewelry."

I tried to follow where she was going with this, but I still wasn't sure. "Where did you find them?"

"Anthony put them in our shed. I found them after he died."

"You think he stole them?"

A small sob escaped, and she nodded. "I do. I think they were stealing them—"

"They?"

"Anthony and Dewayne. I think they were stealing things, selling them, and using the money to buy drugs."

My heart sped. "Did you tell the police this?"

She shook her head. "I was afraid they'd point the finger at me. That my kids would be taken away." Her bloodshot eyes met mine. "You're not going to take my kids away, are you?"

I shook my head. "No. But I do think you should mention this to the police. They want to catch the person who did this, and information like this can help. But it's somehow tied in with the murder."

She stared at me a moment, uncertainty in her eyes. "You really think that?"

I nodded. "Since I'm the former investigator here, I can explain the situation. But only if you want me to."

Finally, she nodded. "Okay, if you think that would be best."

***

I stopped by the station, asked for Chase, and was escorted to his desk.

He and T.J. seemed to be talking rather heatedly about something as I approached. They both backed off from each other when they spotted me, but I could feel the tension between them.

"Holly. What brings you here?" Chase said. His voice sounded tighter than usual.

"I just talked to one of my clients," I started. "She said a couple of things that I thought might help."

"Let me guess — these things point the finger away from you?" T.J. sneered.

"I'm not the one who volunteered to help here. The chief asked," I reminded him.

"Don't talk to her like that, T.J." Anger simmered in Chase's voice.

My breath caught in my throat. I knew I had to somehow douse this fire between the two men before things got out of control.

I raised my hands. "I can handle this." I turned to T.J. "If you don't want my help, I'll leave. I don't have a personal stake in this. I have many other ways I can spend my time."

"That sounds like a good idea to me. Maybe then we can all remain a little more objective here." He cast a searing glance at Chase.

"You need to back off," Chase warned.

"Why? You going to lose it again, just like you did back in Louisville?" T.J. baited.

Chase's face turned red. "You don't know what you're talking about."

"I have friends on the force down there. I know what a hothead you were."

"I don't try to hide the fact that I had a drinking problem, T.J. But that's not who I am anymore."

"So, I'm supposed to rely on you? Someone who might go off the deep end and turn back to the bottle?"

"You're out of line," I said.

A couple of other officers stopped what they were doing and watched the scene in the middle of the office.

"If you don't trust me, request a new partner,"

Chase continued. "I've made peace with my past."

"Maybe that's your problem. Overconfidence. We come across one crime that reminds you of your brother, and you're going to be back where you started."

"Leave him out of this," he muttered. His hands were balled into fists at his sides.

"If you can't handle this conversation, then how are you going to handle seeing it happen in real life?"

"That's enough!" Chase lunged toward T.J.

T.J. charged back.

Before they could get any further, the other officers surrounded them, pulled them apart.

"What's going on here?" a man demanded, emerging from a corner office.

The two men continued to glare at each other, their comrades in arms holding them back.

"Anyone care to explain?" The police captain—at least, that's who I thought it was—stared at everyone.

I stepped back, my heart pounding in my ears.

"Both of you. In my office. Now."

Chase shrugged out of the grasp of the men on either side of him, cast one more scowl at T.J., and then stomped to the office.

This was my cue to leave. Now.

I was only sorry I'd ever come.

CHAPTER 28

I couldn't get the argument out of my head.

The things T.J. had said to Chase were just vicious. He'd been egging Chase on. But why?

Beyond that superficial skimming of the situation, the greater question remained: Was there any truth in T.J.'s words? I knew something had happened in Louisville. I just didn't know the extent of it.

The questions haunted me for the rest of the day. I went through my caseload, but almost as if I was on autopilot. By the time I finished, exhaustion pulled me down, reminding me that I needed to rest.

But, for some reason, when work was over, I found myself standing on Chase's doorstep with a pizza in my hands. I'd gotten his address from my mom, who was the world's best card sender ever. Yes, she still used snail mail, but that also meant she had people's physical addresses.

I knew Chase was home because I saw his truck in the driveway. I could only imagine after what had happened that the commander might have told him to cool it for the rest of the day.

Hopefully, he'd told T.J. the same thing.

I knocked at the door, gathering every bit of grace and etiquette in me. A moment later, Chase jerked the door open, a scowl on his face. The lines around his eyes softened some when he saw me. Not that I noticed.

"Holly," he mumbled. "What are you doing here?"

I thrust the pizza at him. "I knew you had a rough day. I thought some pizza might cheer you up. It has gluten, but you eat that, so it's no problem."

Shut up, Holly. Why in the world was I blathering like a nervous fool?

He stared at the box for a moment before finally taking it. He stepped back and extended his arm behind him. "Want to come in?"

Against my better sensibilities, I stepped inside. His place looked like a typical bachelor pad with minimalist decorations. A Reds poster was the only thing on the wall behind a sofa, blinds the only window covering, and old plastic crates served as end tables.

"You didn't have to come."

I brushed an imaginary crumb off my dress and offered a smile. "I know."

He shut the door and turned to me. His normal shirt and tie were gone. Instead, he wore an old football T-shirt that stretched tightly across his chest, along with some faded jeans. He looked . . . how should I say it? Nice. Very, very nice.

"I'm sorry you had to see that at the station, Holly." Regret stained his voice.

"I'm sorry that happened."

He stared at me a moment before nodding toward the kitchen. "Why don't we go sit?"

I followed him inside, put the pizza on the kitchen table, and sat across from him.

"Can I get you something to drink?"

"Water's great."

He grabbed two bottles from the fridge, twisting the cap off mine before handing it to me. The pizza remained in the box between us. Truth be told, I wasn't that hungry.

"I've made a lot of mistakes in my life, Holly," he started. He sat across from me, his eyes dull and his demeanor heavy.

"We all have."

He shook his head. "I snapped after my brother died. I became obsessed. I ended up losing my job and ruining my marriage."

"Your marriage?" I asked.

He nodded. "I was married for two whole years. I should have never said 'I do.' I was uncertain before saying my vows, but I knew Peyton was ready."

"What happened?"

"We married when I was playing professional football. That career only lasted a year, until I had my knee injury. By that point, she was into living a lifestyle we could no longer afford. I became a cop. She was a hairdresser. She wanted expensive clothes, trips to the Caribbean, a house we didn't have enough money to buy."

"I know marriage can be challenging. All of them are."

He stared off into the distance. "After my brother died, I hardly came home. I was just always looking for answers. My anger was growing. I came home one day, and Peyton was gone. I didn't even go after her. That's how obsessed I was. I'd started drinking to numb my pain."

"You never did find his killer. What happened with Peyton?"

"She filed for divorce. She's remarried now. I haven't really kept up with her, but I hope she's happy. If I could go back and do things over again, I would. But we don't have that luxury, do we?"

"We sure don't. We just have to learn from the past."

He shook his head and looked down at his hands a moment. "To be honest, I don't feel like I ever deserve a chance at certain things again—like love. I messed up big-time. I became the person I'd vowed not to be."

"Everyone deserves another chance. Everyone should be able to learn from their mistakes."

"You're a good listener, Holly." He offered a small, grateful smile. "I think you're in the right profession."

"I love helping people. It's what God created me to do." I took a sip of my water. "How'd you turn your life around, Chase?"

"I hit rock bottom. Lost my wife. My job. Most of my friends. I still had no answers. The police chaplain at the station was the only person who had the guts to confront me about what a mess my life had become. He got me into a faith-based addiction recovery program. I started going to church. It was a slow process, and every time I wanted to give up, this guy—Josh was his name—he'd show up and he wouldn't let me go back."

"Sounds like a great guy."

"A godsend, for sure." He let out a long sigh. "So, as you can see, there was some truth to T.J.'s words. I could be a ticking time bomb."

"Or you could be a reformed soul who's on the straight and narrow. Even people who are changed still make mistakes. You have to accept that. Otherwise, you'll be devastated when you mess up." Part of my internship had been in a drug and alcohol rehab center where I'd led group therapy sessions. I wasn't saying all of this as someone who hadn't seen the devastating effects of addiction. I knew they could destroy people's lives. But I also knew the addictions were entirely possible to overcome.

"Thanks, Holly. I always feel better after I talk to you. You have that effect on people."

"Jamie always says my superpower is kindness."

Chase smiled. "Sounds like a nice superpower."

I rubbed my hands together. "There was another reason I stopped by. I talked to Anthony's mom today, and she said something interesting. I'm not sure if it will help you or not, but I thought I'd let you figure that out."

"Okay."

"I guess both Anthony and Dewayne had been stealing things from local homes and selling them at pawnshops to try and get some extra money. Probably for drugs. She actually showed me some of the items she'd found in the shed behind her house. She hid them before the police found them."

"Why would she do that?"

I shook my head. "Fear? It's like you said — there are segments of the population that have a hard time trusting the police. She thought you might somehow turn this around and make her out to be guilty. She didn't want her kids to be taken away from her."

"She still has the items?"

I nodded.

"I'll see if she'll let me see them. There could be a link, depending on who they stole from. I know there's been a rash of robberies around here lately."

"That's what I was thinking. Maybe Anthony and Dewayne made the wrong person mad. That's why I stopped by the station earlier. I thought you'd want to know."

"This Good Deeds Killer is a real mystery." Chase stood and paced across the room to the window. "I've never seen a case like this. What is he trying to say by cleaning? That he took the victim to the cleaners? Is he making a point to let us know that he's wiped everything down, that there's no evidence?"

I found myself standing and walking toward him. I stood a safe distance away, far enough that I wasn't in his space. "That doesn't seem like something someone involved in a spontaneous act of violence would do."

"You're right. That's why I think these crimes were premeditated. I think the killer is meticulous, I think he knew what he was doing, and I think he wants to make a statement."

"Doesn't sound like anyone I'd want to come across." Familiar guilt pounded at me. Would this be the time to tell Chase my part in all of this? We'd just shared such a poignant moment. He'd opened up. He'd said nice things about me.

One confession and any nice feelings he had toward me would all come crashing down.

"I hate to think that you're somehow connected to this lunatic."

I could hardly swallow. "Yeah, me too."

He looked at me, something changing in his gaze. Was he considering the fact that I could be guilty? Trying to figure out how to break the news to me that he suspected I was involved?

"I know this sounds lame, Holly, but you're going

to make some guy very happy one day."

I let out the breath I held. My relief was instantly replaced with sorrow, though. It didn't look like I was ever going to have the opportunity for that to happen.

"Thank you," I whispered. "But I don't think that's even a remote possibility."

"Why not?"

I shrugged, all my reasons colliding inside my head. Which one was I allowed to share again? "Just a gut feeling."

"Holly, you're beautiful. You're sweet. You're smart. You're what every guy wants in a wife. I'm surprised guys aren't knocking down your door."

His words caused me to flush. "Thank you. It's hard to explain. I've been on dates. I can usually tell after the third or fourth date if I've found 'the one.'"

He leaned closer, a grin tugging at his lips. "The one? To me, it sounds like someone has high standards."

I shrugged, not letting myself be goaded. "There's nothing wrong with standards."

"There is when high standards become unreachable ideals."

I narrowed my eyes at him. "You don't know me as well as you think, Chase Dexter."

I started to pull back when he grabbed my arm. His thumb stroked my wrist. Suddenly all of my senses were on alert. My breathing became shallow as our gazes caught.

"You know me pretty well. At least the equivalent of three or four dates," he mumbled.

Was it just me or was his face getting closer?

I swallowed, my throat burning. His thumb

continued to stroke my arm, sending flurries of electricity scrambling over my skin. "I'd say so."

His hand traveled up my arm to my neck. His fingers splayed there, his touch so warm and comforting that I closed my eyes.

"So if we'd been dating, would you have cut me loose by now?"

I opened my eyes. His face was mere inches from mine. Any smart-aleck response left my mind. Totally and completely.

Then his lips covered mine, slowly, smoothly, hesitantly. When I didn't pull back, he pulled closer. His other hand wrapped around my waist, and my hands reached for his neck.

And for a moment—and just a moment—all of my worries disappeared.

But when they reappeared, they hit me with the force of a hurricane. I couldn't fall in love. Especially not with Chase Dexter. Especially not when I was going to die in a few months. Especially not when I could potentially be the prime suspect in his first case as a detective.

I ripped away, tears flooding my eyes. "I've gotta go."

"Holly, wait—"

I didn't stop to listen to him. I grabbed my purse and fled.

What had I done?

CHAPTER 29

I walked into my house, my heart still pounding.

What had just happened?

Why had I done that?

I should have just stayed away, minded my own business. Like I didn't have enough problems already.

Now I'd just shared my first kiss with a man who'd been my high school crush and lead antagonist. And I had no one to talk to about what had happened.

Of all the people I could have kissed, why Chase? Maybe I shouldn't have allowed myself to be swept away. I shook my head. Nothing was making sense right now. One minute my heart was soaring with joy, and the next I was berating myself.

I sighed, exhausted from my internal conflict.

I didn't turn the lights on as I made my way through the house. I wanted some hot tea. With honey. Jamie had given me some from a local beekeeper, saying something about it helping me with allergies. I didn't even know I had allergies.

I'd make tea, then take a long bath. Tea and baths always made everything better.

In the kitchen, I flipped the light switch.

Nothing happened.

My blood froze.

I slowly turned, looking for a sign of someone. Of something out of place. Of anything else that set off warning bells.

That's when I heard a creak come from the dining room.

My gaze shot across the room.

I couldn't flee upstairs. Only ignorant chicks in horror flicks did that.

To get to the front door, I'd have to pass the dining room.

No way would I do that.

I backed into the living room instead. I made a split-second decision.

I walked to the bookcase and slowly, quietly turned it until I was on the other side. In the library.

I ducked behind the sofa there, in a nice little corner where I felt protected from the world.

At least, I felt protected from the intruder in my house.

I heard something else click.

My heart pounded in my ears and my skin crawled.

I waited for something else to happen.

I waited to see shoes.

I should have run out the back door, I realized. Only then I'd have to run to the gate, which was at the front of the house. By that time, the intruder could have grabbed me there.

In the moment, this had seemed like a great idea.

I pulled out my phone and texted Chase. I prayed he would get it.

Immediately, he texted back.

I'm on my way. You'll be okay, Holly.

I hoped he was right.

***

I was counting the minutes, every cell of my body on alert, waiting for what would happen next. As I bided my time, I saw I had several missed calls. All from my oncologist.

Why couldn't they realize that I didn't want to be poked and prodded anymore?

Just then, my phone buzzed.

I glanced down. My brother was texting me about — what else? — a campaign event.

I texted back: *Busy with other things right now. Like an intruder in the house.*

I figured it couldn't hurt if more than one person knew what was going on, just in case I was never seen again or something. We went back and forth in our texts a moment, and I told him the police were on their way.

I heard another click.

The front door. That's what it had to be.

Had the intruder left? I prayed that was the case.

I continued praying. And counting. And trying not to panic.

My phone buzzed again. It was Chase: *I'm at your house. Where are you?*

I told him I was in the library and that I was okay.

Checking out the rest of the house. Stay where you are.

I wanted to jump out and run to him. But I didn't dare move. Not yet. Not until I knew there was no one between Chase and me.

Time couldn't pass fast enough as I waited for him to check everywhere. I heard him moving throughout the house. I prayed I didn't hear him being hurt. Hear his body hit the ground. Any grunts of pain.

I felt fairly certain the intruder had left. But I couldn't be sure. I hadn't seen anything. I had no confirmation.

My phone buzzed again.

House is clear. I'm coming to you.

The next thing I knew, I heard his voice. "Holly, it's okay. I'm here."

At once, I jumped from my hiding place. I ran toward Chase and threw my arms around him.

"Are you okay?" He pulled me close.

I nodded.

"I checked out the rest of the house. There's no one here."

"Thank you so much for coming."

"Of course."

I saw that look in his eyes again. The look that went beyond friendship. The look that showed he was torn between caring about me and analyzing the way I'd fled from his house earlier.

Another voice sounded at the front of the house. "Holly? Where are you?"

I'd recognize that voice anywhere. It was Alex.

My family's phone tree was in full effect.

***

An hour later, the electricity was back on, Ralph was here, and two uniformed officers were looking for fingerprints.

Chase had faithfully stayed by my side.

The strange thing was that nothing appeared to be taken. Nothing was damaged.

"Are you sure there was someone here?" Alex

asked.

We'd all gathered in a semicircle in the kitchen, and Alex was cross-examining me.

I nodded. "I heard someone. The electricity was out."

"Plus, the front door was open when I got here," Chase said. "I assume that's how the intruder made his getaway."

"But how did he get inside?" Alex pressed.

I shook my head. "I have no idea. I didn't see any signs of forced entry."

"Anyone outside of the family have a key to this place?" Chase asked.

"Mom did lose her keys at that awards banquet for you, Holly," Ralph said. "She assumed she just misplaced them and that it wasn't a big deal, that even if someone found them, they wouldn't be able to identify who they belonged to."

"Maybe she didn't misplace them," I muttered.

Ralph pulled me into a side hug. "I'm just glad you're okay. We've never had any real problems around here before."

Alex poured a cup of coffee. "Good thing Mom's not here. She'd have a heart attack."

She handed Chase the steaming mug, and he accepted.

"Make you not want to be so trusting, Holly?" Alex asked as she fetched another cup of java.

I blinked, surprised at her question. "What do you mean?"

"You're Little Miss Idealist who always sees the best in people. You rethinking that yet?" She took a sip from her mug.

I shook my head. "No, not really."

She rolled her eyes and turned to Chase. "Holly's the one who thinks love can change the world, who thinks simple acts of kindness can build bridges, and who wants to save her first kiss for marriage."

My bottom lip dropped open and my cheeks heated.

She did not just say that.

No!

I didn't dare look at Chase, even though I could feel him staring at me. I knew he'd have questions.

How would I answer them?

"What's wrong?" Ralph asked. "You usually start arguing right about now on why your values shouldn't be criticized."

I shook my head, speechless.

"I think her values sound nice. In my line of work—and with my past—Holly is a breath of fresh air," Chase said.

My heart stopped pounding quite as quickly.

"I have to admit, with what I see every day, her worldview is kind of nice," Alex said. "I'm her big sister. I have to give her a hard time."

"I wish my constituents were that positive," Ralph added.

"Your parents didn't name you Holly Anna for nothing," Chase offered. "I'll take an optimist to a pessimist any day."

"Thank you," I whispered.

Chase stepped closer and squeezed my arm. "You should probably change your locks, Holly. Stay somewhere else tonight until that's done. Please."

I didn't dare look up at him.

Instead, I nodded. "Fine. I'll stay with you, Alex, but just for tonight."

"Great. I'll wait with you until you pack up a few things."

"Actually, I'll stay with her." Chase shifted toward my siblings. "Why don't you both go ahead and go? I'll make sure she's okay."

Alex raised an eyebrow. Instead of a smart remark, she shrugged. "Fine by me. It will give me a chance to spruce up my guest bedroom."

Ralph looked back and forth between Chase and me. "I guess I'll run, too."

I wanted to beg both of them to stay. I didn't want to explain myself to Chase. And, though I knew I wasn't obligated to, I knew I would attempt to do just that.

Queasiness jostled in my stomach as soon as both of them left. Reluctantly, I pulled my eyes up to meet Chase's. I crossed my arms and pressed my lips together, remembering that kiss.

"Is it true?" Chase's eyes looked smoky, intense.

"Is what true?" I wanted to forehead smack myself. Of course I knew what he was talking about. I was buying time, trying to put off the conversation, if only for a few seconds longer.

"You were saving your first kiss for marriage?"

I pulled my arms tighter across my chest. "It's complicated."

"Then give me an uncomplicated version."

"It's really nothing that you should concern yourself with."

"I kissed you tonight, Holly. Of course I'm curious. More than curious, truth be told."

I sucked in a long, deep breath, wishing I could hide under a rock somewhere. I looked away. "I decided in high school that I would save my first kiss for my wedding day."

His eyes widened. "Then . . .? Tonight . . .?"

How did I even approach this? I hadn't intended on kissing him. I hadn't given it much thought at all, really. Maybe that was my problem. I'd stopped thinking and started feeling.

"Things change, Chase. I don't know what else to say."

"I feel like I took something special from you, and I don't say that lightly. I've kissed . . . plenty of girls. I've kissed—" He ran a hand through his hair and stepped back, obviously frustrated. "I've kissed girls who meant nothing to me."

His words were like a slap in the face. I was like nothing to him. "I get what you're saying."

He shook his head adamantly. "No, that's not what I'm saying." He looked toward the ceiling. "What am I trying to say?"

I put my hand on his arm. "Look, Chase, that kiss had no strings attached. You didn't ruin me for life. You didn't destroy my dreams or taint me. Life happens. Views change. I don't know what else to say. Just don't read too much into it. Really."

He stared at me. His mouth opened, like he wanted to say more. But then he shut it again and nodded. "You should get your things."

I stepped toward the stairway, grateful for an excuse to get away. "You're right. I should."

I hurried upstairs, wondering why life had to be so complicated.

CHAPTER 30

I didn't sleep well at Alex's house. Plus, there was the fact that she got up every morning at 5:00 a.m. to run. She came back at precisely 5:30 and drank coffee that percolated, thanks to a timer, while she ran. She fixed steel-cut oatmeal, topped with frozen berries and nuts, along with a green smoothie.

I wished it were my sister's routine that kept me awake, but truthfully I hadn't slept well all night. There were too many thoughts turning over in my mind. I thought about the intruder in my house. Why had he been there? Certainly he had a purpose, yet his motive still wasn't clear.

Then there was my kiss with Chase. I wished I could put it out of my mind, that I could stop thinking about it. But every time I closed my eyes I could feel his warm lips on mine. I could feel his hands drawing me closer. I could feel my heart racing.

All of those images disappeared when I replayed the conversation where he'd learned that he was my first kiss. I wished I were stronger, that I didn't feel a touch of humiliation about the whole incident. But there was something unnerving about it.

I'd been so strong for so long. So why had I let him kiss me? Why hadn't I stopped him? Why Chase of all people? Maybe it was because I realized I might die without ever being kissed, and that seemed like a crying shame.

I couldn't exactly explain that to him, though.

Tired of my thoughts, I pulled a robe on and stomped downstairs. Alex looked way too perky as she read the newspaper at the kitchen table.

"Morning, sis."

I grabbed some coffee and plopped down across from her. "Hey, Alex."

"You look awful."

"Thanks." I ran a hand over my face.

"Are you feeling okay?"

Not really. I hadn't felt well in a long time, and it was only going to get worse from here. "I'm fine. Just a bit overwhelmed, I guess."

"That was so strange what happened last night. The only thing I can surmise is that you walked in in the middle of a robbery. Whoever it was didn't have time to finish what he started."

I nodded, rubbing the edge of my mug. "I suppose that makes sense."

"Either way, it could have turned out much worse."

"Absolutely."

She stood and put her bowl in the sink, rinsing it with some water. "So, what's going on with you and Chase?"

I looked up, surprised. "Me and Chase? Nothing."

"Don't tell me 'nothing.' He couldn't take his eyes off of you last night."

"He was doing his job and making sure I was okay."

She raised her thin eyebrows. "Keep telling yourself that. But, while he couldn't stop watching you, you avoided his gaze like your life depended on it."

I supposed this was what happened when you had an assistant district attorney for a sister. Not much got past her. That worked great for the justice system, but terrible for me. "You're reading too much into it. We're friends. Plain and simple."

"You want to know what the weird thing is?"

I tapped my finger on the table. "I don't know if I do or not."

"I could actually see you two together. I think you could handle each other."

"Handle each other?"

"I mean, you could complement each other. You have enough in common and enough differences, too. The differences make the relationship interesting; the things in common keep the relationship together."

Just then, my cell phone rang. I glanced down, drawing in a breath when I saw Jamie's number. She hadn't talked to me since our argument. Had she finally decided to forgive me?

I stood and paced over to the corner for some privacy. "Jamie?"

"Hey, Holly." Her voice cracked. "I need your help. It's John. We haven't seen him since yesterday morning, and he's not answering his phone. I think something is seriously wrong, Holly."

***

I sat on the couch beside Jamie and squeezed her hand while Mama Val explained everything to Chase.

I couldn't stop thinking about seeing Little T whispering with Abraham that night after I left the youth center. Then John had met up with Little T, and they'd disappeared somewhere together. I hoped I was reading too much into things, but it appeared I wasn't.

"My baby always comes home to check on me. He just wouldn't do something like this." Mama Val dabbed a tissue under her eyes.

"Has anything suspicious happened lately? Has John acted in any way out of the ordinary?" Chase asked.

Mama Val shook her head while Louis patted her hand. "No. Nothing. He was on the straight and narrow. He'd turned his life around."

"Turned his life around from what?" Chase asked.

"He got involved with some bad people in high school. That's when I pulled him out of his public school and enrolled him in a private school. I had to work two jobs to pay his way there. But I didn't want my son to get caught in that trap of being with the wrong people and doing the wrong things."

"I see. And that worked? He stopped hanging out with the wrong crowd?" Chase held a pen and paper in his hands, jotting notes.

She nodded. "It did. He started working part-time at that sports complex. He plays basketball in his free time. He goes to church every Sunday."

Chase nodded. "I'll need a list of his friends. Anyone that I can talk to who might know something."

"I already made one." Mama Val handed him a piece of paper.

Chase stood. "I'll see what I can find out."

"I appreciate it."

I squeezed Jamie's hand one more time. "I'll be right back," I whispered.

I walked Chase outside, all the way to his car,

before saying anything. Honestly, the last thing I wanted to do was to face him right now, to see any more questions in his eyes. But there were bigger issues than my humiliation at stake.

"You doing okay this morning, Holly?" he asked, his voice low and intimate.

I nodded. "Me? I'm fine. I'm the least of my concerns. There's something I thought you should know, though. I didn't want to say it inside, just in case there's nothing there."

"Okay."

"I volunteer at the youth center down on Grand Avenue. When I was leaving the other night, I saw one of the youths — he goes by Little T — whispering to Abraham, the director of the youth center. I ended up following Little T. I saw him meet up with John."

"You followed someone you were suspicious of? That doesn't sound very wise."

I raised my hand. "I know. I didn't think I was in danger. I was just making sure they weren't getting themselves in trouble."

"And if they were —"

"That's beside the point. John hasn't been seen since then. I think they picked up on the fact that I was following them, and I lost them."

"What's the name of this director again?"

"Abraham Willis. He's a nice guy, Chase. He and his wife are barely scraping by, but somehow they have money to go on a cruise to the Bahamas in another week or so. I hate to think the worst . . ."

As soon as the words left my mouth, I regretted them. Abraham was my friend, and I'd just thrown him under the bus. Should I give him a heads-up? Should I talk to him first?

If I did that, and he was guilty, then I'd be tipping him off.

I was just no good at this being-deceitful thing.

"I'll talk to him. I'll be subtle. Okay?" Chase assured me, seeming to read my thoughts.

I nodded. "Thank you. I really think he's a good guy."

"Even good guys can have secrets." His face clouded as he said the words.

Apparently, Chase had a few secrets of his own.

"Thanks again for everything," I told him. "I know you're busy, but I couldn't think of anyone else I'd want to handle this than you."

"I'll be in touch."

I stared at him a moment, remembering the kiss and strangely wanting another one. Did Chase?

His cell phone beeped. His face registered surprise when he looked at the screen. "We just got some results back on those bullets that were fired at you. T.J. is checking it out now."

"What can you tell me?"

"Nothing. Not yet. But we may have some answers for you very soon."

CHAPTER 31

"My mom is cooking," Jamie told me when I came back inside. "It's what she does when she's stressed. We'll have fried chicken, mashed potatoes, homemade biscuits, and everything else under the sun by the end of the day. Save your appetite."

"And you'll eat?"

"I have leftover biscuits made from almond flour, fake-out fried chicken made with ground-up pecans and flaxseed, and for the mashed potatoes—"

"Mashed cauliflower instead. Of course," I finished for her.

We exchanged a smile.

Jamie's smile slipped as we started up the stairs to her room. It was a good time to slip away, since Mama Val was cooking, the little guys were in school, and Louis was playing on his trombone.

"I'm sorry I was terse with you, Holly."

"I'm sorry I spoke when I shouldn't have," I told her.

"You know I want you to speak into my life. We all need people who are willing to tell the truth. We've got to be brave enough to face those opinions, even when they hurt."

We hugged at the top of the steps.

"All of that said, I think you were wrong," Jamie said, twisting the door to her room.

I followed her inside and stared at her a moment. "Was I?"

"Look, it seems like heresy to talk about this while my brother's missing."

"Nothing wrong with distracting yourself."

She nodded. "That's what I'm trying to do. Anyway, I went out with Rex last night."

I blinked, unable to conceal my surprise. "That was fast."

"I know you're supposed to be subtle and play hard to get, but I called Rex right after you left yesterday." She frowned. "Partly just to spite you."

I let that comment slide. "And?"

"He asked if we could meet for coffee between campaign events, and we did."

Was it just a coincidence that Rex had asked out the best friend of his political opponent's sister? Was he fishing for information? Trying to create a media situation? Or was there a chance all of this was real and sincere?

I didn't voice any of that out loud. Instead, I said, "How did it go?"

She smiled. "It was nice, Holly. Really nice. I thought he'd have his game face on the whole time, you know? But he didn't. He was open and honest."

"Tell me more."

"We talked about our upbringing. He talked about being a police officer, about losing his brother, about how he wants to turn the city around."

"Then why's he going into state politics instead of city?"

"He wants to have as wide a reach as possible. He has all of these ideas for programs that could curb the crime in our area."

All the questions I could think to ask her would only make me seem like I had ulterior motives. Things like: Did he ask you to write an article on him? Did he mention my brother at all? Fish for any details?

Instead, I tried to be happy for my friend. "I'm glad you had a good time, Jamie."

She smiled softly. "We're supposed to go out again tonight."

"I'm surprised he has time with the campaigning and all."

Her smile slipped. "It's actually a campaign event."

"Oh."

"I won't go if you don't want me to, Holly."

At first thought, I didn't want her to. But there were other things to consider. "Life is short, Jamie. If this is what you want to do, don't let the election stop you."

She gave me another hug. "Thank you, Holly. That means a lot. It's nice to feel pretty. I always try to be tough, to act like I'm okay with always being single. But there's a part of me that wants the American dream, you know? I want a family to come home to one day. I want to find someone who gets me, who understands me and loves me. Is that so wrong?"

"Not at all."

"Jamie!" Mama Val called upstairs. "Tameka is here."

I blanched. I wasn't the jealous type. I really wasn't. But something about Tameka being here caused not-so-pretty emotions to rise in me.

Life would go on after my death, I reminded myself. I couldn't expect Jamie to never have another best friend. To not ever have someone else to share inside jokes with or to try and fulfill items on a bucket list.

Still, the idea made me more emotional than I'd like to admit.

I glanced at my watch, pretending to be busier than I was. "You know, I should go."

"Are you sure?"

I nodded. "Yeah, but you promise to call me if you need me, okay?"

"Thanks, Holly."

I slipped downstairs, nodding at Tameka on my way out.

Dying was going to be harder than I thought.

***

Back at home, I called a locksmith and waited for him to come out. No way was I staying in this house until I figured out how someone had gotten in and out. A key seemed like the only option, and that meant all of the locks needed to be changed as a safety precaution. As I waited, I paced my house, looking for some kind of a sign as to what had happened.

When I saw nothing, I decided not to waste any more time. Mama Val and I had something in common—we liked to cook when we were stressed.

I pulled down my cookbooks. I'd purchased most of them at thrift stores, and they were from the sixties. I liked the recipes because they contained less sugar and more natural ingredients. I wasn't a health food fanatic like Jamie, but I did try to avoid processed foods whenever possible. And I loved baking.

I found a recipe for lemon pound cake and started mixing, trying to keep my mind off of everything.

Finally, the locksmith showed up.

It should be my dad, I couldn't help but think. He could have switched these locks and not charged me a dime.

At one o'clock, my phone rang. It was Chase. "Good news," he started. "We arrested the person who shot at you."

I braced myself against the counter. "Really? Who?"

"Frank Jenkins."

"Really?"

"Ballistics match the gun that was in his possession. He had a grudge against you and wanted to make you pay for splitting his family apart. That means he's got motive and means."

"How about the break-in at my place? Was he responsible for that?"

"As far as we know right now, he said he has nothing to do with that. We did discover that his house was broken into by those teens, including Anthony and Dewayne. Some of his electronics were stolen and pawned."

"So, is he connected with the murders?" Hope, along with a chill, washed over me.

"We don't know. We're considering that possibility, though. Maybe he was getting payback. He had multiple weapons in his possession."

I nodded. "At least one problem is solved, right? Maybe more."

"Hang tight, Holly. We're going to get to the bottom of this."

***

Making one lemon pound cake turned into making five other cakes. I delivered them to shut-ins from church. I also stopped by the community center and used part of my paycheck to help out some kids who couldn't pay for some sports and dance classes. I made an anonymous donation to the local crisis pregnancy center and sent a whole tray of sandwiches over to my brother's election headquarters for staffers to eat.

I was digging into my savings, but I figured I couldn't take it with me. I might as well put that money to good use before the government decided to take most of it as part of the death tax.

After doing all of that, I stopped by the youth center. I walked in feeling a certain amount of trepidation. Would Abraham suspect me? Did he know I sold him out?

"Hey, hey, hey, Ms. Holly," Little T said. He reached out his hand to give me a high five. "How goes it?"

"It goes just fine. What's going on here?" I slapped his hand and snapped my fingers, just the way the kids had taught me.

"Is that cake?" He stared at the loaf in my hands.

"It sure is. Would you like a piece?"

He licked his lips. "Would I ever. You're going to make some man very happy one day, Ms. Holly. Very happy."

"You staying out of trouble, Little T?"

"You know it."

I leveled my gaze with him. "You promise?"

He put a hand over his heart. "I'd never lie to you, Ms. Holly."

I wasn't so sure about that. "There's a lot of crazy

stuff going on around here."

"Don't I know it?"

"My friend's brother is missing. His name is John Duke. You know him?"

Something clouded his gaze for a minute. "Can't say I do."

"His family is worried sick. If you hear anything, let me know, okay?"

"I will."

I kept walking toward the kitchen. Part of me wanted to drill him more, but I'd always had more subtle ways of doing things. I didn't want him to not trust me anymore. If he knew I'd followed him, he'd never have any faith in me again. "Where is everyone?"

"Abraham's in his office. The rest of the guys are playing basketball out back. None of the girls are here right now."

I handed him the cake. "Why don't you just take this outside? I've already cut it into slices."

"Much obliged." He hurried out the back door.

Good. This would give me a minute to talk to Abraham alone.

I knocked on his door, and he called for me to come in. I ignored my nerves as I stepped into his office.

"Holly. I didn't expect to see you here."

"I just wanted to check on everyone."

He took off his glasses and rubbed his eyes. "It's been an interesting day."

"Why's that?"

"The police stopped by. Apparently, there's a boy missing from the area. They wanted to know if I knew anything about him."

I tried to keep my expression neutral. "Why would

they ask that?"

"I'm assuming it was because of my involvement here at the youth center."

I swallowed hard. "And did you know anything?"

He shook his head. "Not a thing. I don't think this boy has ever been here."

"Hopefully, they'll find him." I shifted. "Abraham, I saw you talking to Little T the other night after I left. It looked heated. Is everything okay?"

He let out a long sigh. "Yeah, Little T is just getting involved with some things he should stay away from. I caught him exchanging a white, powdery substance with someone and confronted him. He tried to tell me he wasn't doing drugs."

"But you didn't believe him?"

"No, I didn't. It's a shame, too, because that boy has so much potential."

I took a step back when he called to me.

"Holly?"

"Yes?"

"There's something I think you should know."

I shifted in the doorway. "Okay."

"I've taken on a part-time job."

I stared at Abraham, processing his words. "What?"

He nodded. "It's true. Donations are down here at the center, plus we didn't get that grant we were trying for. Hannah's been more vocal lately about how hard it is to live on my salary, especially since we want to have another baby. So, I got a job working from midnight until 8:00 a.m. at an infomercial call center."

"Really? I had no idea things were so tight."

He nodded. "I'm making more working at minimum wage at that job than I am here."

"Why's it a secret?"

He sighed. "Sometimes donors don't like it when they feel like the person they're supporting isn't dedicating all of their time to the cause at hand. I was trying to keep it quiet. There's something about being in ministry that seems to make people think that money is inconsequential."

"I didn't know you were struggling so much. I'm sorry, Abraham. There's no shame in getting paid a fair wage."

Sirens cut through the air, and I bristled.

It wasn't just one siren. It was a lot of sirens, rushing down the road right outside the youth center.

My first thought was John.

Please let him be okay, I prayed silently.

"Listen, I've got to go. I'll check in later."

I hurried to my car, desperate to find out what was going on.

CHAPTER 32

I slowed as I pulled into a cul-de-sac. There were two ambulances, three police cars, and even a fire truck blocking the road farther down. I spotted a brown sedan and realized that Chase was here, too.

I stopped my car and stared at the run-down house. I'd never been here before. This wasn't the home of one of my clients. But I had a feeling that I knew exactly what was inside: heartbreak.

I climbed from my car, walked to the police line, and waited. I prayed. I hoped I was reading too much into this. I longed for this murder streak to be over, but in my heart I knew it wasn't.

The city was facing a terrible serial killer, and I was somehow mixed up in all of it. It was enough to make me feel light-headed.

Thirty minutes into my stakeout, EMTs wheeled someone out on a gurney. A sheet covered the body. I knew what that meant.

The Good Deeds Killer had struck again.

Lord, please watch over this family. Place your hand of comfort on them. Bring the person behind this to justice.

Two hours after I arrived, Chase ducked under the police line and made his way toward me. He took my elbow and led me away from the crowds.

"How'd you know to come here?" he asked.

"I was out and I heard the sirens. I was hoping I

was wrong, but my gut told me I wasn't."

"Your client?"

I shook my head.

"Your business card was inside the home."

I sucked in a deep breath. "That can't be possible."

"T.J.'s bent on bringing you in for questioning. He said my relationship with you is clouding my judgment."

"Do you want me to come in?" I trembled at the thought. I was a terrible liar. I'd pour out the whole story. Which they wouldn't believe was the whole story, of course.

"I'll hold him off. In the meantime, get out of here. Okay?"

I nodded and went back to my car.

***

Instead of going home, which I didn't want to do, I went to Jamie's. It was nine o'clock at night, but her family was all night owls. Her dad was always playing at some jazz club downtown, and the evenings were the only time Mama Val could grab a minute to herself.

Mama Val answered the door when I knocked. "Holly! Not used to seeing you out here this late at night."

"I hope you don't mind. I wanted to check on all of you. Any news?"

"Come on in, child. No, there's no news. I'm just trying to trust that the good Lord is handling all of this. There's not much else I can do."

"Prayer is for the strong, not the weak. Isn't that what Pastor Melvin said?"

"Oh, Holly. You are so right." She put her hand on my back. "You'll never believe who is here."

"Who?"

I stopped at the entryway to the den. Before she could answer, I spotted a familiar figure sitting on the couch beside Jamie.

"Rex Harrison," I mumbled.

"Now, don't you take this personally. My Jamie is walking on clouds," Mama Val whispered.

I nodded and put on my best happy face. "Jamie. Rex. I hope I'm not interrupting."

Jamie was practically glowing. "No, you're fine. Rex heard about what happened and stopped by to see how I was doing."

I looked at Rex, trying to keep my expression neutral. "You heard about John? Is it on the news?"

"No, I still have friends within the police department, though. I heard the last name and worried that John might be related to Jamie. I was right."

I sat across from them. "Your mom just told me there are no updates."

Jamie's smile dimmed as she nodded. "It's true. I hope he's just being stupid and irresponsible. Is that too much to wish for?"

"I hope for the same," I told her.

I felt Rex studying me. I might have—just maybe—scowled. What kind of politician tried to strike up a romantic relationship right before an election?

"Anything new with you?" Jamie asked.

"Someone broke into my home, they caught the guy who shot at me, and there was another murder," I told her. "Someone down on State Street."

"The Good Deeds Killer?" Her eyes widened.

I nodded. "It appears that way."

"I'll get back to the other things you said in a moment," Jamie started. "Who could be doing this? Killing all of these people in our little neighborhood? Gangs and drugs kill enough of those guys. We don't need a serial killer going after them, too."

I'd give anything to figure out that answer. "It all seems to point back to drugs. That's what I hear every time I turn around."

"An angry drug dealer taking it out on his minions?" Jamie asked.

"Drug dealers don't seem to have an affinity for cleaning homes before they leave after killing someone." I shrugged. "I don't know. Maybe a gang initiation?"

"That's a scary thought." Jamie shivered. "Maybe none of us are safe."

"I also heard that these kids had been breaking into homes, stealing things, and pawning them. Maybe the police are looking in the wrong direction entirely. Maybe this is some homeowner retaliating." Should I be saying all of this in front of Rex, I wondered? I figured he knew most of it already or he could find out. Right now, he sat quietly, listening.

"Obviously, that's more complicated than most people assume," Jamie said.

"I guess this guy has influence and connections." I tried not to look at Rex, for fear he was guilty. Then I remembered that someone with his status would have to be pretty desperate to manufacture drugs and sell them while running for state office. "This isn't just some kid off the street."

"Then who is it?" Jamie asked.

"It's someone who knows how to use chemicals to alter organic substances and make them practically lethal, in the least psychedelic. It's someone who has connections with these kids."

"I can see you two would make great junior detectives. And I'm not being sarcastic." Rex leaned forward. "Tell me about the victims."

I ran through my mental checklist. "They all worked different jobs. Two went to the same high school but really didn't seem to know each other. None of them go to the same church or seemingly have any affiliation. Except they did all play basketball."

"Together?" Rex asked.

I shrugged. "Usually at the community court down off of Grand."

Rex flinched. I almost didn't catch it, but I could see his wheels turning.

"What are you thinking?" I asked.

He shook his head, something close to melancholy coming over him. "It's probably nothing."

"Share anyway. We'll let you know if it's nothing," Jamie said.

He leaned toward us, his elbows perched on his knees. "One of my campaign sponsors is trying to clean up his image. He's been playing basketball down in the Hill. In fact, he paid to have the whole court redone not long ago."

"Who is it?" I held my breath as I waited for his response.

"Orion Vanderslice. Even worse: he knows exactly how the manufacturing process works. That's what he's in the business of."

Jamie and I exchanged a glance. Could Rex be right?

Even more: Was he being the bigger person and putting his campaign in jeopardy for the sake of finding a killer?

Maybe I had let my own bias play too harshly in my feelings toward the man. Maybe he was a good guy after all.

CHAPTER 33

Brian was waiting for me on the porch when I pulled up to my house.

I glanced at my watch.

It was past ten at night. What in the world was he doing here?

Then I remembered him going to that warehouse. Visiting with Desiree.

Maybe having Brian here wasn't a great idea, especially with my mom being out of town.

I slowed my steps on the sidewalk as he stood from the iron chair on the porch. "Brian. What are you doing here?"

He stepped toward me. "I heard about everything going on. I wanted to make sure you got inside okay. Ralph told me about the break-in."

I nodded, but my heart didn't slow down. Not enough, at least. "That was thoughtful of you."

He cocked his head. "I'm a thoughtful kind of guy." He reached for my arm to help me up the steps.

Why did I feel so nervous? Did I really believe that Brian could be behind these murders? The idea was crazy.

"You're shivering," Brian said. "We should get you inside."

My mind raced but came up with no graceful way to deter him from entering my home. I made the quick decision to trust him. I only hoped I didn't get killed in the process.

My hands still trembled as I stuck my key in the lock. It clicked, and I pushed the door open. To my relief, the lights flickered on when I hit the switch.

I scanned the interior of the house. Everything looked clear.

Brian appeared behind me.

I knew the heart was a strange thing, but mine, at the moment, twisted when I realized I'd much rather have Chase here.

It made no sense that I trusted Chase and I feared Brian. When all the facts were laid out, Brian's past was squeaky clean. He'd always treated me well. He'd bent over backwards to make me feel like a lady.

Chase, on the other hand, had rejected me publicly. He had a history of drinking. A slight leaning toward having a temper.

Brian closed the door behind him. "So, I did have slight ulterior motives for stopping by."

To kill me?

I gulped. "Did you?"

Quickly, I moved toward the kitchen. At least I could grab a knife. I'd have a fighting chance.

He reached into his pocket. I waited to see a gun or something else equally threatening.

Instead, he pulled out his phone, typed something in, and held it up. "Look what went viral today."

I leaned closer. It was a picture of me talking to Rex Harrison that day down at the Serpentine Wall.

I frowned. "Oh, that."

"Fraternizing with the enemy?" He cocked his head to the side, accusation in his eyes.

I couldn't tell if he was being playful or serious. The guy was tightly wound sometimes, and he took life very, very seriously.

"I wouldn't call it that," I told him. "I just happened to run into the man. People, of course, had their cameras ready . . . she said with a touch of disdain to her voice."

Brian grinned. "You're cute when you refer to yourself in third person, you know."

I crossed my arms and shoved my hip against the kitchen counter. "Why does this matter? Is my brother losing points or something?"

"The election is only a few days away. Your brother has been losing a little of his lead every day. I worry about him. He's staked a lot on this election. If he loses . . ."

"What? What will happen if he loses?"

"I think he's buried himself in his work since Melinda died. I don't know what he'll do with himself if he doesn't win."

"Melinda died a long time ago. I know he misses her — she was his wife, for goodness' sakes — but I think he's moved on."

He shrugged. "Maybe you're right. It was just one theory."

Brian always said things with a purpose; he wasn't one to speak off the top of his head. So why had he said that? I'd have to think on it for longer. "Why's Ralph losing his lead? Nothing's changed."

Brian let out a quick puff of air through his nose. "But everything has changed. People are scared because of this Good Deeds Killer. They look at a guy like Rex Harrison, a former police officer, and see someone who knows how to protect our area. He's always been an advocate for the poor. I'm afraid they see your brother as a starched-shirt politician."

I bit my lip. Ralph wasn't like that. He'd make a great state senator, and I knew he'd look out for the interests of the people. But Rex was charming and charismatic in his own right. I could see how people would fall for him, just like Jamie had. Heck, after today, I'd almost put my faith in him. Not many politicians would be willing to implicate a man who'd practically single-handedly funded their campaign.

Brian put away his phone and stared at me a moment. "Do me a favor and try to avoid any more candid shots with Rex, especially ones where you look like you're enjoying yourself. That's the last thing we need."

I might as well lay everything out there . . . everything except the fact that I'd broken into someone's home, that is. "There is a small problem, Brian. Apparently, Jamie and Rex are kind of dating."

His eyes widened. "You're joking?"

"I wish I were."

"Why would she do something like that? Does she want to ruin this election?"

"I think you're overstating it a bit, don't you?"

He began pacing. "Is he trying to find out our secrets?"

"I think he might really like her. Unfortunately."

Brian swung his head back and forth. "Not with this guy. This guy only cares about winning."

"So you think he's dating someone who appeals to the people in the demographic he's targeting." I could read Brian like a book. He calculated the returns on his relationships like most people calculated their investments. I doubted he could fathom the fact that not everyone did the same.

"Yes! And that would be a brilliant move on his part. Didn't you tell your friend to stay away? At least until after the election?"

"She has free will. I can't make her do anything. Besides, she's flattered to get the attention."

Brian ran a hand through his thinning hair. "Women."

"You're overthinking this. Ralph can stand on his own two feet. He just needs to keep being strong on the issues he's known for. Forget about Rex."

"If only it was that easy. I may have to pull my wild card."

I froze in anticipation. "What's that?"

"I have an idea. I've got to think it through. But I think it's an angle that will really make readers sympathize."

I let out a sigh. It was Melinda, wasn't it? "I hate politics. I really do. They complicate life. I just want people to do what they say. I'm tired of these games."

"Unfortunately, you have to play them to win. Speaking of which, tell your friend Jamie not to spill anything."

I shrugged, maybe a little too dramatically. "There's nothing to spill. I don't sit down and talk strategy with her."

He glanced at his watch. "I've got to go. I've got essays to read."

"Essays?"

"I've been tutoring some kids, prepping them for college. One of the things we work on is college applications."

I sucked in a breath. Maybe Brian did have a connection to the murder victims. I hated to think the worst of people, but . . . could Brian be the Good Deeds Killer?

CHAPTER 34

I left early for work the next morning, just so I could swing past the warehouse where I'd seen Brian.

Orion. Orion was behind these crimes. That's what I told myself. But Brian still remained on my mind.

I'd known for a while now that the person responsible for the murders had recognized me and that they were most likely someone I knew, someone I'd spoken with before. That's why Brian still seemed like a viable candidate for the position of Murderer. But Orion seemed like a possible candidate, as well.

I slowed as I approached the warehouse. Everything was quiet out here. There were no cars or people loitering outside.

Should I check the place out? It was broad daylight, which added some security. Besides, my days were numbered anyway.

I made a split-second decision to pull into the parking space. Moving quickly, I climbed from the car. My heels clicked on the cement around the building as I hurried toward the front door. Looking both ways and spotting no one, I tugged at the door.

Nothing. It was locked.

I hurried to the other side, searching for a window that was low enough to allow me to peek in. Again, there was nothing.

But there was a Dumpster.

It wasn't my smartest move ever, but I found a couple of boxes, pushed them together, and used them as steps so I could reach the top of the Dumpster. I had to move carefully, because of my heels, my dress, and my knack for clumsiness.

I grabbed the windowsill and pulled myself up. My gaze barely skimmed the top.

I tried to see inside, but dark shrouded the interior. I couldn't make anything out.

Which meant all of this effort was for nothing. I had no more of an idea what was going on inside this building now than I'd had before I came.

I sighed and turned to get down.

That's when I heard the *blip-blip* of a police cruiser.

I looked up in time to see T.J. climb from his unmarked police sedan.

***

"Holly Paladin. Fancy seeing you here." T.J.'s hands went to his hips as he stared at me.

And he didn't even bother to help me down.

I carefully took a step, only the boxes collapsed. I nearly tumbled onto the ground, but I caught myself on the edge of the Dumpster.

Dirt smeared across the skirt of my dress, and my ankle throbbed.

But I hadn't fallen. Not totally, at least.

I wiped the dust off my skirt and raised my chin, trying to seem like this was totally normal, something that I did every day. That everyone did every day, for that matter. "Hi, T.J."

He stared at me, accusation in his gaze. "Can I ask

what you're doing?"

I shrugged nonchalantly. "Just checking out the old building."

"You couldn't wait until it opened?"

"Nope." I refused to break my gaze.

His eyes narrowed. "What are you really doing, Holly?"

"Social work kind of things that concern privacy. I can't tell you details." In the broadest sense, I supposed that was true. Still, guilt pounded at me.

"Is that right?"

"Of course. Now, I've got to get to work." I tried to hurry past him, but he caught my arm.

"We found a partial print on the scrub brush at another victim's place. It's not enough to bring you in, but I think you're involved in these murders somehow, Holly."

I raised my chin, a strange sense of strength rising in me as I stared T.J. down.

"I'm watching you," he continued. "One wrong move, and I'm bringing you in. Do I make myself clear?"

I jerked away from him and continued back to my car. He'd followed me, I realized. That's the only way he could have happened past at the exact moment I was here. It was too big of a coincidence.

It wasn't until I was inside with my doors locked that my breathing slowed.

That had been close. Really close.

***

I went through my routine at work, trying to wrap

up some of my paperwork, as it was an office day.
During my lunch break, I pulled out a sack lunch and
grabbed a copy of the local newspaper.

The headline caught my eye: Rex Harrison Cuts Ties
with Orion Enterprises.

I skimmed the article. Apparently, in yesterday's
paper, something came out about Orion Enterprises
having shady business practices, underpaying workers,
and being behind on paying their taxes.

This would be Brian's doing, if I had to guess.

So today, Rex Harrison was disassociating himself
with the company. I was sure it helped that Rex seemed
to suspect Orion of possibly being involved in these
local murders, as well.

I did an Internet search on Orion. His mug shot
came onto my computer screen. Even in his publicity
pictures, the man didn't smile. There was a certain
gleam in his eyes that made me wonder what was
going on inside his head.

Was this the face of a killer? Caligula? I didn't
know. I'd only met the man once. But if he was
manufacturing Cena, he could be making millions off
of it. Some people never seemed to have enough money
and would do anything for more.

Would that be his motivation?

I shook my head. I just wasn't sure. He did fit the
description as far as having influence.

"Holly?"

I looked up and saw Doris standing there. "Yes,
ma'am?"

"I need you to start logging your hours."

I blinked. "What?"

She scowled. "I know Helen might love you, but all

of this sick time you're taking? I smell something fishy. I won't have our company's funds wasted."

"I'm not wasting the company's time. I get my job done. I work late if I have to."

"That used to be the case. Lately, you're running around doing everything you can to get out of work."

"Helen gave me permission to help the police find this killer."

She slapped a paper on my desk. "You're coming in late, taking long lunches, and leaving early. You're not reliable."

I stared at my boss, trying to get a read on her. Finally, I asked, "What are you saying?"

"I'm saying, I don't care who your family is or who you're dating or who you've blinded with your empyreal goodness."

"I'm not dating anyone, nor am I a saint."

She raised her chin skeptically. "Yeah, I know that. Apparently, there are others who don't. Consider this your final warning. Helen won't let me fire you, but I can make your life miserable."

As she walked away, I shook my head. Why was it that people either seemed to love me or hate me? There were very few in-betweens.

Having my supervisor hate me wasn't a good thing. Maybe I should just quit this job. I had no idea what I'd do. Maybe I would work for my brother if he won this election.

Then I remembered the families I helped. I couldn't let them down. I could put up with Doris for their sakes . . . I hoped.

I sighed just as my cell phone rang. I recognized Jamie's number. I glanced in Doris's direction, saw she wasn't looking, and answered quietly. No need to stir things up any more. "What's going on?"

"Can you meet for lunch?"

I glanced at Doris again. She glanced back my way, and I slid down in my office chair for a moment. "This may not be the best day."

"Please. It's about John."

Why was I worrying about job security right now? I was dying, for goodness' sakes. "Where do you want to meet?"

CHAPTER 35

I sat across from Jamie at some organic restaurant that mostly served salads and soups. I'd already eaten, so I only ordered a water. Jamie was already munching on some organic greens.

"Did they find John?" I asked. Hope rose in me, but despair was hot on its tail.

She shook her head. "Not yet. I've been talking to some of his friends. No one seems to know where he went or what happened to him."

"I'm sorry, Jamie."

"I was hoping you'd go with me to talk to one more."

I nodded. "Of course. Who?"

"Little T."

My face paled. "You think he has something to do with this?"

"I know they've hung out a couple of times. I know Little T likes you. Maybe he'll open up."

I let out a long breath. "Of course I'll talk to him. I don't know how open he'll be, though."

"That's great, because he's meeting me here. Now."

I blanched, surprised at the encounter. "I guess you were counting on me to say yes."

"I can't stop thinking about the police finding John with three bullets to his chest, Holly. Just like those other guys. At first, I thought my brother was just being irresponsible and he'd gone somewhere or gotten back into drugs. Now I'm not sure."

I glanced at my watch. "When's Little T coming?"

"Five minutes."

I took a sip of my water, trying to formulate a plan of action.

"I saw the article today on Orion," Jamie started. "Brian actually tried to get me to write something about his unethical business practices and his ties with Rex."

That was news to me. "Really? I guess you said no."

Jamie's jaw tightened, her disposition that of a severe thunderstorm warning in its final moments. "He said he would report my dad if I didn't."

I bristled. "What?"

She nodded. "It's true. He said Robbie — a guy in my dad's band — is under the age of twenty-one, and he's played in some clubs with strict age limits. Brian said he could press charges against the band."

"Why didn't you tell me this sooner? I would have talked to him, set him straight. He can't do that!"

"He did do it."

"Jamie, I'm so sorry. I had no idea. You've got to believe me."

She nodded. "I believe you. I talked to my dad, and he said the owners of the jazz club approved it, so he didn't think it was a big deal. I just don't want to see my dad have to go through this hassle, you know? He's a good guy. You know he wouldn't do anything illegal — not on purpose, at least."

"I'm going to talk to Ralph about this."

"Don't bother. Not right now. Not until the election is over. And, just in case you're wondering, I didn't tell Rex about this."

"That wasn't my biggest concern, Jamie."

She nodded. "I know. But stuff like that could ruin a campaign. As much as I love a good expose, I don't want that at the expense of my friendship with you."

"Thank you, Jamie."

"It's the same reason I didn't write the article on Orion. I don't like it when stories get personal. There are things more important in life than winning elections."

"I agree."

Just then, the door opened and Little T walked in. He smiled when he spotted me. "If it isn't Ms. Holly. Fancy seeing you here." He slid into the booth beside me. "So, to what do I owe the pleasure of this meeting?"

Jamie nodded toward me. How did I even approach this? "Little T, I need your help."

"Anything for you, Ms. Holly."

"When was the last time you saw John?"

"Who's John?"

"Remember, I talked to you about him before? He's Jamie's little brother."

"I'm sorry. I don't know a John." He shrugged nonchalantly.

I locked my gaze with him. "Little T, I saw you with John on the night before he disappeared. I'm hoping you can tell me where he is before something happens to him."

All the warmth left his face and he drew back. "You saw me?"

"I was leaving the youth center. I saw you with him."

His face clouded. I figured he was probably

remembering the car that followed him and putting it together that that was me.

He finally looked at me again. "There's a guy I know by the name the Disciple. Maybe that's who you're talking about."

I glanced at Jamie. "The Disciple?"

"He was named after one of the twelve."

My heart sped for a minute. That had to be John. "What do you know about him?"

"I took him to talk to someone about making some extra money."

"Who? Who did you take him to?"

"Ms. Holly—"

"It was Caligula, wasn't it?" I wanted to lecture him about aligning himself with people like that, but this wasn't the time.

He shrugged. "Maybe."

"What happened?"

He shrugged again. "I don't know. I dropped him off. That was that. I was just the courier."

"Where did you drop him off?" Jamie demanded.

I could see Little T starting to shut down again, and I placed my hand on his arm. "It's okay. We're just worried. Please, anything can help."

"It was a warehouse downtown."

I remembered Brian's visit to that warehouse. Could it be the same place? "Address?"

He spouted off a different address than the location where I'd seen Brian. I made a mental note to call Chase after I left here and ask him to check it out.

"Who was he meeting?" I asked.

"He wears a mask. If you see his face, you die. Just like those other guys."

***

I worked extra late at the agency that evening, trying to appease Doris, although I was beginning to resent her more than anything.

I'd called Chase on my way in to work and told him about my conversation with Little T. He'd promised to check out the warehouse and encouraged me to stay safe.

By the time I got home, it was dark outside. I shoved my key into the lock and lumbered into my house. I just needed some time to rest, some time to chew on everything I'd learned.

I dropped my keys onto the table in the foyer, kicked off my shoes, put my purse on the shelf, and started toward the living room. For once I was actually glad my mom wasn't home, because I needed a moment.

Everything in my life felt like it was in turmoil right now, and I felt overwhelmed, to say the least.

John was missing, my job was on the line, my time on earth was ticking away, and everything in general just felt out of whack. Even more, I had no idea what to do about it. The issues had become far greater than the fact that I'd been at that first crime scene.

I fixed myself some tea with honey and walked toward the living room.

I stopped in my tracks when I saw blood on the floor.

I held my breath as I followed the trail.

It led to my couch.

CHAPTER 36

Slowly, I peered over the back of the couch.

A man was there. Lying down. Bleeding.

I gasped when I saw his face.

John. It was John. Jamie's brother.

I dropped my tea and ran to him. "John? Are you okay?"

I shook him, and he moaned.

He pulled his eyes open, each movement lethargic. "Shh. No one can know I'm here."

"What happened?"

"Stabbed . . ." His voice trailed off, and his eyes started to close again.

"I should get you to the hospital." I started to get up, but John grabbed my arm, his grip viselike.

"No one can know I'm here. If they find me . . . they'll kill me." His gaze locked with mine.

I froze, uncertain how to proceed. "How about Jamie? Can I call Jamie?"

He swung his head back and forth. "She . . . can't . . . come."

"Why? Why not?"

"Watching . . ."

I leaned closer as his voice faded out again. "Watching who? Who's watching who?"

His face distorted with pain. "They're watching you. Watching my house. Looking for me."

"You're not making any sense." I shook my head, trying to comprehend what he was getting at. Who was watching me?

"Please. Help." He let out a desperate cry and began writhing.

"Help? I want to help. But how?"

He stayed silent.

"John? Stay with me." I shook him, unwilling to let him lose consciousness.

He moaned.

There was only one thing I could think to do. One person who could help. "I'm going to call a friend. He's trustworthy. I promise. But you need help I can't give you. Okay?"

He stared at me and said nothing. He was fading fast, I realized.

With panic, I picked up my phone and called Chase. My hands trembled along with my voice when Chase finally answered.

"Holly? What's going on?" His voice sounded light, unaware.

"I need you to come over. Now."

"Are you okay?" Instant worry gripped his tone.

I glanced at John. "Yeah, it's a long story. Listen, come dressed in normal clothes, okay? No work stuff. You'll understand when you get here."

"I'll be right over."

***

I saw Chase pull up and waited until he was halfway up the sidewalk before opening the front door. I ran out to greet him, planting a kiss on his lips before throwing my arms around him.

"Wow. What was that for?" His eyes widened.

"Just play along," I whispered. "Act like you're here to see me."

After a brief moment of thought, his arms squeezed tighter around my waist and he pulled me off my feet. When he set me back down, his fingers intertwined with mine. We walked hand in hand into the house. Just like a couple in love, ready to spend the evening together. That's what I was counting on, at least.

As soon as I closed the door, I turned all of the locks and my smile disappeared.

"John is here. He's hurt. He needs help."

"John? Jamie's brother? Did you call 911?" Chase bristled.

"I can't. He's hiding from someone. He said they're watching me. If they find him, they'll kill us both."

His eyebrows furrowed together. "Take me to him."

I led him into the living room. "I wrapped up his wound and gave him some water. He'd faded in and out of consciousness. I don't know what to do."

Chase knelt beside him, surveying his wounds. "He needs a doctor."

"That's what I told him. He refused. Made me promise not to take him."

"We've got to clean this wound out. Get me some towels. Boil some water. I need a first aid kit."

Chase worked for the next hour to clean John's wound. John managed to wake up enough to take some pain medication and drink some water, and then he faded again.

When we'd done all we could, Chase and I sat on the floor across from John, monitoring his breathing. I prayed over and over again that he would be okay.

My fingers itched to call Jamie. She'd want to know. But John didn't want to put his sister's life in danger. He didn't want to lead the bad guys here, either. That meant that my hands were tied. I was between the proverbial rock and hard place.

"You did well, Holly." Chase patted my leg. His hand stayed on my knee.

"Thanks. I didn't know what to do."

"Did John say anything else?"

I shrugged, leaning back against the chair behind me. "That if they find him, they'll kill him."

"Who's 'they'?"

I shook my head. "I have no idea. Did you check out the warehouse, by chance? Were there any answers there?"

"We did. It's owned by Orion Enterprises. There was nothing suspicious there."

I frowned, dropping my head back onto the cushion. "Another dead end. Yet it's not. Orion keeps coming up over and over again."

"I find it hard to believe he would be involved in something like this." Chase ran his hand across his face.

"Are you telling me that you've never been surprised at a culprit before?"

He sat up straighter. "I've been surprised plenty of times. People can do the most unexpected things for the most unexpected reasons. I'm sure you've seen that as a social worker."

"Plenty of times."

"Holly, I know I shouldn't say this . . ."

I waited, anticipating exactly what this was about.

". . . but I'm not sure who I can trust. I can't help but

wonder if this Caligula guy might be a police officer."

That was not what I'd been expecting. I jolted upright. "Why would you think that?"

"I think things are being covered up. I wrote a ticket to Orion Vanderslice for reckless driving about a month ago. I can't find any record of it. Plus, all the fingerprints we collected at the crime scenes for the Good Deeds Killer? They're gone."

"Wow. Who do you think it could be?"

"I'm going to sound really crazy now, but I've wondered about the chief."

I held back my gasp. "Why?"

"He's been acting different lately. Quieter. Snappier. He disappears to his office a lot. Sometimes I don't think he's concerned enough about this serial killer we have on the loose. I think he should call in the feds—the FBI, the DEA. But he seems strangely calm."

I let his words sink in.

"Don't let this go beyond you and me, okay? I probably shouldn't be saying any of this, but I just don't know who I can trust. Except you."

I remembered my role in all of this, and guilt again gnawed at me. I said nothing, though. I was beginning to realize that I coped best by avoiding anything unpleasant. Things like cancer, even.

"Thanks for trusting me, Chase. I'll keep my mouth shut."

He offered a grateful smile. "Thanks, Holly."

I stared at John, whose chest rose and fell steadily. "What now?"

"Now we wait. We hope that he's okay."

Chase put his arm around my shoulder and pulled my head onto his chest. I didn't argue. It felt good to be held close, to feel cared about and protected.

I must have drifted to sleep, because the next thing I knew I was being jostled awake as Chase moved.

"He's coming to," Chase muttered.

I blinked. A glance at the windows told me it was still dark outside. How long had I been out? It didn't matter.

We scrambled toward John. He pulled his eyes open. After a few minutes, he pushed himself up.

"How are you feeling?" I asked, kneeling beside him.

He looked dazed for a moment before nodding. "Better, I think."

"I cleaned your wound. Gave you some makeshift stitches," Chase said.

John squirmed. "I remember. It didn't feel good."

"Sorry, it was the best I could do."

He nodded and sat up even more. "Sorry about the couch."

I looked down at the deep red stain on my mom's cheerful yellow cushions. "Don't worry about it. I know a crime scene cleaner who can give me some tips on getting that out." My friend Gabby wouldn't mind helping me from across the miles.

Chase sat in the chair across from him. "John, can you tell me what's going on?"

"A friend of a friend told me about this great job offer where I'd make three times the money for half the work. I knew it sounded too good to be true. I picked this guy up. It was the only way I could meet with the boss."

"Was this boss Caligula?" I asked.

John glanced at me, his face darkening. "I didn't

know that until I got there."

"What happened when you got there, John?" Chase asked.

He sucked in a long, shaky breath. "He took me to this dark alley, in the back door of a building, down some steps, and into this room. There was a man waiting there."

I held my breath, waiting to hear what happened next. Could this be the break we'd been waiting for? Would we finally have some answers?

"He wore this mask. A ski mask. His voice was disguised."

"Was he tall? Skinny? Fat?" Chase asked.

John shook his head. "It was dark. He was wearing a coat. I think he was on the taller side, but I can't be sure. Anyway, he told me I could start selling Cena for him. He needed some more distributors. I had no idea my friend was talking about drugs when he mentioned a job opportunity. I would have never gone if I'd known."

"What happened next?" Chase asked.

"I told him I wasn't interested and tried to leave. These guys who worked for him grabbed me. Told me that no one gets this far and walks away. If I knew what was best for me, I'd take the job."

"And you said?" I asked.

He shook his head again, squeezing his eyes shut and touching his bandage. "I told him no way. I walked away from that kind of life. I don't want to battle those demons again. He wouldn't take no for an answer, though. Finally, I told him I'd do it. Only, I had no intention of doing it. I just wanted to get out of there."

"So he let you walk away?" Chase shifted, leaning

closer.

"He said I was in a trial period. He started mumbling about people forgetting the good and only remembering the bad. I had no idea what he was talking about. Anyway, he gave me some Cena and told me who to deliver it to. He told me if I didn't do it, I'd die."

"How'd you end up here?"

"I ran. I thought I could get away, and I did for a little while. But they followed me when I left my house. Roughed me up. Took me back to Caligula. He said that no one crosses him. That's when he pulled out the knife." John squeezed his eyes shut. "He didn't want to kill me. He wanted to scare me into doing what he wanted."

I leaned closer. "Then?"

"I don't even know how much time went by. They gave me some drugs, and I passed out. Caligula left. When I woke up, the guys he'd left to guard me were high and totally out of it. When they turned their backs, I managed to slip past them. Once I was out, I ran."

"Do you remember where the warehouse was?" Chase continued. "Could you take us back there?"

John shook his head. "They gave me some of that drug. It hadn't worn off when I left. Everything was spinning. I passed out in someone's car on State Street. Woke up, and some of the drug had worn off. That's when I knew I had to keep running."

"How do you know you weren't followed?" I asked.

"They would have killed me off by now if they knew where I was."

"Who were you supposed to deliver that Cena to?" Chase questioned.

"Some punks. High schoolers. Users."

"I'm going to need that address," Chase said.

John rattled it off.

"Why'd you come here, John?" I asked, still trying to put the pieces together.

"I knew you were the only one who could help me. That's why."

CHAPTER 37

We kept an eye on John for the rest of the evening, and he seemed to stabilize. Finally, at 6:00 a.m. Chase stood.

"If we don't want to raise suspicions, I think I should go. I've got to figure out a few things now, considering what I learned from John. Knowing that he made it to State Street can narrow our search perimeters."

Someone could easily run from the warehouse where I'd spotted Brian to State Street.

"Do you think John will be okay?"

"As long as he stays on the down low, I think he'll be all right. Staying here all day will only arouse suspicions, though. I'll make sure an officer patrols past this area. I'll just say some people reported some suspicious activity."

I nodded and walked Chase to the door. Thankfully, it was Saturday, so I didn't have to worry about going to work and Doris today.

"Thank you for everything, Chase. I don't know what I would have done without you."

He smiled that smile that melted my heart every time. "Anytime, Holly."

He opened the door and stepped onto the porch. I followed after him, ignoring the cool breeze and the brittle air.

"I hope I didn't put you in an awkward position, Chase. I know you have a sworn duty here."

His lips pulled into a tight line. "I'll figure out something. It's officially my day off, so I can buy a little time."

I thought about that warehouse again. "There's one more place I think you should check out. I'd like to go with you, though."

His eyebrows knit together. "Is that a good idea?"

I shrugged. "I'm not sure what's a good idea anymore."

He finally nodded slowly. "Let me go home and get cleaned up. How about if I come to pick you up in an hour?"

I flashed a smile. "That sounds great."

He leaned down and planted a soft kiss on my lips before pulling me into a long hug. "Trying to make it look real, you know?"

This was part of the cover, I remembered. I tried to tell my heart that, but it refused to listen and continued to beat out of control.

He kissed my forehead before walking back to his truck.

I looked over in time to see Mrs. Signet shaking her head. "Your mom's not going to like this. You having a guy over all night? I thought more of you."

I opened my mouth to explain but stopped. Instead, I slipped back inside. I had bigger worries at the moment.

***

I pointed to the warehouse where I'd seen Brian

enter and depart. "There."

"You think this is where they took John? Why here?"

I was going to have to tell him the whole truth. I didn't want to. I didn't want to do anything to put my brother's campaign on the line. But there were other things to consider, mainly people's lives.

As Chase pulled to the side of the street, I sucked in a deep breath and spilled everything. "I saw my brother's campaign manager come here the other day."

"I'm still not seeing the connection, Holly."

"His name is Brian. Brian would do anything to win."

"You think he'd manufacture and sell drugs? How would that help him to win the election?"

I shrugged. "Influence people? Bribe them? I don't know. I just know that Brian isn't the type to frequent a warehouse."

"Maybe he was picking up some brochures for the campaign."

"It was just weird. That's all I know to say. Something didn't feel right about all of it. The answers could be waiting for us inside."

Chase leveled his gaze with me. "You'd put your brother's election on the line for this?"

I nodded, confident this was the right thing, yet still feeling slightly queasy. "If that's what I have to do."

"You're sure?"

I nodded again. "Yeah, I really want some answers, even if it makes people in my life look really bad."

"Let's go, then."

I tried to push away the niggle of anxiety that swept through me as I approached the building. I pictured opening the door, seeing Cena being manufactured, seeing Brian in charge of the whole operation.

"Should you get a warrant? I could talk to Alex . . ."

He shook his head. "There's not enough evidence to justify a warrant. All we're going on here is a hunch."

I frowned, realizing this whole thing might be futile.

Chase turned the handle and the door opened. A brightly lit room waited in the distance. I wasn't sure why I'd expected something dingy and shady.

I stayed at the door while he crept inside, his gun drawn.

That's when I heard someone appear behind us.

I turned and saw a man standing there.

CHAPTER 38

"Can I help you?" he asked.

The man wore a white dress shirt, faded black pants, and scuffed-up shoes. I braced myself, excuses forming on my lips but nothing escaping.

Chase held up his badge. "Cincinnati PD. We had a report of a suspicious incident here, and I came to check it out."

He turned to me. "And you are?"

"Holly," I offered.

"A ride along," Chase explained. "Who are you?"

"Dean Andrews. I'm renting this facility. Can I ask about the nature of the call? What kind of suspicious incident happened here?"

"Someone thought they saw a suspicious person loitering outside of the building. What is this place, Mr. Andrews?"

He stuck his head outside, looked up and down the street, and then closed the door. He nodded toward an interior door. "Let's go to my office."

I stepped from the lobby into the huge warehouse and spotted . . . casino-style games against the walls? Was this a secret gambling operation?

"We're a support group for recovering gamblers," Dean Andrews explained.

"What?" The question slipped out before I could stop it.

He nodded. "It's true. We have various meetings here throughout the week."

"What's with the games, then?" Chase asked.

"They're a part of our therapy. That's all. We learn to overcome gambling by facing our addictions, by saying no. It makes us stronger." He looked at Chase. "But I assure you that nothing illegal is going on."

"Why here? Why a warehouse instead of some office? Better yet, why not a counseling facility?" I asked.

He raised an eyebrow at me. "I thought you were a ride along. Whatever. We like to maintain our privacy. A lot of our members are people who are admired in society: CEOs, a few professional athletes, political figures. You get the point. The last thing they want is for people to catch wind of this. It's also the reason why there's no signs on the building."

"Do you have any paperwork? Business license?" Chase asked.

"Of course. Let me go grab them." The man disappeared into the back.

"Well, I guess this was a bust," I muttered, disappointed. At least now I knew. Brian had a gambling problem. Was that his secret? Maybe someone who took risks like that wasn't the best person to run an election campaign.

"You were following your instincts. At least we can rule this out now."

I nodded, just as Dean came out from the office with some papers in his hands. Chase looked them over and nodded.

"Thanks for speaking with me, Dean," Chase started.

"I'd appreciate your discretion."

Chase nodded. "Will do."

***

Once back in the car, I shook my head, my thoughts spinning. I'd just majorly wasted Chase's time. Maybe I was a great CPS investigator, but a terrible detective.

"I need to go check on John," I told Chase.

"I'll come with you."

We pulled up to my house, I unlocked the door, and we stepped inside.

Everything was quiet.

"John?" I called.

No response.

Chase pushed me behind him.

All the lights were off. There was no sound. No movement.

What was going on?

My mind jumped to the worst places. Places of death and pain.

Dear Lord, please be with him.

I glanced at the couch as we approached.

"Stay here, Holly," Chase ordered.

I nodded and backed against the wall, continuing to pray. A moment later, Chase came back downstairs and put his gun away. "There's no one here."

"Where did John go?"

"My guess? He left. There are no signs of struggle. He probably started feeling better and figured it was too risky to stay."

I released my breath. "He shouldn't have done that."

"People react in funny ways when they're in danger."

I raked my hand through my hair. "What am I going to tell Jamie?"

Chase squeezed my arm. "Listen, let's go grab some lunch and clear our heads. How about some Cincinnati chili? How's that sound?"

My stomach grumbled in return. "It sounds good."

***

Lunch was a nice distraction, except for the fact that I wasn't hungry. I'd merely picked at my food.

"What's going on in that head of yours, Holly?"

"I just want to find this guy. I want this to be over with. I'm tired of one person having so much control over the people in this city."

"We're doing everything we can."

I nodded. "I know. Believe me, I know. This isn't a reprimand to you or anyone else on the police force. Whoever is behind this has pulled me into it. I'm tired of living like this."

He leaned closer. "So, who do you think is behind this?"

I let out a sigh. "Well, I thought maybe Brian, but apparently he just has a gambling problem."

"Who else?"

"I considered Abraham, but he was just working a second job. I thought about Rex, but he has an alibi for at least one of the murders."

"Rex? You really thought he could be Caligula?"

"Maybe I was blinded by my own dislike of the man. I just keep thinking about who this has to be.

270

Someone who has contact with youth. Someone who has connections and influence. Someone who knows me."

"Wait—someone who knows you? Why would you say that? And do you mean someone who knew you prior to the crimes?"

I'd just admitted too much, hadn't I? I nodded. "Yeah, I think this person knows me. He knew who my social work clients were. He stole the mop and bucket and broke into my house."

"That could be unrelated," Chase offered.

I could tell he didn't believe it either.

"Want to hear something strange?" Chase asked.

Did I ever. I leaned closer. "Of course."

"I found a receipt the other day. It fell out of T.J.'s pocket. I started to give it back to him when I realized it was for a mop and bucket. I visited the store, and they sell the exact same kind that's being left at crime scenes."

My eyes widened. I'd never even considered T.J. as a suspect. But Chase thought something could be going down at the police precinct. T.J. could be that person.

"Are you sure he wasn't just checking to see where the supplies were bought?"

"He could be. But why didn't he tell me? That would be something important in the investigation."

"That's a great question." Chills went up my spine. I glanced across the restaurant just in time to see a man be seated. It was the guy I'd seen with Katrina!

Chase followed my gaze. "What is it?"

"That man. I saw him with one of my former clients. I'm pretty sure I saw him at one of Rex's campaign rallies, as well."

"Is that significant?"

I shook my head uncertainly. "I'm not sure. There's just something about him." Could he have been the man I'd spotted that day when I'd been nearly shot at the bank?

"His name is Evan Stewart. He works for the mayor, but he comes into the office sometimes."

"Upstanding guy?"

Chase shrugged. "I can't say. I don't know enough about him. But I can keep an eye on him, to see if there's anything suspicious about him."

I nodded. "That sounds like a good idea."

"Listen, I've got to get back to work. How about if I drop you off at Alex's?"

As Chase paid, I stepped outside onto the sidewalk to get some air.

Just as my feet hit the cement, a car swerved around the corner. Headed straight toward me.

I dove toward the building, hoping I'd make it out of the way in time.

CHAPTER 39

Chase hadn't stopped scowling since he'd rushed outside and seen what had happened.

He'd tried to get a license plate number, but it was too late. Instead, he helped me up, concern all over his face.

I'd insisted I was fine, just a little embarrassed. He'd taken a report and then driven me home so I could get cleaned up.

"You're going to be sore tomorrow." He stood in the entryway to my house, towering over me. "Why don't you go upstairs and take a bath? I'll wait down here."

"I'm sure you have better things to do." I pulled out a dining room chair and tried to sit down, but my back ached too much.

"No, I insist. Please go. Turn on your music. Relax. It can do a body good."

He'd wanted to call an ambulance, but I'd told him I was fine.

Finally, I nodded. I headed upstairs, thinking a long, hot bath just might be the medicine I needed. I started the water, pulled up my favorite playlist on my phone's music player, and grabbed a change of clothes.

Every time I closed my eyes, I saw images of the car headed toward me. I hoped T.J. could find the driver of that car. Or would his loyalty toward Rex mean hatred toward anyone who opposed the man? People like me, the sister of Rex's political opponent? I didn't know.

I poured some Epsom salt into the bath and then lowered myself there. I listened to Ella Fitzgerald sing "Someone to Watch Over Me" and closed my eyes.

I was supposed to go to a campaign rally tonight. But I suddenly felt tired and overwhelmed. Maybe I'd stay in for the rest of the evening and take it easy for once. I'd been running around like crazy lately, and where had it gotten me? Nowhere.

The longer I stayed in the bath, the more convinced I became. It was like my body was shutting down.

My heart rate steadily increased, and my breathing felt labored, like I couldn't pull a deep breath into my lungs.

Was my anxiety getting the best of me? Was everything catching up with me? I wasn't sure.

Usually baths made me feel relaxed.

Suddenly, I froze. Was that a noise I'd heard? Something downstairs? Maybe a door opening.

Had Chase left? Had someone else entered?

Maybe T.J. was finally here, with the evidence he needed to haul me to prison.

The room began spinning, a blur of turquoise and blue.

I had to get out of here.

Now.

I dragged myself from the tub. Once out, I could barely stand. My legs felt rubbery. I managed somehow to pull my clothes on.

My head was still spinning as I opened the door. I held onto the wall.

Something wasn't right, I realized.

Was it the cancer? Was it choosing this moment to stake a claim on my body?

I took a step and everything went black.

CHAPTER 40

I pulled my eyes open, my subconscious feeling as if it was being vacuumed out of a vortex. Or as if I was Alice being dropped into Wonderland.

Only this wasn't Wonderland.

I blinked.

I was in the hospital.

Everything rushed back to me. The end was getting closer, I realized. Though I'd had amazing peace about this only a month ago, right now tears rushed to my eyes. What had changed?

Chase's face suddenly appeared. No, not just in my mind. He was here. Beside my hospital bed. Beside me.

"Holly?" He stood, peering over me. "You're awake."

"How's my hair look?" It was my lame attempt at a joke.

He hooked a piece behind my ear. "Beautiful. Just like you."

My cheeks flushed. Those darn cheeks. "Thanks. You didn't have to wait here, you know."

He lowered himself beside me. "I wanted to." He stared at me another moment. Was it my imagination or were those tears in his eyes? "You could have told me, you know." His voice sounded hoarse and thick.

"Told you what?" My heart pounded in my ears. I knew the answer.

"The doctor let it slip. He assumed I knew. Holly . . ." His voice caught.

I shook my head as tears filled my eyes. I'd managed to be so relatively unemotional about this for so long, but now everything was coming to the surface, and I didn't like it one bit.

"What did he tell you?"

"That you had a condition. A life-threatening condition."

I dabbed under my eyes with a tissue. "That's all?"

He nodded, his intense gaze still on me. "That's all. I was hoping you might tell me the rest."

I shrugged, trying to pull myself together. "There's not much to say."

"I'd say there's a lot to say."

I squeezed my eyes shut. I'd been living in denial for too long now. I didn't even know how to talk to people about my health. "I have a rare form of cancer. I probably won't live another year," I blurted.

Moisture glimmered in his eyes. "Oh, Holly . . ."

"It's not a big deal. I've lived a good life."

"There are amazing treatments out there—"

I shook my head. "I don't want to go that route. I don't want to put myself through that. I watched my dad go through it, and it's just not worth it."

"But for your family . . ."

I shook my head again. "They don't know."

He stood up as if he'd sat on a hot stove. "They don't know? Holly, how could you not tell them?" He began pacing, shaking his head, squeezing the skin between his eyes.

"They have so much going on, Chase. There's my sister's wedding and my brother's running for office.

They're still getting over my dad's death. I didn't want to throw anything else on them."

"Throw something on them? Holly, this isn't news that you've quit your job or gone broke gambling. This is your life. They'll want to know."

My chin trembled. "I don't want to spend the rest of my life with people feeling sorry for me and looking at me with pity and thinking I'm fragile. I want to go out strong. I'm not afraid of dying, Chase." At least, I wasn't until today. A tear slipped down my cheek.

Suddenly, Chase was back at my side. He sat beside me and pulled my head into his chest. That's when the tears started pouring.

And Chase held me, wiping away every single one.

***

I'd already seen what felt like twenty million doctors. But when my oncologist, Dr. Henderson, walked into the room, I knew I'd seen one too many. There was no way to avoid him here.

I didn't even try to smile as I glanced up at him. He was a small man with small glasses and a soft voice. Whenever I saw him, my entire body tensed and my throat went dry.

"Holly, good to see you're awake. How are you feeling?" He stood at the foot of the bed.

"I've been better."

He glanced at some papers on his clipboard. "I just got the results of your blood work back, Holly. Is it okay to discuss things now?" He glanced at Chase.

Great, *now* the man cared about privacy.

"Go ahead," I told him. At this point, what else was

there to hide?

"We were afraid your symptoms were caused by your disease. However, your blood work showed high levels of amphetamines in your system."

"Amphetamines?" I questioned. "That's a drug. I don't do drugs."

He squinted at me. "That's why I thought it was odd. Are you sure there's not something you want to tell us?"

I nodded. "Positive. I don't know . . ."

Chase shook his head on the other side of me. "Holly, did you put anything in your bath?"

"Just some Epsom salt and a little essential oil."

"That's why someone broke into your house, Holly. That day when nothing was stolen? They switched your bath salt for something else."

I rubbed my cheek. "You think someone would do that?"

"What other explanation is there?"

I shook my head. "There's not."

"Should I call the police?" the doctor asked, glancing between me and Chase.

"I am the police," Chase told him.

"Very well, then. The good news is that this should be out of your system soon, Holly. The bad news is that we want to keep you until tomorrow for observation."

"Got it."

He lowered the clipboard, and I knew exactly what was coming. "And I really need you to come back into the office for some more follow-up appointments. Haven't you gotten my messages?"

"I've just been busy."

"You've got to take time for yourself."

I shrugged. "I really don't know what there is to discuss. I have my end-of-life plan."

"I realize checking off items on your bucket list is important, but there could be a more effective way of doing things." He glanced at Chase and paused. "However, we should talk about it another time."

When the doctor walked away, Chase's face came into view. I saw the concern in his eyes, and it nearly broke my heart.

"Why is someone targeting you, Holly?"

I shook my head. "I'm not one hundred percent certain." I stopped myself, tired and exhausted from keeping things hidden. "Actually, Chase, there's something I need to tell you."

"Okay."

"Why don't you sit down?"

Nausea roiled in my stomach. It may have felt like we had the start of a relationship. But this was going to turn everything upside down.

"When I heard I had only a year to live, I decided to make some drastic changes in my life."

Chase's phone beeped.

He hit a button without ever breaking eye contact. "Keep going."

"I originally had this bucket list that included falling in love and traveling to Europe and photobombing tourists at a Reds game." I shook my head. "Anyway, I realized that life was too short for that. I wanted to make a difference—"

His phone beeped again. "Just ignore it," he insisted.

"Maybe you should check it, Chase. Just in case it's something important for work."

"You sure?"

I nodded, partly relieved I didn't have to finish telling my story and partly disappointed.

"I'm sorry, Holly. Just one minute."

I nodded as he slipped into the hallway. He appeared a moment later with a new excitement in his eyes.

"Holly, there's been a break in the case. I really want to hear—"

"Go, Chase."

"Are you sure?" Doubt lingered in his gaze.

I nodded. "I'm positive. We can have this conversation later."

"I hate to leave you."

"I'll call Jamie."

He planted a kiss on my forehead and then hurried toward the door. "I'll check on you later. I promise."

"Just don't get yourself killed. That's all I care about."

"I won't."

***

"Bath salts?" Jamie asked. "Are you serious? This whole world has gone mad."

I nodded. "I know. Thanks again for coming to sit with me, by the way."

She nodded. "No problem. All I was doing was sitting home and worrying anyway."

I wanted to tell her that I'd seen John. But I'd promised John I wouldn't. My friend looked so worried. The options battled inside me.

"Have you seen Rex anymore?"

"We were supposed to meet for coffee tonight. I canceled."

"You didn't have to do that for me."

"Sure I did. I wouldn't leave you here by yourself, Holly. You're like my sister. Speaking of which, have you told your brother or sister about your condition?"

"I texted them and let them know I wouldn't make it tonight. I don't want to worry them."

"You're always so worried about worrying other people. Sometimes you just have to let the truth play out and let people worry about their own selves."

I stared at my friend for a moment. "You really think that?"

She nodded. "Of course I do. You always try to protect people, Holly. That's admirable, but there comes a time you have to let people go through painful things. It will make them stronger in the end."

"Then there's something I need to tell you. Please don't hate me." I wasn't at all certain about this decision.

"I don't know if I could ever hate you, Holly."

"I saw John," I blurted.

She froze. "What?"

I nodded. "He's alive. He showed up at my house."

She stood, her entire body tense. "When?"

"Friday night. He'd been stabbed. I helped to get him cleaned up. He made me promise not to tell anyone."

"Why would he do that?"

"He said it would put you in danger."

"Why did he go to you?"

"He knew I was working with the police on this. He thought I might be able to help."

She crossed her arms. "And were you?"

I shook my head. "I don't know. Some guys tried to manipulate him into selling drugs. He told them no. They got rough with him, but he somehow got away. He's been on the run since then."

"What do you mean, since then?"

"He left my house, Jamie."

She shook her head. "I can't believe you didn't tell me."

"Jamie . . ."

"You knew how worried I was."

"It was difficult—"

"Not nearly as difficult as wondering if your brother might be dead."

"Jamie, he made me promise," I tried to explain.

"How could you do this? I thought you were my friend."

"I am your friend. Jamie, you know I am."

She glanced at her watch. "You know what? Maybe I have time for that coffee after all."

As she left the room, tears squeezed at my eyes. What a mess, and it was all my fault.

CHAPTER 41

"Alex asked me to come and check on you. I told her that the doctors here were perfectly capable of caring for you," William said. He was my sister's fiancé, an average-looking guy with an even temperament and premature worry lines on his forehead.

"Thanks for coming," I told him. "It's kind of you."

We did the normal chitchat, and I thought I was free and clear. He didn't seem the least bit suspicious that something may be wrong with me other than bath salts and a serial killer on my tail.

"Do you mind if I look at your charts, Holly?"

My throat tightened. I'd been so close. I knew if he took one look at my medical history, he'd know something was wrong. Yet, if I refused, he'd only grow concerned.

With hesitancy, I nodded.

He picked up the clipboard and scanned the stats there, reviewing my information. His eyebrows drew together and he shook his head. "This can't be right."

I said nothing.

He looked at me, the lines on his forehead deepening. "Holly?"

I pressed my lips together and nodded. I wanted more than anything to deny it, but I couldn't. William knew the truth.

"Oh, Holly." He tilted his head, speechless for a moment. "Does . . . does Alex know?"

"I haven't told anyone yet."

"Really . . .?" He shook his head. "Cancer?"

"There are no good treatments for the particular variety I have. I always have to be unique, you know. So, anyway, I'm just accepting it and living my last days to the fullest."

He glanced at the chart again and shook his head. "Holly, could I review your charts? I'm not an oncologist, but my best friend from med school is. I'd just like to take a look."

"Look all you want. I don't have any hope for a different diagnosis, though."

"And there may not be one. But I'd like just to review this. I've never heard of this kind of cancer, even."

"It's rare."

"I do hope you'll tell your family soon, Holly."

I filled my lungs with a long breath before nodding. "I will. I promise."

Just then, someone knocked at the door. I looked up and saw Chase there. William excused himself as Chase came and sat beside me.

"Where's Jamie?"

"She couldn't stay." My heart thudded with the words. "It was nice to have a little quiet."

"I've got good news."

"I could really use some good news right now."

"We just arrested Orion for the murder spree plaguing the city."

I blinked in surprise. "What?"

He nodded. "It's true. Someone came forward with

information to implicate Orion. We discovered the drug was being manufactured on the bottom level of one of his old warehouses. He had connections with each of the boys due to the basketball league he started."

"Did he own up to the charges?"

Chase shook his head. "No, he's denied them, but that's normal."

"That's great news."

"I wanted to come and tell you myself. It still doesn't explain why he chose you to take the fall by stealing the mop and bucket, but that may just be one mystery we never figure out."

I nodded.

"I've got to go attend to some more details. I'll stop by in the morning, though. At least you can rest easy now that this guy will be behind bars."

"That sounds great, Chase. Thank you."

***

I tossed and turned all night, partly because I was in the hospital hooked up to machines and partly because of the turmoil churning in my life.

Of course, one of those major sources of turmoil should now be eliminated, but I just couldn't come to terms with Orion being arrested.

Sure, he'd been on my suspect list. Sure, he had motive, means, and opportunity. But somehow everything felt too easy.

Brian had been a suspect, but he'd just had a gambling problem.

Abraham had been a suspect, but he'd just taken on

a part-time job.

I'd halfway suspected John, but he'd nearly been a victim of the killer himself.

Rex had crossed my mind, but he'd been the one who'd turned over the information to nail Orion, even though he might lose campaign money.

I supposed I could be overthinking this whole thing. Maybe I was just looking for things to worry about. That's how my life felt sometimes.

The other fact remained that, because I'd kept everyone in the dark about my illness, I lay in the hospital room by myself right now. Unless you shared your problems with other people, you couldn't expect them to help you carry the burden. I'd dug this hole for myself, and now I had to live with it.

I also had to live with the fact that my best friend wasn't speaking to me. Maybe we were growing farther and farther apart. We hardly ever fought, yet this week we'd had two major ones. Was God preparing Jamie to not have me in her life anymore?

"Hey, sis." Alex stuck her head into the room. She held up a flowered overnight bag. "I brought you some clothes."

I'd had no choice but to call my sister. Not unless I wanted to go home in a hospital gown, which I didn't.

I sat up. "Thank you. I'm so ready to get out of here."

She crossed her arms. "You could have called last night, you know."

"I know, but you had Ralph's campaign rally."

"There's more to life than politics." She sat down across from me. "So, someone put bath salts in your actual bath salt?"

I nodded. "Strange, huh? It's the same stuff that's connected with Cena."

"I wish people realized how messed up drugs can make you. Then maybe they would think twice — both the users and the dealers."

"There's too much money in it for people to give it up."

She shook her head. "You heard about Orion Vanderslice?"

"Isn't that crazy?"

"No one can believe it. I mean, everyone knows he's not the friendliest guy and that he's money hungry. But who would have thought he'd sink this low?"

"I heard he was manufacturing the drugs in his warehouse."

Alex nodded. "He claims ignorance. He probably *didn't* know exactly where the drugs were being made, most likely on purpose as a safety precaution."

I shook my head. "I still think it's crazy. I mean, making drugs is one thing. But cold-blooded murder? That's a whole different story."

"I agree. People will go to desperate measures to protect their futures, even the CEO of a successful company. He got himself in a bad position and was scrambling to get out."

Why wasn't I going to desperate measures to ensure I might have more of a future?

"Listen, how about if I help you get cleaned up? I know you still have a few hours until you're discharged."

I smiled. "That sounds great. No baths, though. Only showers for a while."

***

At lunchtime, I insisted Alex should leave. She wanted to wait, but I knew that even though it was Sunday, she had a busy schedule. I really was okay with being alone in the hospital.

What I wasn't okay with was the change in my thoughts about dying.

About my choice to be alone in all of this.

In my realization that secrets could hurt people.

Put it all together, and I was melancholy when Chase arrived at two.

"I'm sorry I couldn't be here earlier," he started. "We've been busy trying to wrap this investigation up."

"How's it going?"

He nodded. "Good. We found purchase order forms for Orion Enterprises, signed with Orion's signature, for chemicals used to make Cena. It proves he knew about the drugs. He has no alibi for the nights of the murder. He employed two of the boys who were killed."

"Wow. I'm glad it came together."

"Me, too."

"You look nice," Chase told me, glancing up and down at my dress. "You don't miss a beat, do you? Even being here in the hospital, you still look like a million bucks."

"I do like feeling like a lady."

"You are a lady, Holly."

I bit back a frown. "At least one person thinks so."

"You have others who don't?"

"Apparently, I cause strong emotions in people.

Good and bad emotions. Lately, a lot more bad emotions."

"I can't see it."

I smiled. "You're kind."

"I'm honest."

I stood. "The doctor just discharged me about thirty minutes ago. I'm ready to go."

"Perfect. Your chariot awaits."

A nurse brought a wheelchair into the room and walked with us as Chase pushed me down to the entrance. Once we were in his car, he turned to me. "Where to, my lady?"

"Anywhere but my house."

"Want to hang out at my place for a while? As you know, it's nothing fancy."

I smiled. "Yeah, nothing fancy sounds perfect."

The day was unseasonably warm. Chase kept a hold on my hand as we walked inside. "I have something I think you'll like."

He led me through the house and out the back door. I blinked at what I saw there. Party lights were strung from the posts of a pergola over the back deck. A nice grill and a comfy-looking love seat were there.

"Nice."

"I can't take the credit. The previous owners did this. I think they liked their parties." He pulled out a chair. "Want to sit?"

I shook my head. "Not really. Too much sitting lately."

He walked over to a box and opened it up. "I know you love your old music, but I happen to think music from the sixties reigns supreme. Despite that, I did find some Nat King Cole."

A moment later, "When I Fall in Love" gushed through the speakers. He clicked the lights on overhead and took a step closer.

"You care for a dance?"

A tremble took over my limbs, and it wasn't because of my disease. "Sounds nice."

His arm went around my waist, and he took my hand in his. Gently, we swayed back and forth to the music. Something about his touch made me crave it even more. He was warm, and for just a moment, I felt safe. He leaned down until we were cheek to cheek.

As the lyrics of the song washed over me, I had to hold my tears back. The nostalgia nearly did me in, and I wanted to capture this moment forever.

Dancing with Chase like this was what I'd dreamed about, ever since high school. And it was even more perfect than I'd envisioned.

He pulled back, his face dangerously close to mine. He leaned toward me, and I felt certain he was going to kiss me.

I closed my eyes.

His lips hit my cheek instead of my lips, though. He lingered there, softly pressing his lips into my skin.

"Holly—"

"Yes?" I whispered.

"I want to kiss you."

"Then why don't you?"

His lips covered mine and he drew me closer. I wrapped my arms around his neck, totally swept away in the moment. He pulled back, sighing in my ear.

"Why now?" he mumbled.

"What do you mean?"

"I mean, all these years of liking you—"

I recoiled in surprise. "You haven't liked me all of these years."

"Sure I have." His eyes twinkled. "I just thought you were out of my league."

"Oh, Chase." Could I have really misread things so badly?

"So, all these years of liking you, I finally have you in my arms, and now . . ."

A lump lodged itself in my throat. "Let's not talk about that."

"You have to talk about it sometime, Holly."

"Why ruin the moment?"

We swayed back and forth.

"Maybe we should get married," he whispered.

I stopped. "What?"

He grinned and shrugged. "It's on your bucket list, isn't it?"

"You've got to stop joking like that."

"Who says I'm joking?"

My cheeks flushed. "Chase, that would be crazy."

He looked in the distance. "Is it crazy? You know better than anyone how short life is."

I imagined being with Chase as I lived out my final days. I imagined the feeling of protection I always felt when I was with him. I thought about waking up to his arms around me.

I contrasted those images with those of living in my mom's house. Going to work every day for a supervisor who hated me. Continuing on, feeling surrounded by people yet surprisingly alone.

Chase won by leaps and bounds.

"What would you do if I said yes?"

"I'd say, let's go."

"No preacher would marry us in a day."

"Maybe he could write us in for later this week. You're thinking about it, aren't you?"

"It's tempting."

"Just give in, Holly. Do something for yourself. You're always so concerned with others."

I nodded. "After the election is over, if we both haven't decided this crazy whim is just that, then let's do it."

He picked me up and spun me around.

Maybe my first kiss would only be shared with the man I married after all.

CHAPTER 42

I spent the night at Alex's. I just couldn't stand the thought of staying in the other house by myself.

Chase and I had spent the rest of the day yesterday at his place. We'd watched old movies and ordered pizza and just enjoyed being together.

He'd driven me to Alex's place, kissed me good night, and promised to call me today.

I'd awoken early, poured some coffee, and plopped myself on Alex's couch to watch the news.

The headline story was about Rex. How he'd turned over key information that had led to the arrest of Orion. How he was a hero.

I dreaded talking to Ralph or Brian today. I couldn't begin to imagine how many percentage points he'd drop.

Just then, Ralph's picture came on the screen.

"In other news, Ralph Paladin's family was given a devastating blow recently when they found out that sister Holly Anna Paladin has been diagnosed with terminal cancer."

I sat up straighter. What? I could hardly breathe.

Brian's face came on the screen. "As you can imagine, the family is devastated. Holly is doing well, though, and she's insisting that her brother go forward with his campaign."

My mouth dropped open. I glanced at my cell

phone. It was dead, and that was probably a good thing. My phone was going to be ringing off the hook. I had to talk to Alex and Ralph before they heard this.

Or did Ralph already know?

How did Brian know?

I rubbed my temples.

Tomorrow was election day. It appeared that both candidates were pulling out all of the stops.

Alex's phone rang. I jumped up to answer, but she must have just gotten out of the shower and grabbed it.

I braced myself. Sure enough, she stomped down the stairs a few minutes later, her eyes wide and on me. She wore a robe, and her hair was pulled up in a towel. Based on the water sprinkled across her face, she hadn't even had time to dry off.

"Is it true?" she demanded.

"Alex—"

"Don't do that mumbo jumbo where you give a long-winded explanation before answering. I just need a yes or no."

I squeezed my eyes shut. "Yes."

I waited for a lecture. For anger. For accusation.

Instead, my sister threw her arms around me and didn't let go. "I can't believe it. Why didn't you tell me? You're my baby sister."

"I didn't want to worry you. Especially not with the wedding coming up."

"Why have you been carrying this alone? I could have been there for you. Throughout meetings and decisions and heartbreaks."

"I was going to tell everyone. After the election and wedding. Those deserve to be happy times."

She hugged me again. When she pulled back, I saw

the tears in her eyes. She carefully wiped them away with the edge of her robe. "This is going to take a while to sink in. You told Brian?"

I shook my head. "I have no idea how he found out."

"Well, Ralph is going to give him a piece of his mind. Then I'm going to jump in. How could he do this to us?"

"Anything to win. I guess he milked the Melinda story for all it was worth and he needed something new."

"Holly, I just don't know what to say. I have so many questions." She shoved the phone in my hand. "But first you have to call Ralph."

***

Two hours later, Alex left. I insisted that she should. She told me she was going to wrap up things at the office and then come home early. She would take today off to be with me, and tomorrow because it was election day. I figured there was no need to argue with her.

I found my phone, plugged it in to charge, and checked my texts. I had a whole slew of them, mostly from people who'd watched the news. *Awesome.*

I had some damage control to do.

My eyes stopped at an email from Doris. "I heard the news. Why don't you take some medical leave? You've got it coming. I think it would be best for everyone's sakes."

My jaw dropped open. I was pretty sure she was just looking for a way to get me out of the door.

Impulsively, I emailed back. "That sounds like a

great idea, Doris. I think I will take some time off. Indefinitely. I'll talk to Helen about this as soon as possible."

Life was too short to deal with people like Doris. I'd find another way to help those families.

I got ready for my day, not feeling at all optimistic. Just as Peggy Lee started singing "Is That All There Is," the doorbell rang.

Who now? I prayed it wasn't the press. Knowing my luck, that's exactly who it would be.

When I opened the door, I was surprised to see Jamie standing there.

"I don't know what's wrong with me lately, Holly," she started.

"What are you talking about?"

She shook her head. "Can I come in?"

"Of course." I opened the door wider. "How'd you know I was here?"

"Your cell is going straight to voice mail. I called Chase instead."

"How do you have Chase's number?"

She shrugged. "He gave it to me when my brother disappeared. Of course. Did you think I was stalking him or something?"

"Just curious." I closed the door and ushered her to the couch. "What's going on?"

She hit her hands against her hips and sighed. "I don't know why I'm letting my insecurities get the best of me, Holly. It's like the old, fat me who didn't believe in herself still pushes to the surface sometimes. I automatically think the worst of people. Something about being around Rex brought that out in me."

I swung my head back and forth, regret gripping

me. "I should have told you about John. I just didn't
know what to do. He made me promise and—"

"You were between a rock and a hard place. I
should have tried harder to understand. I just . . . I just
feel like you're leaving me, and I'm trying to hold on
and control everything else in my life." Tears
glimmered in her eyes.

"How's that working for you?" I whispered.

"Terribly." She sniffled before letting out a weak
chuckle.

My heart ached with loss. "I'm sorry, Jamie. I really
hate messing up. Like, really hate it."

She nodded. "Girlfriend, I know."

We hugged each other.

Part of me wanted to jump in and tell her
everything: *Did you see the news story about Rex? About
Ralph? Chase and I could be getting married.*

Instead, I stayed quiet.

"There's something else I need to tell you." Jamie's
lips pulled into a tight, trepid line.

I nodded. "Okay."

"But I need to wait until Chase gets here."

"Chase is coming?" It was the first I'd heard of it.
My apprehension deepened.

She nodded and glanced at her phone. "He should
be here any minute—"

Just then, the doorbell rang again.

"I've got it," I insisted.

Sure enough, Chase stood on the porch. He stepped
inside, gave me a quick kiss, and nodded at Jamie in
the background.

"I saw the news," he muttered.

I frowned. "Yeah, we're trying to get to the bottom

of it. I don't know how Brian found out."

"What a way for your family to hear, huh?" His voice sounded low, sympathetic.

"I've been doing damage control all morning. My whole family will be here this evening so we can talk. My mom's even coming back early from her trip."

"Do you want me to be here with you?"

Some of my tension melted away. "Yeah, I'd really like that."

"Something you two want to tell me?" Jamie asked behind me.

I turned around, pulling my hand from Chase's chest. I hadn't even realized it was there. I pointed back and forth between the two of us. "We're kind of . . ."

"Together," Chase finished, wrapping an arm around my waist.

Jamie's eyebrows shot up. "Nice. I like that news."

"Me, too." Chase straightened. "Now, what's going on, Jamie? You said you needed me to stop by?"

She nodded, any of her delight from just seconds ago disappearing from her features. "Can we sit at the table?"

"Of course," I told her.

We all settled at the round table, watching as Jamie pulled out her laptop. She started typing, her frown deepening with each keystroke.

"So, I was working on some of those after-election articles," she began. "I started doing a piece on Rex's high school days. I justified it, thinking as long as we weren't officially dating that there was no breach of ethics. Anyway, I thought it would be cool to talk to some of his old teachers and classmates. His English teacher lives in Pittsburgh now, so I called her."

I nodded, anxious to find out where she was going with this. "Okay."

"Well, she said all of these nice things about Rex. He was charismatic, had a hard upbringing, rose above all of it. Then she started telling me that she'd just gone through some old papers and she found one he'd written. He was apparently obsessed with Roman times."

"What are you getting at, Jamie?" Chase asked.

Uncertainty wavered in her eyes as she met Chase's gaze. "The paper he'd written was on Caligula and how he was misunderstood."

Cold washed over my entire body. "You mean, you think Rex is Caligula?"

"I don't know what I mean, Holly. I just know that something doesn't feel right." Concern tightened her features.

"Why would Rex risk everything for this?" I shook my head, trying to gather my thoughts. "I remember a couple of weeks ago Brian said that his campaign was in serious financial trouble. They didn't have enough money. Would he have gone this far?"

"What about Orion? The evidence against him is pretty incriminating," Chase said. "It's hard to refute."

"What if Orion was set up?" I asked. "You said the chief was anxious to put a lid on this case. Maybe the chief isn't covering up anything, but what if he inadvertently helped Rex?"

"Rex's schedule gave him the perfect alibi, though," Chase said.

"Good point," I said.

Chase's phone beeped. "You guys, I have to get this. It's T.J."

I nodded.

Chase rose and paced into the kitchen to answer. The next thing I heard was "What are you talking about? Why are you still on this witch hunt?"

Jamie and I glanced at each other.

Finally, Chase hung up. He paced over to me, a knot between his eyebrows. "That was T.J. He just said someone reported an anonymous tip. They said you were at Dewayne's house on the night he died."

The blood drained from my face. "Someone reported that?"

Chase nodded. "That's crazy, isn't it?"

Jamie and I exchanged another look.

"What are you saying, Holly?" Chase stared at me, confusion in his gaze.

I desperately wanted to make that look — that brief moment of doubt — disappear from his gaze. But I couldn't lie. Not anymore.

"I tried to tell you," I started. My throat went dry and I felt queasy all over.

His eyes widened, and he took a step back. "Wait. Are you about to say that you were there?"

"I —"

He held up a finger, tension straining his features. "How . . .? Why didn't you . . .? What were you doing . . .? You know what — don't tell me anything. I don't want to have to lie to my captain."

"But —" I started again.

"Really. Don't say anything." His gaze held mine, leaving no room for argument. I saw the disappointment there. Maybe even distrust.

I sighed, feeling defeated. I'd ruined everything, hadn't I? "What does this mean?"

Chase locked his jaw. He closed his eyes and shook his head, as if still trying to reconcile his image of me with this new information. "It means that T.J.'s looking for you, Holly. I told him you weren't at home. He wants to bring you in."

Adrenaline surged in me. "We've got to find the evidence to nail Rex first."

"I'm glad that's your biggest concern and not spending the rest of your life in jail." Chase raked a hand through his hair and started pacing. "It's bad enough that I'm going to lose you to cancer. But to this?"

I stood, desperately wishing I could rewind my life. "Chase . . ."

He didn't say anything, just pulled me into a hug. Some of my tension melted, but I had the pressing urge to cry.

"I'll give you guys a minute," Jamie started.

I stepped back, keeping one hand on Chase's arm and drawing on every last ounce of my strength. "We don't have a minute, guys. We've only got a little bit of time to figure this out."

Chase's jaw hardened again. "No one has seen this guy, this Caligula, so that makes it hard to identify him. Just knowing Rex wrote a paper on him isn't enough evidence to do anything with."

"So we find something that is," I said. "He framed Orion somehow."

"Maybe Orion will sell him out," Jamie offered.

"My guess is that Orion has a really big secret he's hiding, and Rex knows it and is blackmailing him," I said, pacing as I tried to sort my thoughts.

"I can go talk to Orion," Chase said. "I'll see what I

can get out of him. You two keep digging around online."

I nodded. "Sounds like a plan."

Chase kissed my cheek. "And stay away from T.J."

He hurried toward the door. When he opened it, a figure was already standing there.

CHAPTER 43

"T.J.," Chase started. He moved in front of the doorway, blocking it. "What are you doing here?"

"Did you forget that all the police sedans are equipped with GPS? It let me track down exactly where you were. I figured you'd be with your little girlfriend."

Dread pooled in my stomach. I stood, partly wanting to back away and partly wanting to show T.J. he couldn't bully me.

I chose to stand up for myself. I charged toward the door, unwilling to let Chase take the fall for this. "I didn't do anything wrong."

"Then why have you been hiding the truth?" T.J. asked.

"T.J., you have no right to be here." Chase started to push himself in front of me, but I stood my ground.

T.J. continued to stare at me. "You're blinded by love, my friend. I think Orion had an accomplice this whole time. Holly was his 'inside woman' who told him about the families' schedules, who helped him get in and out."

"Why would I do that?" My voice somehow remained even.

"You tell me." T.J. gave me the death glare.

"I'd have no reason to do that. It would gain me nothing."

T.J. didn't back down. "Maybe he coerced you into helping."

"Again, he has nothing to hold over me." I held his gaze.

"No one's that squeaky clean," T.J. insisted.

"Back off." Chase shoved him away.

I could see the fire in Chase's eyes, and I knew I had to turn this around before things got out of control. "I do think you got the wrong guy, though."

T.J.'s attention snapped toward me. "What are you talking about?"

"I think the real perpetrator was right in front of your eyes the whole time. Your former partner. Rex Harrison."

He let out a short, hard laugh. "You think Rex is behind these murders? You're crazier than I thought."

"He wrote about Caligula in high school," Jamie added.

"A high school paper doesn't prove anything," T.J. insisted. "Rex would never be behind something like this."

"Not even if his campaign was in trouble? If he needed more money?" I asked.

"He got Orion to invest in him."

Another thought struck. "What if his brother left this formula for Cena and Rex decided to finish out his work?"

T.J. flinched.

"There's one other thing I didn't have a chance to tell everyone," Jamie said. "Apparently, Rex consistently takes forty-five minutes to himself at each of his campaign events. People always said it was to help him find his center, some kind of New Age–

sounding mumbo jumbo. But, based on where his events took place on the nights of the crimes, that would be just enough time for him to slip away and do the deeds."

"Conjecture. It still doesn't prove anything," T.J. insisted.

"Do me a favor." I looked at Chase and T.J. "Talk to Orion. See what he's hiding. There's got to be a reason he's hiding it. I think he made a deal with Rex and then Rex sold him out. Just see what you can find out."

T.J. shook his head and backed up. "I'll tell you what I'm going to do. I'm going to go talk to the chief right now. All of you will be in jail by the end of the day. Mark my words. Even you, Chase."

***

"You should go," I told Chase. "Disengage yourself from all of this. I don't want to get you in trouble."

"But you want to get me in trouble?" Jamie called in the distance.

I ignored her for a second. I'd have time to talk to her in a moment.

"I'm not leaving you, Holly," Chase said.

"You just got this job. You just got back on your feet. I'm not going to take that from you."

"How about me?" Jamie quipped.

"Jamie, you'll be applauded for your journalistic skills and determination. That's the difference between a journalist and a detective. Detectives have more rules to abide by."

"True that." She leaned back in the chair and kept tapping away at the computer.

Chase squeezed my arm. "Holly, I appreciate your concern, but I'm a big boy. I'll make my own choices. Right now, I'm staying with you."

I smiled as relief filled me. Spontaneously, I leaned forward and planted a kiss on his cheek.

"Thank you, Chase." I walked back over to Jamie. "Jamie, that day at the Serpentine Wall, you told me that Rex had a brother who committed suicide, right?"

She nodded.

"What kind of a career did he work again?"

"He was an engineer of some sort. Why?"

"Can you find out what kind?" I asked.

"Of course." She typed something. "Why are you asking?"

"Because if Rex is behind all of this, how did he get his hands on the drug? Did he confiscate it from someone he arrested? Did he stumble upon it somehow?" I shook my head. "I'm not sure."

"You guys, check this out." Jamie turned the computer toward us. "His brother was a chemical engineer. Rex just happened to be working in Cincinnati when the suicide happened."

"What are you getting at?" Chase asked.

"Well, his brother lived in Cincinnati. What are the chances that Rex covered up something?" Jamie shrugged. "I also just hacked into the police records—"

Chase ran a hand through his hair and closed his eyes. "Please don't say stuff like that in front of me."

"It turns out his brother had a gambling problem."

"That's not a crime," I pointed out.

"No, but it is when you're engaged in illegal gambling operations. Apparently, Rex wasn't able to wipe everything off of his brother's records. But it wouldn't surprise me if there was something he was covering up."

***

"I've got to go take some pain medicine," I told Chase and Jamie. "I'm feeling a little sore."

Neither of them questioned me when I left the room. But I had to execute my next move quickly. Quietly, I grabbed my keys and I walked out the back door.

I remembered the talk I'd heard Rex give at the youth center. He'd mentioned something about his brother owning a big house with lots of land.

It sounded like the perfect place for some secret operations.

Someone had to find evidence to nail Rex.

Since I was the one with mere months to live, I made the most sense. I couldn't stand the thought of anything happening to either Chase or Jamie. I knew they'd try to talk me out of this or insist that they come also. I couldn't let that happen.

What I was about to do was illegal and iffy. I wouldn't let them get any more mixed up in this.

I rushed to my car, cranked the engine, and pulled out of the driveway. My heart raced as I sped down the road.

I had the address of Rex's brother on my phone. I looked down at it now. It wasn't too far away. Thank goodness. It was a long shot, but this was the only plan of action that made any sense to me.

I had to face the fact that I could be arrested soon. Because of my actions, Chase could lose his job. I didn't have any time to lose.

It only took forty minutes to pull up to the house. There were no cars there. I pulled around to the back of the building, just in case.

My limbs trembled as I stepped out. I checked the doors. They were all locked. But that wasn't a problem.

I reached into my purse and pulled out my lock picking kit.

It was too bad going to jail wasn't on my bucket list. I'd be well on my way, since I now had a long list of offenses to my name.

The door clicked. I'd done it. I quickly put away my kit and turned the knob. "Here goes nothing," I muttered to myself.

I stepped inside the house. It was all dark and all quiet. I'd seen the low windows outside the house and knew there was a basement here. That was the first place I'd check; it made the most sense.

I tiptoed through the kitchen, holding my breath in the dead silence of the space. I spotted a doorway and pulled it open.

Just a closet.

My heart still pounded in my ears. I tried another doorway.

It led to a staircase.

Bingo!

Slowly, carefully, I lowered myself onto the first step.

There was so much that could go wrong here. Fear coursed through me. I had to just get this over with. Do what I needed to do and get out of here.

When I reached the bottom of the stairs, I turned on the light.

What I saw blew my mind.

Before me were tables with various kinds of lab equipment. There were flasks and burners and beakers. In the corner, boxes were stacked high.

Moving quickly, I hurried across the room and peeked inside. I pulled out a bag filled with a white powder. Cena.

My theory was right.

Rex's brother had come up with a formula for these wildly popular synthetic drugs. He'd sold them to pay off his gambling debts, an addiction he never got over.

The man probably *had* killed himself, but I wondered if it was a planned action or if he'd overdosed. I bet Rex was first on the scene. He'd discovered his brother's body; he'd discovered his brother's creations.

And he'd seen the opportunity to make money. A lot of money. Enough money to eventually fund his campaign.

He'd covered up the crime, reported his brother's death as a suicide, and then set to work on his own evil plan. This had been years in the making.

I pulled out my phone and snapped some pictures — just the evidence we needed — and emailed them to Chase and Jamie. This was the proof we'd been looking for.

"I can't believe you'd stoop this low," someone said behind me.

I turned and saw T.J., his gun raised and pointed at me.

I gasped, wondering if I'd had the wrong bad guy all along.

CHAPTER 44

"What do you think you're doing?" T.J. demanded.

"I'm discovering the evidence you failed to find." I looked behind him, swallowing hard. He blocked my only way out of the room.

T.J. glanced around the room. "This is quite the operation."

"I would have never guessed you were behind it," I muttered. "I knew you were a jerk, but I didn't think you were a criminal."

He tightened his face in surprise. "You think I'm the guilty one?"

"I know you bought a mop and bucket."

He squinted. "I was confirming that you'd purchased them at that very store."

"Why didn't you tell Chase, then?" I asked.

"Because I didn't think I could trust him. I thought he could be working with you."

I took another step back, still not totally believing his story. "But you're here now. This is your headquarters, isn't it?"

"I don't know what you're talking about. I've never been here before in my life."

"Why are you here now, then? With your gun raised?" I asked. Just then, my cell phone vibrated in my purse. Had Chase and Jamie gotten my messages?

"Because I followed you," he snarled. "My gun is

raised because I'm still not sure what side of the law you're on. You just broke into someone's house. Someone else's house."

"This is Rex's brother's house."

Some of the arrogance left his face. "His brother is dead."

"Exactly. This is Rex's now. It's also the focal point of drug operations. Orion was just a cover-up. Rex is the real bad guy."

He shook his head, rebellion in his gaze, a refusal to see the truth. "I don't believe that. Rex was a good cop."

"Rex knows how to charm people," I said.

T.J. still didn't budge. "I've called in backup. They'll be here soon to arrest you."

"I think you're both trespassing," a new voice added.

My head jerked upward. Rex slowly, confidently made his way down the stairs, a gun in his hands.

T.J. turned toward the sound, his weapon still aimed. "Rex."

I held my breath, waiting to see how things would play out.

Rex, looking cool and unruffled, reached the bottom level and stared at me. "I underestimated you. I should have offed you while I had the chance."

"Tell me this isn't true, Rex," T.J. pleaded.

I could see the truth washing over his features.

"There are people trespassing on my property. I can't have that happen," Rex said. "I have the right to defend my property."

"Is that right, Caligula?" I said, trying to keep him talking, trying to buy some time.

He smiled, and my bones suddenly felt brittle. I was looking at pure evil. This man didn't seem to have a soul.

"No one sees Caligula and lives. No one," he muttered, pacing the room.

"Tell me this isn't true, Rex. Tell me you're not behind all of this," T.J. said.

He sighed. "I'll have to make sure your body isn't found until after tomorrow's election. Can't have your brother getting the sympathy vote. Now, out to the woods. Both of you."

"Rex, don't do this," T.J. urged. "I don't want to take you down."

"You won't have to." Rex suddenly pulled the trigger. Three times.

T.J. dropped to the ground.

I gasped in horror, disbelief filling me. Rex had just shot his friend. There was no doubt he'd do the same for me.

"Now, you. Get outside. I was really hoping not to have to do that in here. It's much harder to move the body."

"I'm going," I mumbled. I started up the steps, my hands raised.

My mind raced. Visions of the future filled my head. Images of a future with Chase. Of a full, happy life.

Those pictures were followed by smiling portraits of all of the kids I'd helped so far in my career. All the families I still had to help. I had to fight, I realized.

Rex shoved me through the kitchen, toward the back door. My chances of escape were diminishing quickly.

"You couldn't leave well enough alone, could you?" Rex muttered.

"I just can't believe you're such a hypocrite. Preaching the evil of drugs while manufacturing them."

"You know what's not fair? Losing an election because you don't have the funding. The rich can't always win. It's not fair for the rest of us."

"You framed the one person who helped you with funding. Sounds like a dumb move on your part."

"He had it coming. Orion was so twisted he had no hope."

"Let me guess—you caught him doing something illegal, then held it over him as leverage."

He snorted. "You're a smart one, Holly Anna. Not entirely the optimist I'd hoped you'd be."

I turned to face him, praying he'd see me as a person. "You'll never get away with this."

"Wrong. When I'm in office, I'll have even more power to bury this whole thing."

"You obviously don't know my family that well. Besides, I already sent the evidence that implicates you to the media. You're done, Rex. You're never winning this election."

The first real sign of emotion flashed across his face. Anger.

"Outside. Now!" He shoved me out the door.

"One more question," I started, desperate to buy time. "How'd you know about the secret cubbyhole in my attic? You left the buckets and mops at my house and then stole them again."

"Oh, that's easy. When I left the buckets there, I installed a camera so I could see how you reacted. I also saw where you hid them, which worked out quite nicely, wouldn't you say?"

"Why do I have a feeling you didn't do any of that? You had your people do the work for you, didn't you?"

"Only the minor stuff, like breaking and entering, switching out bath salts, shooting at you and framing that poor Frank Jenkins. There was only one person I could trust with the major tasks, and that was myself."

We reached the woods. I tried to slow my steps, but he kept pushing me along. "Your connection to the city and therefore the police station was Evan," I muttered. "Who works for the mayor."

He chuckled. "Very good. I got Evan to schmooze with Katrina. She was starting to ask too many questions and needed a distraction. They started dating. He let her use his very nice car, gave her a necklace. Women can be bought, I don't care what anyone says."

I nearly stumbled over a root, but he pulled me back up by my hair. I yelped in pain, but tried to rein myself in. "Jamie couldn't be bought. Sorry you were so wrong about her."

"She is quite beautiful and also easy to charm. I wanted an inside scoop on you—for both underworld and political reasons."

I was about to chide him for being so shallow. Before I could, someone rushed from around the oak tree in front of us, tackling Rex. They both fell onto the ground.

Chase. It was Chase.

"You should have stayed out of this," Rex muttered.

Chase swung at Rex's gun, trying to knock it out of his hands.

A bang ripped through the air.

Pain sliced into my shoulder.

And it was with complete clarity that I realized I didn't want to die. From a gunshot wound or cancer.

I had way too much to fight for.

But just as the thought entered my mind—just as I saw Chase pin Rex to the ground—I blacked out.

CHAPTER 45

I woke up in the hospital. Was this the end? Now that doctors were doing all these tests on me, would they discover that the cancer had spread? Wasn't that the real reason I'd avoided the doctor's appointments? I didn't want to face reality.

Chase was beside me, leaning over my bed with worry in his eyes. "Holly, you're awake."

"What are you doing in here?"

He shrugged. "They let me stay, but only in an official police capacity. I have to take your statement, and such. Plus, I had ulterior motives. Everyone's anxiously waiting outside for you, though."

I couldn't help but smile.

Chase wiped my hair back from my face, his eyes tender and soft. "Are you okay? You gave me a good scare."

"I don't know. Am I okay?"

"The doctor said your shoulder should heal fine. The bullet just skimmed it, but you lost quite a bit of blood."

I nodded. "That's good news."

"In other news, you're never allowed to do that again. You scared me to death."

I squeezed his hand. "How'd you get there so quickly?"

"You're not the only one good at reading people. I

got suspicious when you slipped away. I figured you might want to be a martyr. I stepped outside just as you pulled out of the driveway. I lost you . . . initially. But then I got your text. Luckily, I wasn't that far away."

"It's a good thing you were around."

"And it's a good thing for the city that you were around."

My smile slipped. "What happened to Rex?"

"He's in jail. There was more than enough evidence to nail him. Orion finally confessed that Rex pulled him over for driving under the influence. It was his third offense. He would have gone to jail. Rex said he would let him off the hook if Orion would do him a favor. He had no idea that Rex was Caligula."

"Did he really shoot all of those people?"

Chase sighed, long and hard. "He had people helping him. He seemed to be the master of holding leverage over people, including your friend Little T. Little T—also known as Arthur McGinnis—owned up to everything."

Another life wasted, I realized. I hated to see it. "And T.J.? Is he okay?"

"He was wearing a bulletproof vest. He's going to be just fine." Chase pulled back. "You have a lot of family members who'd really love to see you. You up for it?"

I nodded. "Send them in."

My family and Jamie flooded into the room. I answered all of their initial questions and insisted I was okay and defended what I'd done. My mom stood at my bedside, tears in her eyes. I knew we needed to talk later.

Ralph turned to Chase. "How about you? Are you

still on the squad?"

Chase nodded. "I am. The chief actually looked pretty impressed, probably because his wife's favorite employee was involved."

"Former employee. I quit. Besides, you're still on the squad because they see what a good detective you are. Without you, they would have never nailed Caligula. Or, Rex, I should say."

Alex shook her head, pushing her glasses higher. "What are you doing for a job now?"

I shook my head. "I have no idea, but I'm sure something will come up."

"You can always come work for me. I think Rex is officially disqualified for this senate race," Ralphie offered.

"I'll keep that in mind. Now, don't you need to get back to your election headquarters? It is election day."

He glanced at his watch. "I still have some time."

"What happened with Brian?" I asked.

"Besides the fact that I fired him?" Ralph said. "He claimed he found out about your . . . condition because he stopped by the hospital to visit you and overheard a conversation between you and your doctor."

"And I found out why he was visiting Desiree," Jamie added. "He claims he was campaigning in the neighborhood."

"And John?"

Jamie grinned, practically beaming. "He came back home last night when he heard that Rex had been arrested. He was lying low, trying not to be discovered. I should apologize because he stole the key to your place, the one you gave me when your family went on vacation last year and I watered your plants."

"That's great news. I'm glad John is okay."

Silence fell for a minute.

Finally, my mom shook her head. "You should have told us."

Regret pressed on me. "I know. And I'm sorry. I just didn't want to ruin anyone's big moment. The election. The wedding."

"You're always thinking of other people. That's what we love about you, Holly. But sometimes, people have to think of you, too," Alex said.

Chase squeezed my shoulder.

I nodded. "I know. I'm going to do just that. I promise."

If there was one thing I'd learned as I'd faced an even more imminent death, it was that I wasn't ready to leave my loved ones yet.

***

Everyone dealt with loss in different ways, I realized. I dealt with the potential of losing my life by living in denial and doing crazy things I would otherwise never do.

Ralph dealt with losing Melinda by pouring himself into his work.

Chase had dealt with losing his brother by drinking.

Rex had dealt with the loss of his brother by carrying on his legacy.

It was time that I found a better way to deal with my circumstances, though.

Chase stopped me before we walked into the doctor's office. "The election's over," he reminded me.

"I realize that." I smiled.

"You know what that means, right?"

"That Ralph is now our state senator?" I teased.

"I think there's something else on your bucket list you're going to be able to cross off. Let's go to the justice of the peace. Today."

"You would really do that?"

He nodded. "With you? I'd do anything. Even almost lose my career."

I ran my hand down the edge of his jaw, soaking in every inch of his face. I pushed away the doubts that wanted to emerge. Getting married after less than seven days in a whirlwind romance? It was crazy. But I didn't have time to do the typical date-a-year/be-engaged-for-six-months thing.

I had to stop overthinking things. The stress caused by my experience with Rex had probably diminished the time I had left on earth even more. "Yes, let's do it."

He grinned and covered my lips with his. "Now, let's go see what the doctor has to say."

I was taken back for my appointment almost as soon as I walked inside. I introduced Chase to William as we sat across from him, the desk between us.

"I wish you'd come to me earlier, Holly," William started.

"It wouldn't have made a difference," I told him.

"It would have. Holly, you don't have cancer," William said.

I blinked, certain I hadn't heard him correctly. "How can you say that? My doctor said—"

"I don't care what he said. You were misdiagnosed. I mean, I still have more tests to run. But your doctor based very affirmative results on very subjective tests."

"How could that happen? There were multiple tests

run."

"There have been instances of people who've been diagnosed with this disease undergoing chemo and actually dying from treatments, only in the end to find out they didn't have this disease. Sometimes, doctors want to make a name for themselves by being on the threshold of treating a new disease. I happen to know of two other people who've been diagnosed with this disease. They have your same doctor."

My mouth dropped open. "So I'm healthy? Why am I so tired, then? What about my skin?"

"I think you have panniculitis. That's the inflammation of the subcutaneous adipose."

I stared at him. "What?"

"I'll get to the bottom line. It's curable. Very curable."

My mouth gaped open. "Are you serious?"

"I wouldn't joke about something like this, Holly." There was no hint of amusement in his gaze.

I gasped and looked at Chase. He threw his arms around me. "That's great news."

I nodded. "It is."

"Like I said, I still want to do more tests. But Holly, your doctor had it wrong. I'm certain of that."

And now, I was out of a job, I'd given away most of my savings, and I'd almost been arrested.

I closed my eyes as I realized the implications.

Chase seemed to read my thoughts and squeezed my hand.

"Talk to my nurse. We'll line up the rest of the tests. I know a specialist you can see."

I smiled. "Thanks, William."

"Anything for my future sister-in-law."

Chase and I were silent as we walked from the doctor's office. It seemed like we should be rejoicing, but instead both of us seemed to be in shock.

"Chase—"

"Holly—"

We both started at the same time.

"You first," I said.

"We shouldn't get married."

I nodded, relief filling me.

"I could be the man you needed me to be for a year. But I can't be that person for the rest of your life."

"What do you mean?"

"I have too many skeletons in my closet. Too many things I need to work out."

"So you were just marrying me because you felt sorry for me?"

He reached for my arm. "No. By all means, no. I'd like nothing more than to marry you. The fact is that you deserve someone better than me."

"I'll be the judge of that." I frowned. "But I have to agree that we shouldn't get married. It was a crazy whim that seemed like a great idea when I thought I only had months to live."

His shoulders visibly relaxed. "So you agree?"

"Absolutely."

"How about we back up a few steps and start from the beginning? Maybe with a date?"

I grinned. "I'd like that very much."

"Friday at seven? I can pick you up."

I looped my arm through his. "It's a date."

###

If you enjoyed *Random Acts of Murder*, check out these other Holly Anna Paladin Mysteries:

Random Acts of Deceit (Book 2)

"Break up with Chase Dexter, or I'll kill him." Holly Anna Paladin never expected such a gut-wrenching ultimatum. With home invasions, hidden cameras, and bomb threats, Holly must make some serious choices. Whatever she decides, the consequences will either break her heart or break her soul. She tries to match wits with the Shadow Man, but the more she fights, the deeper she's drawn into the perilous situation. With her sister's wedding problems and the riots in the city, Holly has nearly reached her breaking point. She must stop this mystery man before someone she loves dies. But the deceit is threatening to pull her under . . . six feet under.

Random Acts of Malice (Book 3)

When Holly Anna Paladin's boyfriend, police detective Chase Dexter, says he's leaving for two weeks and can't give any details, she wants to trust him. But when she discovers Chase may be involved in some unwise and dangerous pursuits, she's compelled to intervene. Holly gets a run for her money as she's swept into the world of horseracing. The stakes turn deadly when a dead body surfaces and suspicion is cast on Chase. At every turn, more trouble emerges, making Holly question what she holds true about her relationship and her future. Just when she thinks she's on the homestretch, a dark horse arises. Holly might lose everything in a nail-biting fight to the finish.

Random Acts of Scrooge (Book 3.5)

Christmas is supposed to be the most wonderful time of the year, but a real-life Scrooge is threatening to ruin the season's good will. Holly Anna Paladin can't wait to celebrate Christmas with family and friends. She loves everything about the season — celebrating the birth of Jesus, singing carols, and baking Christmas treats, just to name a few. But when a local family needs help, how can she say no? Holly's community has come together to help raise funds to save the home of Greg and Babette Sullivan, but a Bah-Humburgler has snatched the canisters of cash. Holly and her boyfriend, police detective Chase Dexter, team up to catch the Christmas crook. Will they succeed in collecting enough cash to cover the Sullivans' overdue bills? Or will someone succeed in ruining Christmas for all those involved?

Random Acts of Greed (Book 4)

Help me. Don't trust anyone. Do-gooder Holly Anna Paladin can't believe her eyes when a healthy baby boy is left on her doorstep. What seems like good fortune quickly turns into concern when blood spatter is found on the bottom of the baby carrier. Something tragic — maybe deadly — happened in connection with the infant. The note left only adds to the confusion. What does it mean by "Don't trust anyone"? Holly is determined to figure out the identity of the baby. Is his mom someone from the inner-city youth center where she volunteers? Or maybe the connection is through Holly's former job as a social worker? Even worse —

what if the blood belongs to the baby's mom? Every answer Holly uncovers only leads to more questions. A sticky web of intrigue captures her imagination until she's sure of only one thing: she must protect the baby at all cost.

If you enjoyed *Random Acts of Murder*, you might also enjoy The Squeaky Clean Mystery series:

Hazardous Duty (Book 1)

On her way to completing a degree in forensic science, Gabby St. Claire drops out of school and starts her own crime-scene cleaning business. When a routine cleaning job uncovers a murder weapon the police overlooked, she realizes that the wrong person is in jail. But the owner of the weapon is a powerful foe . . . and willing to do anything to keep Gabby quiet. With the help of her new neighbor, Riley Thomas, a man whose life and faith fascinate her, Gabby seeks to find the killer before another murder occurs.

Suspicious Minds (Book 2)

In this smart and suspenseful sequel to *Hazardous Duty*, crime-scene cleaner Gabby St. Claire finds herself stuck doing mold remediation to pay the bills. Her first day on the job, she uncovers a surprise in the crawlspace of a dilapidated home: Elvis, dead as a doornail and still wearing his blue-suede shoes. How could she possibly keep her nose out of a case like this?

It Came Upon a Midnight Crime (Book 2.5, a Novella)

Someone is intent on destroying the true meaning of Christmas — at least, destroying anything that hints of it. All around crime-scene cleaner Gabby St. Claire's hometown, anything pointing to Jesus as "the reason for the season" is being sabotaged. The crimes become more twisted as dismembered body parts are found at the vandalisms. Someone is determined to destroy Christmas . . . but Gabby is just as determined to find the Grinch and let peace on earth and goodwill prevail.

Organized Grime (Book 3)
Gabby St. Claire knows her best friend, Sierra, isn't guilty of killing three people in what appears to be an eco-terrorist attack. But Sierra has disappeared, her only contact a frantic phone call to Gabby proclaiming she's being hunted. Gabby is determined to prove her friend is innocent and to keep Sierra alive. While trying to track down the real perpetrator, Gabby notices a disturbing trend at the crime scenes she's cleaning, one that ties random crimes together — and points to Sierra as the guilty party. Just what has her friend gotten herself involved in?

Dirty Deeds (Book 4)
"Promise me one thing. No snooping. Just for one week." Gabby St. Claire knows that her fiancé's request is a simple one she should be able to honor. After all, Riley's law school reunion and attorneys' conference at a posh resort is a chance for them to get away from the mysteries Gabby often finds herself involved in as a crime-scene cleaner. Then an old friend of Riley's goes missing. Gabby suspects one of Riley's buddies might be behind the disappearance. When the missing woman's mom asks Gabby for help, how can she say no?

The Scum of All Fears (Book 5)
Gabby St. Claire is back to crime-scene cleaning and

needs help after a weekend killing spree fills her work docket. A serial killer her fiancé put behind bars has escaped. His last words to Riley were: *I'll get out, and I'll get even.* Pictures of Gabby are found in the man's prison cell, messages are left for Gabby at crime scenes, someone keeps slipping in and out of her apartment, and her temporary assistant disappears. The search for answers becomes darker when Gabby realizes she's dealing with a criminal who is truly the scum of the earth. He will do anything to make Gabby's and Riley's lives a living nightmare.

To Love, Honor, and Perish (Book 6)
Just when Gabby St. Claire's life is on the right track, the unthinkable happens. Her fiancé, Riley Thomas, is shot and in life-threatening condition only a week before their wedding. Gabby is determined to figure out who pulled the trigger, even if investigating puts her own life at risk. As she digs deeper into the case, she discovers secrets better left alone. Doubts arise in her mind, and the one man with answers lies on death's doorstep. Then an old foe returns and tests everything Gabby is made of — physically, mentally, and spiritually. Will all she's worked for be destroyed?

Mucky Streak (Book 7)
Gabby St. Claire feels her life is smeared with the stain of tragedy. She takes a short-term gig as a private investigator — a cold case that's eluded detectives for ten years. The mass murder of a wealthy family seems impossible to solve, but Gabby brings more clues to light. Add to the mix a flirtatious client, travels to an exciting new city, and some quirky — albeit

temporary—new sidekicks, and things get complicated. With every new development, Gabby prays that her "mucky streak" will end and the future will become clear. Yet every answer she uncovers leads her closer to danger—both for her life and for her heart.

Foul Play (Book 8)

Gabby St. Claire is crying "foul play" in every sense of the phrase. When the crime-scene cleaner agrees to go undercover at a local community theater, she discovers more than backstage bickering, atrocious acting, and rotten writing. The female lead is dead, and an old classmate who has staked everything on the musical production's success is about to go under. In her dual role of investigator and star of the show, Gabby finds the stakes rising faster than the opening-night curtain. She must face her past and make monumental decisions, not just about the play but also concerning her future relationships and career. Will Gabby find the killer before the curtain goes down—not only on the play, but also on life as she knows it?

Broom and Gloom (Book 9)

Gabby St. Claire is determined to get back in the saddle again. While in Oklahoma for a forensic conference, she meets her soon-to-be stepbrother, Trace Ryan, an up-and-coming country singer. A woman he was dating has disappeared, and he suspects a crazy fan may be behind it. Gabby agrees to investigate, as she tries to juggle her conference, navigate being alone in a new place, and locate a woman who may not want to be found. She discovers that sometimes taking life by the horns means staring danger in the face, no matter the consequences.

Dust and Obey (Book 10)

When Gabby St. Claire's ex-fiancé, Riley Thomas, asks for her help in investigating a possible murder at a couples retreat, she knows she should say no. She knows she should run far, far away from the danger of both being around Riley and the crime. But her nosy instincts and determination take precedence over her logic. Gabby and Riley must work together to find the killer. In the process, they have to confront demons from their past and deal with their present relationship.

Thrill Squeaker (Book 11)

An abandoned theme park. An unsolved murder. A decision that will change Gabby's life forever. Restoring an old amusement park and turning it into a destination resort seems like a fun idea for former crime-scene cleaner Gabby St. Claire. The side job gives her the chance to spend time with her friends, something she's missed since beginning a new career. The job turns out to be more than Gabby bargained for when she finds a dead body on her first day. Add to the mix legends of Bigfoot, creepy clowns, and ghostlike remnants of happier times at the park, and her stay begins to feel like a rollercoaster ride. Someone doesn't want the decrepit Mythical Falls to open again, but just how far is this person willing to go to ensure this venture fails? As the stakes rise and danger creeps closer, will Gabby be able to restore things in her own life that time has destroyed—including broken relationships? Or is her future closer to the fate of the doomed Mythical Falls?

Swept Away, **a Honeymoon Novella (Book 11.5)**
Finding the perfect place for a honeymoon, away from
any potential danger or mystery, is challenging. But
Gabby's longtime love and newly minted husband,
Riley Thomas, has done it. He has found a location
with a nonexistent crime rate, a mostly retired
population, and plenty of opportunities for relaxation
in the warm sun. Within minutes of the newlyweds'
arrival, a convoy of vehicles pulls up to a nearby house,
and their honeymoon oasis is destroyed like a
sandcastle in a storm. Despite Gabby's and Riley's
determination to keep to themselves, trouble comes
knocking at their door — literally — when a neighbor is
abducted from the beach directly outside their rental.
Will Gabby and Riley be swept away with each other
during their honeymoon . . . or will a tide of danger and
mayhem pull them under?

Cunning Attractions **(Book 12)**
Politics. Love. Murder. Radio talk show host Bill
McCormick is in his prime. He's dating a supermodel,
his book is a bestseller, and his ratings have
skyrocketed during the heated election season. But
when Bill's ex-wife, Emma Jean, turns up dead, the
media and his detractors assume the opinionated
loudmouth is guilty of her murder. Bill's on-air rants
about his demon-possessed ex don't help his case. Did
someone realize that Bill was the perfect scapegoat? Or
could Bill have silenced his Ice Queen ex once and for
all? Gabby Thomas takes on the case, but she soon
realizes that Emma Jean had too many enemies to
count. From election conspiracy theories to scorned

affections and hidden secrets, Emma Jean left a trail of trouble as her legacy. Gabby is determined to follow the twisted path until she finds answers.

While You Were Sweeping, a Riley Thomas Novella
Riley Thomas is trying to come to terms with life after a traumatic brain injury turned his world upside down. Away from everything familiar—including his crime-scene-cleaning former fiancée and his career as a social-rights attorney—he's determined to prove himself and regain his old life. But when he claims he witnessed his neighbor shoot and kill someone, everyone thinks he's crazy. When all evidence of the crime disappears, even Riley has to wonder if he's losing his mind.

Note: *While You Were Sweeping* is a spin-off mystery written in conjunction with the Squeaky Clean series featuring crime-scene cleaner Gabby St. Claire.

The Sierra Files:

Pounced (Book 1)

Animal-rights activist Sierra Nakamura never expected to stumble upon the dead body of a coworker while filming a project nor get involved in the investigation. But when someone threatens to kill her cats unless she hands over the "information," she becomes more bristly than an angry feline. Making matters worse is the fact that her cats — and the investigation — are driving a wedge between her and her boyfriend, Chad. With every answer she uncovers, old hurts rise to the surface and test her beliefs. Saving her cats might mean ruining everything else in her life. In the fight for survival, one thing is certain: either pounce or be pounced.

Hunted (Book 2)

Who knew a stray dog could cause so much trouble? Newlywed animal-rights activist Sierra Nakamura Davis must face her worst nightmare: breaking the news she eloped with Chad to her ultra-opinionated tiger mom. Her perfectionist parents have planned a vow-renewal ceremony at Sierra's lush childhood home, but a neighborhood dog ruins the rehearsal dinner when it shows up toting what appears to be a fresh human bone. While dealing with the dog, a nosy neighbor, and an old flame turning up at the wrong times, Sierra hunts for answers. Her journey of discovery leads to more than just who committed the crime.

Pranced (Book 2.5, a Christmas novella)

Sierra Nakamura Davis thinks spending Christmas with her husband's relatives will be a real Yuletide treat. But when the animal-rights activist learns his family has a reindeer farm, she begins to feel more like the Grinch. Even worse, when Sierra arrives, she discovers the reindeer are missing. Sierra fears the animals might be suffering a worse fate than being used for entertainment purposes. Can Sierra set aside her dogmatic opinions to help get the reindeer home in time for the holidays? Or will secrets tear the family apart and ruin Sierra's dream of the perfect Christmas?

Rattled (Book 3)

"What do you mean a thirteen-foot lavender albino ball python is missing?" Tough-as-nails Sierra Nakamura Davis isn't one to get flustered. But trying to balance being a wife and a new mom with her crusade to help animals is proving harder than she imagined. Add a missing python, a high maintenance intern, and a dead body to the mix, and Sierra becomes the definition of rattled. Can she balance it all — and solve a possible murder — without losing her mind?

The Worst Detective Ever:

Ready to Fumble
I'm not really a private detective. I just play one on TV. Joey
Darling, better known to the world as Raven
Remington, detective extraordinaire, is trying to
separate herself from her invincible alter ego. She
played the spunky character for five years on the hit TV
show Relentless, which catapulted her to fame and into
the role of Hollywood's sweetheart. When her marriage
falls apart, her finances dwindle to nothing, and her
father disappears, Joey finds herself on the Outer Banks
of North Carolina, trying to piece her life back together
away from the limelight. A woman finds Raven—er,
Joey—and insists on hiring her fictional counterpart to
find a missing boyfriend. When someone begins
staging crime scenes to match an episode of Relentless,
Joey has no choice but to get involved.

Reign of Error
Sometimes in life, you just want to yell "Take two!" When a
Polar Plunge goes terribly wrong and someone dies in
the icy water, former TV detective Joey Darling wants
nothing to do with subsequent investigation. But when
her picture is found in the dead man's wallet and
witnesses place her as the last person seen with the
man, she realizes she's been cast in a role she never
wanted: suspect. Joey makes the dramatic mistake of
challenging the killer on camera, and now it's a race to
find the bad guy before he finds her. Danger abounds
and suspects are harder to find than the Lost Colony of
Roanoke Island. But when Joey finds a connection with
this case and the disappearance of her father, she

knows there's no backing out. As hard as Joey tries to be like her super detective alter ego, the more things go wrong. Will Joey figure this one out? Or will her reign of error continue?

Safety in Blunders
(coming soon)

Carolina Moon Series:

Home Before Dark (Book 1)
Nothing good ever happens after dark. Country singer
Daleigh McDermott's father often repeated those
words. Now, her father is dead. As she's about to flee
back to Nashville, she finds his hidden journal with
hints that his death was no accident. Mechanic Ryan
Shields is the only one who seems to believe Daleigh.
Her father trusted the man, but her attraction to Ryan
scares her. She knows her life and career are back in
Nashville and her time in the sleepy North Carolina
town is only temporary. As Daleigh and Ryan work to
unravel the mystery, it becomes obvious that someone
wants them dead. They must rely on each other—and
on God—if they hope to make it home before the
darkness swallows them.

Gone By Dark (Book 2)
Ten years ago, Charity White's best friend, Andrea, was
abducted as they walked home from school. A decade
later, when Charity receives a mysterious letter that
promises answers, she returns to North Carolina in
search of closure. With the help of her new neighbor,
Police Officer Joshua Haven, Charity begins to track
down mysterious clues concerning her friend's
abduction. They soon discover that they must work
together or both of them will be swallowed by the
looming darkness.

Wait Until Dark (Book 3)
*A woman grieving broken dreams. A man struggling to
regain memories. A secret entrenched in folklore dating back*

two centuries. Antiquarian Felicity French has no clue the trouble she's inviting in when she rescues a man outside her grandma's old plantation house during a treacherous snowstorm. All she wants is to nurse her battered heart and wounded ego, as well as come to terms with her past. Now she's stuck inside with a stranger sporting an old bullet wound and forgotten hours. Coast Guardsman Brody Joyner can't remember why he was out in such perilous weather, how he injured his head, or how a strange key got into his pocket. He also has no idea why his pint-sized savior has such a huge chip on her shoulder. He has no choice but to make the best of things until the storm passes. Brody and Felicity's rocky start goes from tense to worse when danger closes in. Who else wants the mysterious key that somehow ended up in Brody's pocket? Why? The unlikely duo quickly becomes entrenched in an adventure of a lifetime, one that could have ties to local folklore and Felicity's ancestors. But sometimes the past leads to darkness . . . darkness that doesn't wait for anyone.

Light the Dark (a Christmas novella)
Nine months pregnant, Hope Solomon is on the run and fearing for her life. Desperate for warmth, food, and shelter, she finds what looks like an abandoned house. Inside, she discovers a Christmas that's been left behind — complete with faded decorations on a brittle Christmas tree and dusty stockings filled with loss. Someone spies smoke coming from the chimney of the empty house and alerts Dr. Luke Griffin, the owner. He rarely visits the home that harbors so many bittersweet memories for him. But no one is going to violate the

space so near and dear to his heart. Then Luke meets
Hope, and he knows this mother-to-be desperately
needs help. With no room at any local inn, Luke invites
Hope to stay, unaware of the danger following her.
While running from the darkness, the embers of
Christmas present are stirred with an unexpected birth
and a holiday romance. But will Hope and Luke live to
see a Christmas future?

Cape Thomas Series:

Dubiosity (Book 1)
Savannah Harris vowed to leave behind her old life as an investigative reporter. But when two migrant workers go missing, her curiosity spikes. As more eerie incidents begin afflicting the area, each works to draw Savannah out of her seclusion and raise the stakes — for her and the surrounding community. Even as Savannah's new boarder, Clive Miller, makes her feel things she thought long forgotten, she suspects he's hiding something too, and he's not the only one. As secrets emerge and danger closes in, Savannah must choose between faith and uncertainty. One wrong decision might spell the end . . . not just for her but for everyone around her. Will she unravel the mystery in time, or will doubt get the best of her?

Disillusioned (Book 2)
Nikki Wright is desperate to help her brother, Bobby, who hasn't been the same since escaping from a detainment camp run by terrorists in Colombia. Rumor has it that he betrayed his navy brothers and conspired with those who held him hostage, and both the press and the military are hounding him for answers. All Nikki wants is to shield her brother so he has time to recover and heal. But soon they realize the paparazzi are the least of their worries. When a group of men try to abduct Nikki and her brother, Bobby insists that Kade Wheaton, another former SEAL, can keep them out of harm's way. But can Nikki trust Kade? After all, the man who broke her heart eight years ago is anything but safe...Hiding out in a farmhouse on the

Chesapeake Bay, Nikki finds her loyalties—and the remnants of her long-held faith—tested as she and Kade put aside their differences to keep Bobby's increasingly erratic behavior under wraps. But when Bobby disappears, Nikki will have to trust Kade completely if she wants to uncover the truth about a rumored conspiracy. Nikki's life—and the fate of the nation—depends on it.

Distorted (Book 3)
Coming soon

Standalones:

The Good Girl

Tara Lancaster can sing "Amazing Grace" in three harmonies, two languages, and interpret it for the hearing impaired. She can list the Bible canon backward, forward, and alphabetized. The only time she ever missed church was when she had pneumonia and her mom made her stay home. Then her life shatters and her reputation is left in ruins. She flees halfway across the country to dog-sit, but the quiet anonymity she needs isn't waiting at her sister's house. Instead, she finds a knife with a threatening message, a fame-hungry friend, a too-hunky neighbor, and evidence of . . . a ghost? Following all the rules has gotten her nowhere. And nothing she learned in Sunday School can tell her where to go from there.

Death of the Couch Potato's Wife (Suburban Sleuth Mysteries)

You haven't seen desperate until you've met Laura Berry, a career-oriented city slicker turned suburbanite housewife. Well-trained in the big-city commandment, "mind your own business," Laura is persuaded by her spunky seventy-year-old neighbor, Babe, to check on another neighbor who hasn't been seen in days. She finds Candace Flynn, wife of the infamous "Couch King," dead, and at last has a reason to get up in the morning. Someone is determined to stop her from digging deeper into the death of her neighbor, but Laura is just as determined to figure out who is behind the death-by-poisoned-pork-rinds.

Imperfect
Since the death of her fiancé two years ago, novelist Morgan Blake's life has been in a holding pattern. She has a major case of writer's block, and a book signing in the mountain town of Perfect sounds as perfect as its name. Her trip takes a wrong turn when she's involved in a hit-and-run: She hit a man, and he ran from the scene. Before fleeing, he mouthed the word "Help." First she must find him. In Perfect, she finds a small town that offers all she ever wanted. But is something sinister going on behind its cheery exterior? Was she invited as a guest of honor simply to do a book signing? Or was she lured to town for another purpose—a deadly purpose?

Complete Book List:

Squeaky Clean Mysteries:
#1 Hazardous Duty
#2 Suspicious Minds
#2.5 It Came Upon a Midnight Crime (a novella)
#3 Organized Grime
#4 Dirty Deeds
#5 The Scum of All Fears
#6 To Love, Honor, and Perish
#7 Mucky Streak
#8 Foul Play
#9 Broom and Gloom
#10 Dust and Obey
#11 Thrill Squeaker
#11.5 Swept Away (a novella)
#12 Cunning Attractions
#13 Clean Getaway (coming soon)

Squeaky Clean Companion Novella:
While You Were Sweeping

The Sierra Files:
#1 Pounced
#2 Hunted
#2.5 Pranced (a Christmas novella)
#3 Rattled
#4 Caged (coming soon)

The Gabby St. Claire Diaries (a Tween Mystery series):
#1 The Curtain Call Caper
#2 The Disappearing Dog Dilemma

#3 The Bungled Bike Burglaries

Holly Anna Paladin Mysteries:
#1 Random Acts of Murder
#2 Random Acts of Deceit
#3 Random Acts of Malice
#3.5 Random Acts of Scrooge
#4 Random Acts of Greed
#5 Random Acts of Fraud (coming soon)

The Worst Detective Ever:
#1 Ready to Fumble
#2 Reign of Error
#3 Safety in Blunders

Carolina Moon Series:
Home Before Dark
Gone By Dark
Wait Until Dark
Light the Dark (a Christmas novella)

Suburban Sleuth Mysteries:
#1 Death of the Couch Potato's Wife

Stand-alone Romantic-Suspense:
Keeping Guard
The Last Target
Race Against Time
Ricochet
Key Witness
Lifeline
High-Stakes Holiday Reunion
Desperate Measures
Hidden Agenda

Mountain Hideaway
Dark Harbor
Shadow of Suspicion

Cape Thomas Series:
Dubiosity
Disillusioned
Distorted (coming in 2017)

Standalone Romantic Mystery:
The Good Girl

Suspense:
Imperfect

Nonfiction:
Changed: True Stories of Finding God through
Christian Music
The Novel in Me: The Beginner's Guide to Writing and
Publishing a Novel

About the Author:

USA Today has called Christy Barritt's books "scary, funny, passionate, and quirky."

Christy writes both mystery and romantic suspense novels that are clean with underlying messages of faith. Her books have won the Daphne du Maurier Award for Excellence in Suspense and Mystery, have been twice nominated for the Romantic Times' Reviewers' Choice Award, and have finaled for both a Carol Award and Foreword Magazine's Book of the Year.

She's married to her Prince Charming, a man who thinks she's hilarious—but only when she's not trying to be. Christy's a self-proclaimed klutz, an avid music lover who's known for spontaneously bursting into song, and a road trip aficionado.

When she's not working or spending time with her family, she enjoys singing, playing the guitar, and exploring small, unsuspecting towns where people have no idea how accident prone she is.

Find Christy online at:
www.christybarritt.com
www.facebook.com/christybarritt
www.twitter.com/cbarritt

Sign up for Christy's newsletter to get information on all of her latest releases here:
www.christybarritt.com/newsletter-sign-up/

If you enjoyed this book, please consider leaving a review.